WHITE LOTUS: A NOVEL OF EGYPT'S FALL

Part I of the White Lotus Trilogy

LIBBIE HAWKER

RUNNING RABBIT PRESS

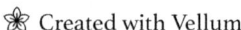 Created with Vellum

I

SLAVE

❧ I ❧

THE TRADER

DORICHA FOLDED HERSELF AGAINST THE COLD, CRUMBLING mudbrick of the room's inner wall. Pulling her knees up to her chest, she wrapped her arms around thin legs. Shin bones pressed hard against the tender flesh of her inner forearms—bones near as sharp as knife blades, cutting with the force of her hunger. The threadbare cloth of her tunic was stiff with grime and soot, but a stab of fear went through her on the tunic's behalf. Soon even that dirty scrap, like every other good thing she had once had, would be taken away from her—and beneath her only garment she felt very naked, very frail. Doricha rested her chin on her knobby knees and listened.

The voices came from beyond the frayed yellow curtain, a stained and moth-eaten thing that separated one end of the single-room apartment from the other. On Doricha's side lay the family's lone sleeping mat—a single hard, flea-specked pallet for all five of them—and above the cold patch of shadow where Doricha crouched, the apartment's only window. Shutterless, with its ripped drapery pulled back to let in the sour stink of back-district Tanis, the window also admitted the sounds of the crowded alley outside: the loud clatter of an ass's hooves on the hard-packed lane; gruff shouts of men haggling over some cheap, shoddy wares; a child screaming shrilly as its mother scolded and whipped it. Doricha furrowed her brow, concentrating on the voices beyond the curtain—her mother's voice, and that of the silky, erudite man, a perfect stranger who had appeared that morning in the back district, asking directions to the stacked, leaning row of hovels where Doricha and her family now lived. He was as incongruous amid the piss-soaked alleys as a peacock in a tumbledown hen house.

"She hasn't yet begun to bleed," Melaina said. Doricha could hear the pain in her mother's words—a now-familiar thickness that had first appeared six months prior, when Doricha's father had been killed by bandits. "And that's why it must be now. If it's now... if I do this thing now, the gods forgive me, then she'll have time to be trained, won't she? Trained up proper and cultured, like, so she'll know what to expect. So she can have a chance. That's what the women told me... the ones who said I ought to... I ought to..."

"And that's what you want, isn't it?" the strange man said in his smooth, rich voice. "You want her to have a chance."

"Isn't that what every mother wants?" Melaina choked on the words. "The gods forgive me."

"You needn't take on so," said the man. "You're right to make the transaction now, while she is still a child. The training she will receive at this young age will—"

"What they talking about, then?" Aella piped up. Doricha's six-year-old sister looked as solemn as a priestess of Isis. She huddled on the sleeping mat, one arm wrapped around each of the twin boys, trying to keep their little brothers silent and still. Aella's once-golden hair was dull and stringy, her small body thin as a twig, her eyes glazed by hunger. But she managed to keep Bolin and Belos quiet, and for that Doricha was grateful.

"Hush," Doricha whispered. "Can't hear 'em if you're talking, can I?"

She caught the tail end of the man's words. "—I do have a reputation, madam, and I uphold it with pride. I am well known throughout Egypt—and beyond, I dare say—for making and managing the finest *pornae* in the land."

Doricha's breath caught in her throat. She hugged her legs tighter still, but she felt more exposed than ever. *So it's come to this, then.* The man was a trader of pornae. Street-walkers—whores. Doricha knew she had no cause to feel either surprised or hurt. This was a sensible progression, after all—a natural bend in the hard, rocky road their lives had taken ever since her father's death. It was no more than she ought to have expected.

But knowing that did little to quell her fear. A wave of nausea swelled in her gut; she squeezed her eyes shut, blocking out the sight of the small, dirty room that was their home—for how much longer, without Father to earn the few *hedj* per week this rough shelter cost them? She tried to take solace in the darkness behind her eyelids, but she couldn't shut out the stink of back-district Tanis, the piss and rotting refuse in the alleys, the close, cloying smell of unwashed bodies and hunger and despair. With her eyes closed, even over the din outside and the smooth voice of the silk-draped pimp, over her mother's stifled sobs, Doricha imagined she could hear the breaths and heartbeats of little Aella and the twins. Such tiny things, all three of them. Small and brave and uncomplaining. Mother's only goal after Father died was to see the family back in Thrace, and safe once more. To keep moving north, to find some way across the sea, until at last the family stood again on good, reliable Thracian soil. Thrace—their homeland, where once life had been good, where once, when Doricha was a little girl, they had wanted for nothing. Those sunny, contented days of her early childhood seemed a thousand years in the past.

I'm all Mother has left to barter—my family's only asset. She listened again to the soft murmur of her imagination—Aella and the little boys breathing in and out, in and out, their thready pulses beating in time with her own, for after all, they were one family, one blood.

Most of us will get back to Thrace, and that must be enough for you, Mother. It will be enough for me.

Beyond the curtain, Melaina spoke up, loud and indignant. The sudden shift in her mother's emotions made Doricha's eyes snap open. "You would think, sir, that the Pharaoh would do more to help people like us, so it wouldn't come to this."

The sound of footsteps crossing the dirt floor—a light, confident tread. That was the man, then, not Mother. "Do you mean," he said, "the poor? Egyptian Pharaohs have never done much to succor the poor. Not enough, at any rate."

He passed the yellow curtain. Through a rip in its cloth, Doricha caught one fleeting glimpse of him: curling black hair, skin of a deep olive tone, a sharp, hooked nose on a face that was still rather young. And his clothing! Though she could see him for only the briefest of moments, still Doricha could not help but see the richness of his well-draped tunic: its color bright as the sun, the careful red embroidery of angular keys crossing over one shoulder.

"I don't mean the poor, sir," Melaina said. "I mean Greeks. Well—we're Thracian, of course, but it's near enough, isn't it?"

The man, out of sight now, gave a low, sympathetic chuckle. "It is."

"It's said the Pharaoh loves Greeks more than he loves his own Egyptians."

"I cannot disagree with such a rumor. Our present king of Egypt admires all things Grecian. His over-fondness for the Greeks has given many good native-born Egyptians cause to speak against him."

"But he doesn't admire us enough to help us. So many of us stranded here, after we came down to Egypt to do good, honest work, but found the work all dried up with the river."

"The river itself isn't dried up, madam." The man said it with a hint of amusement in his voice, tolerance for Melaina's rural ignorance. It made Doricha's hackles raise. "Just a few of the river's arms here within the Delta region. This is not unheard of; many times throughout history, the river has silted over its various Delta arms and carved new paths through the soil."

"That's as may be, but the change was enough to send my husband and me into poverty. Not enough work to be had in any of the places where we were told to look for it. And four children to feed, gods help us. What were we to think?"

"And, I presume, by the time you reached Egypt there wasn't enough coin left to travel south beyond the Delta, to seek out your fortune in places where the river is far more reliable."

"Yes, sir," Melaina said. Her voice was soft with defeat. "That was the way of it."

"Madam, I have heard the same sad story many times. More times than I can count, alas. Greeks, once hopeful, stranded in Egypt and forced into slums with no way to get back home."

"It's not right, that the Pharaoh won't do a thing to help us."

"No," the man said quietly. "It's not right. On that, we certainly agree. But you are fortunate after all, Madam. The gods have given you a daughter of the right age. She provides you with a solution to your troubles—a way out."

Doricha swallowed hard. Her mother maintained that strained, trembling silence.

"Shall we have a look at the girl now?" the man suggested at length.

Still, Melaina did not speak.

Doricha could all but see her mother, one pale hand clutching the neck of her ragged tunic, face turned away and head ducked in shame. She couldn't allow her mother to continue in such distress. The time had come to take whatever she could—her future, the family's safety—into her own small hands. Doricha drew a deep breath and pushed herself up from the hard earthen floor.

"Where you going?" Aella asked. The boys squirmed in her arms, whining softly, struggling to break free and follow their big sister.

"Stay put," Doricha told the twins. To Aella she whispered, "Don't worry. I won't leave without saying good-bye. But I've got to go to Mother now and help her out, you see? Otherwise, she'll never do it herself."

Aella's dirt-smeared brow furrowed in confusion. "Leave? What you talking about, then?"

"Stay put," Doricha said again. She pushed past the yellow curtain before Melaina could summon her. She would spare her mother that pain, at least—calling her daughter out to be sold like a donkey in the market.

Melaina made a thin, faint sound as Doricha came through the curtain, somewhere between a sigh and a cry of agony. But the girl did not look at her mother. She kept her eyes on the tall, lavishly dressed man as he turned toward her. He stood with chin cupped in hand, assessing Doricha in a stiff, business-like silence. She watched his face, his shrewd eyes, as he took stock of her. She seemed to see herself through the trader's appraising stare. The narrow, straight frame of a child who was still many months—if not years—from adolescence; the delicate bones that pressed through skin and tunic, making awkward angles of her shoulders. The unimpressive height—even if six months of hunger had not stunted her growth, Doricha knew the gods had never intended her to grow tall. Skinny legs with prominent knees, the firm, resilient flesh of youth wasting away. Bare feet with dirt under the toenails. Doricha drew herself up and stood as proudly as she could—she hoped she looked proud—though she knew no back-district rat had any cause for arrogance or poise.

The man stepped toward her. At close range, the smell of him overwhelmed Doricha—a rich spice of sandalwood, myrrh, and ginger, like the fine cleansing oil she had once tested at a market stall, rubbing it into her wrist and sniffing deeply until her head was dizzy, and then the oil merchant had lunged at her with a stick and a shower of curses and driven her away. The unfamiliar decadence of the whore-trader's scent made Doricha feel warm and cautious at the same time. He was from an entirely different world than she, as far apart from Doricha's reality as the Pharaoh was from his Egyptians, or as the gods were from mortal men. Even when her family had been safe in Thrace, so many years ago, they had never been wealthy enough to comb expensive oil through their hair.

Gently, the trader lifted Doricha's chin. He turned her face this way and that, considering the angles of her features in the room's dim light.

"Very pale complexion," he said. "Though tender—she is freckled from the sun, I see. Those green eyes will be an asset— exotic. Not many women in Egypt have light-colored eyes. And her hair. It's neither golden nor red, but somewhere in between. How would one describe hair like this, I wonder?"

Melaina, turned away and shuddering as she held back her sobs, made no reply.

The man answered his own question. "Rose gold. I've seen smiths in the south of Egypt who work with rose gold. Very fine, rich stuff."

Doricha fought to keep her expression neutral, plain—to keep the spite and tears from her eyes.

"My name is Iadmon," he told her, still holding her chin.

Doricha didn't know what to say, so she kept her silence. But she held Iadmon's dark eyes steadily with her own. *I am not afraid*, she tried to tell him with her unflinching stare. She hoped Iadmon believed her. She barely believed herself.

"I think she will do nicely," Iadmon said to Melaina, releasing his grip on Doricha's chin. "She is thin and dirty, but proper feeding and a good bath will take care of that."

Melaina stood with her back turned to them both, huddled in upon herself. Doricha watched her mother shake with the rhythm of her silent weeping. Then she turned to Iadmon and caught him once more by the eye.

"Will I fetch a high enough price that they'll make it back to Thrace?" she asked.

Melaina gasped and turned toward Doricha, reaching out to clutch her eldest child. "No, I can't! I've changed my mind, sir. I can't let my girl go. Not for this!"

Doricha moved away from her mother's hand. She did not allow Iadmon's gaze to slip from her own. "You must pay enough that they can all get back to Thrace—my mother, my sister, and the two little boys. Otherwise, I won't go with you. And if you cheat my family after you take me away, I'll run off and you'll never see me again, and you'll have wasted all your money."

For a moment, Iadmon did not speak. He only watched her steadily, those dark eyes prying, assessing. Then a slow, amused smile curled one side of his mouth. Bracing hands on hips, Doricha sniffed sharply to make her point, and again the pimp's rich smell filled her head.

Iadmon leaned close to her, speaking quietly and with a smile —as if the conversation were a secret, intimate thing, and one held between friends. "Little girl, how much money do you think you're worth?"

Though his smooth, cultured voice never roughened, there was no mistaking the mockery in his words. Doricha chose to ignore the subtle sting, and answered as if he had asked the question honestly. "I guess the only figure that matters is how much *you* think I'm worth."

Iadmon straightened. "Clever child," he said, so softly that Doricha almost didn't hear him. The faint trace of mockery left his eyes entirely—the thin, wry curve of his smile, too. A more contemplative stillness settled over him. His dark brows lowered for a moment; he seemed to deliberate with himself. Then he nodded once and held out his hand. "Worth enough to get your family back to Thrace, and then some. You have my word on that.

No need to run off and waste my money. I'll see to it that they can leave Tanis this very day, if you like."

Doricha lowered her eyes, considering Iadmon's hand. It was soft-skinned, untroubled by work, unlike the cracked palms and callused fingers of her father's hands. But in its bigness and its confident, untrembling posture, she saw that he was strong despite his life of ease. Iadmon was a powerful man—maybe even a great man. Doricha hoped he would be as good as his word. She slapped her palm against his own, and he caught her fingers in his grip. Warm, hard, unflinchingly certain, his big hand shook her small and frail one.

Doricha knew with sudden force, with a sting of tears in her eyes, that she couldn't go back through the yellow curtain—couldn't look at Aella and the twins again. She couldn't say good-bye, because it would be forever. They would go home to Thrace, but she would remain in Egypt with this tall, rich-smelling man. The family would be parted now, but as long as Doricha avoided that terrible word—goodbye—then she might still pretend she would see her family again, someday, somehow.

She swallowed the lump in her throat and turned to her mother. Melaina's eyes were puffy and red, her mouth twisted with a terrible agony. Tears cut shining tracks through the grime on her cheeks.

"Tell the little ones I love them," Doricha said, startled at the steadiness of her voice.

Iadmon's hand landed gently on Doricha's back, between her thin shoulder blades. He pressed her toward the door.

"No," Melaina cried again. "I've changed my mind, sir!"

"I'll send my man with your money in less than two hours," he said. He didn't look back at Melaina as he ushered Doricha out of the hovel. Doricha didn't look back, either. "I am as good as my word."

Melaina's pitiful weeping filled the single, small room. It spilled out after them as Doricha and Iadmon stepped over the threshold. Doricha heard the clatter of wooden rings as the yellow curtain was knocked aside. "Doricha!" Aella cried, and her feet pounded against the earthen floor as she ran.

Iadmon's hand tightened on the back of Doricha's neck. "Don't turn around, child." His voice was not unkind. "Not now. At times like these, there's nothing one can do except keep going."

❧ 2 ❧

TO MEMPHIS

DORICHA'S BREATHS CAME SHORT AND HARSH AS SHE WALKED ALONG beside the whore-trader. Iadmon's hand remained on the back of her neck, guiding her firmly toward an inescapable fate. But his grip wasn't necessary. Doricha's bare feet slapped on the earthen lanes and mudbrick courts of Tanis, brisk and unhesitating despite her fear. If this Iadmon proved to be as good as his word, then her sale would see the family back to Thrace, where they might find cousins to offer them charity, might cobble together some means of scratching out a new life. Doricha told herself that her family's safety was the only thing that mattered now. She told herself she would do whatever she must to protect her little sister, the twins, and even her sad, broken mother. She would not run from Iadmon, nor resist the fate toward which he propelled her.

When they emerged from the shadowed alleys of the back district, the air was not as close, and the hot Egyptian sun raised odors of dry dust and donkeys' dung from the roads—much more pleasant smells than those that pervaded the slums. Iadmon seemed to relax a little as they left the poor district behind. He drew a deep breath and let it out with a sigh of contentment, of finality, as if cleansing his lungs and his conscience of unpleasant things. His grip on Doricha's neck softened.

"We are going to the docks," he told her as they paused at the edge of a marketplace, allow a wagon to roll past.

The wagon's bed was laden with a heap of honey-gold wheat as high as a Thracian mountain. Grain dust drifted in its wake, glittering in the mid-day sun. The market rang with the high, sharp shouts of hawkers and fairly quaked with the rumble of carts' and hand-barrows' wheels. At any other time, Doricha would have delighted at the bustle, the variety of sights and sounds. But now she only watched the wagon with dull, stinging eyes as it rolled away. When Iadmon pressed lightly on the back of her neck, she stepped forward again, responsive and mindless like an animal trained to the harness.

"What is your name?" Iadmon asked.

"Doricha, Master. I must call you Master now, I suppose."

"That would be well. For now."

They walked on in silence for a moment. As soon as she'd told him her name, a tightness had seized Doricha's chest. She wondered at it, examining the thick pressure, the insistent squeeze in her gut, trying to understand its source—and all at once, she knew it. "Will you take my name away? Give me another one instead?" That would be far worse than losing her grimy, ragged tunic. The thought made her sick to her stomach.

Iadmon glanced down at her, his dark brows lifting in surprise. "Do you want me to give you another name?"

"No." Her throat closed, and she had to breathe deeply several times before she could speak again. "No, Master, but I think now it doesn't matter one bit, what I want."

"You're an intelligent girl, Doricha." There was approval in his voice—pride, even. Self-congratulation on a purchase well made.

"I don't know much of slaves," Doricha said. "But I reckon I am one now, and that's all there is to it."

She paused. Iadmon waited in silence for her to speak,

leading her out of the sun and into a shaded alley. At the end of the alley she could see the gray-brown smoothness of the Nile's waters, dazzling in the sun, reflecting its strong glare into the alley's cool shadows. Squinting, she said, "I reckon from now on you'll tell me what to think, what to do... even what my name must be, if you take a fancy to change it."

Iadmon's soft chuckle surprised her. His hand lifted from the back of her neck, then returned, patting her gently, as a man might do to a favorite horse or hound. "I see no point in changing your name, Doricha. Have no fear on that account."

There was no one in the alley but the two of them. The narrow walls funneled toward them the compelling, faintly salty smell of the sluggish Delta waters. The moisture in the air was soothing against her sun-struck skin.

"I didn't tell them goodbye," Doricha said suddenly, not understanding why she said it. She could expect no sympathy from Iadmon, her new master. Her owner.

But he watched her as they walked along. She could feel his gaze upon her, quietly observant, curious—and not without compassion. "Do you regret that?" he finally asked.

"I didn't think I could do it without crying and frightening the little ones out of their wits. Only, before I came out to see you, I told my sister Aella I would say goodbye."

"You knew you were to be sold?"

"Of course. I heard you talking to my mother." She added belatedly, with a little anxious jump of her shoulders, "Master."

"Do you understand why your mother did it?"

"She didn't do it," Doricha replied. "I did. She wanted to call it off. You remember, Master."

He nodded, sighed. "Yes. You're quite right, of course. It never gets any easier, persuading parents to give up their children."

Doricha was silent for a moment. When she was certain of keeping the bitterness from her voice, she said, "Then why do you do it, Master?"

"Someone must trade in spices, if the people of the world are to have flavor for their meat. Someone must trade in cloth, if the people of the world are to have garments to wear. Someone must trade in slaves—and I am that someone. Do not resent your mother, Doricha. She is a good woman who found herself in a dark and desperate place."

"I won't, Master—I don't. Even if she hadn't tried to call the sale off, I wouldn't resent her then, neither."

"Either," Iadmon corrected.

Doricha blinked up at him, confused.

"You will learn to speak properly, with time. It will be a necessary part of your training, to speak with culture and refinement."

She swallowed hard. She knew what pornae did—any child from the slums had seen the transactions that took place in alleys and alcoves, up against the dry mudbrick walls with skirts pushed up around hips. She didn't see that fine-and-fancy speech had anything to do with *that* sort of business.

They emerged from the alley's far end, stepping out into the bright light once more. Doricha squinted all the harder as the glare throbbed in her eyes. The sudden urge to sneeze tickled inside her nose. The docks were crowded with men carrying wares to and from the many long boats with their high, curving prows and brightly painted hulls. The men weren't the only ones who worked the docks, of course. Pornae leaned against crates and warehouse walls, dressed in garish colors, their faces painted in parodies of fine ladies' more elegant and subdued styles. They called out now and again to the deck-hands and fishermen: "Just ten hedj for one up against the wall, boys!" "I'm half price if you're quick and hard!"

Iadmon led Doricha across the flat limestone pavers of the quay. A grand boat was moored a little apart from the others, its hull painted vibrant red with a great, blue-and-white eye staring out from its prow. Doricha was not skilled at reading, but as she and Iadmon made for the red ship, she had time enough to puzzle out the Greek letters etched on its hull and highlighted in glimmering gold leaf: *Samian Wind*.

As they neared the *Samian Wind*, a man came swiftly down the ramp to greet Iadmon. Though he wore a tunic nearly as fine as Iadmon's own, he bowed with an obsequious air that marked him at once as a slave—or a servant, at best. The man was short of stature, barely reaching Iadmon's shoulder. He had a stocky body, a shuffling gait, and a curious way of holding his head and neck—thrust forward and tipped slightly to the side—that suggested either great curiosity or a defect of the spine. Perhaps both. His tight black curls and deep-brown complexion suggested African blood, and Doricha noted that his face still looked rather youthful. He couldn't have been more than a dozen years older than she.

"Aesop," Iadmon said to his servant, "get into my cask and weigh out two hundred hedj. I shall draw a map for you. Follow it, and you'll find a red-haired Thracian woman with three small children, two of them twin boys. You must give her the money within two hours' time."

Doricha flushed; her legs trembled as relief swept powerfully through her. Two hundred hedj would certainly be enough to see Mother and the children back to Thrace, and to set them up comfortably once they reached home. Iadmon had kept to his word, after all.

Aesop nodded, but turned a wide-eyed, disbelieving stare on Doricha. "Two hundred for this little one, Master?"

"And worth every bit. Trust me on that count."

Aesop straightened—as much as the kink in his back would allow—and smiled openly at Doricha. She liked his smile. It was honest and warm; it put her at ease, as much as anything could just then. "I always do trust you, good Master. I'll do as you instructed, straight away." He returned to the boat's ramp, but paused at its foot, giving Doricha one more lingering, assessing look. Then he climbed up to the boat's deck and disappeared into its heavily curtained cabin.

Iadmon took Doricha by the shoulders, turning her gently to face him. "Child, do you understand what has happened today?"

"Yes, Master." She struggled to look at Iadmon, fought not to drop her gaze in shame. "I'm to be a whore now. Like them." Doricha nodded toward the garish, laughing pornae who strolled along the quay.

Smiling, his eyes alight with sly speculation, Iadmon shook his head. "Before I'd seen you for myself, I admit that I had intended to make of you a common porna. But once I met you, Doricha, I thought better of it. You have more potential than that."

She swallowed, watching his face intently, sensing that her master had more to say.

"You have such thoughtful eyes, and your bearing is so very confident, so naturally poised. There is great intelligence in you, and the capacity for yet more learning. You are as bright as you are beautiful. It's a rare combination."

She couldn't stop herself from lowering her face then, staring down at the dirt that caked her feet and ankles. "Reckon I must be very dull indeed then, Master, for I'm not much to look at. I know as much."

Iadmon's deep laughter rumbled in the close space between them. "That's where you're wrong. You are like a tarnished bit of silver now: dirty, but you'll shine again with a bit of polishing. In fact, I intend to make you shine brighter than you ever thought possible. Do you know what a *hetaera* is, Doricha?"

She looked up at him again, shaking her head mutely. She had never heard the word before.

"A hetaera is a woman who entertains men. Not only with her body, but intellectually, aesthetically. *Hetaerae* enjoy a very rare status. They alone, among all Greek women, may converse openly with men in public forums. Only the hetaerae may move about freely without male chaperones. They may even own property and participate in government. Such status is more than even the luckiest well-born girls can dream of. Intelligent as you are, surely I don't need to tell you that for a girl like you—found in the back alleys of Tanis, sold by your starving mother—such a great opportunity will never come again."

Doricha's heart pounded at Iadmon's words. Her mouth was suddenly dry. "No, Master. You needn't tell me."

"I won't lie to you, Doricha. I've no need to deceive you. This will not be an easy path. If we are to root rustic Thrace out of you and replace it with something more cultured and refined, then you must have rigorous training. The hours of your learning will be long and difficult. But that will not be your only challenge. You must face competition, too. There are many hetaerae in Egypt these days—and elsewhere in the world, too. Many of them have advantages you lack: good blood and well-placed families; money to pay for the best tutors, the best clothes, the brightest jewels. You must learn to shine brighter than they if you hope to reach your full potential. And you should strive to reach it, Doricha, for a hetaera who does well may earn enough coin to buy her freedom from her master. In a few short years, you could be a free girl again."

Doricha's eyes widened. The breath stopped in her throat.

"If any hetaera wishes to do *that* well," Iadmon said, "she must distinguish herself. I have been in this business a long time; believe me when I tell you that it's not easy to stand out, to win the affection and trust of rich men who can help you, who can give you the coin you will need. And all the other hetaerae in the world, Doricha—all those other women will be trying just as hard as you, competing for the same men, the same gold. Women can be hard-willed... cut-throat."

She bit her lip.

"I am taking a gamble on you, child. If you become the entertainer I believe you can be—if you live up to the potential I see in

you—then you will make me very wealthy *and* will win your freedom, too."

"Are you not very wealthy already, Master?"

Iadmon laughed softly. "Here is your first lesson about
wealthy men—heed it well: rich men always desire more riches.
That has ever been the way of the world, since the gods first made
it. In that regard, I am no different from any other rich man. But
you won't only enrich me, Doricha. Nor will you merely buy back
your freedom. You may also send money to Thrace—to see to the
needs of your family."

Her heart pounded all the harder. "I... I reckon I'd like that
very much, Master."

"Good," he said. "It's always best to have some motivation,
some reason to work especially hard. If you succeed, you will
make us all rich—even your mother and the rest of her children.
But if you fail, Doricha—if you are not strong enough to face the
other hetaerae, to fight for the wealth that could be yours—you
may find yourself knocked down to the status of a common
porna. Or worse, you may end up in the river, dead at the hands
of some rival who is fiercer and cleverer than you. I think I've
judged you well, and you are sharp enough to rise to the task. But
are you brave enough to make a good attempt? Brave enough to
learn the ways of a hetaera?"

Doricha wrapped her thin arms around her body, holding
back a shiver. "Do I have any choice, but to try?"

Iadmon smiled again, that slow, silky curve of his lips. "You do
not have a choice—not truly. But I will tell you something else,
child: you are an investment. I am prepared to sink a considerable
cost into you, to wager much on this gamble called Doricha. I
speak not only the two hundred hedj I paid your mother, but of
all the costs that are yet to come: good food, a safe home, fine
clothes, the best tutors money can buy. I won't push you harder
than I think you can bear, for that would only snuff you out, like a
lamp's flame in a persistent wind. I didn't become rich by wasting

my money. All I expect in return for my investment is that you will not squander my time."

Doricha's brow furrowed. She drew a ragged breath. "That seems... reasonable enough, I reckon. Master."

"Very good." Iadmon turned, gesturing to the ramp—to the *Samian Wind*, ready at its moorings. "Then let's be aboard, and off. A new life awaits you. A new venture awaits us both."

"We're leaving Tanis, Master?"

"Of course," Iadmon said with a dismissive shrug. "A man like me doesn't live in a backwater such as this."

"Then where do you live, Master, if I may ask?"

Iadmon climbed the ramp with eager steps. Doricha trailed behind, holding her thin arms out stiffly to balance on the swaying plank of wood.

"In Memphis, girl. Memphis—the greatest city in the world!"

BEHIND THE WALL

IADMON GESTURED OUT OVER THE RAIL OF THE *SAMIAN WIND*, ONE grand sweep of his arm to take in the whole deep-green swath of the Nile Valley that spread before them. That carpet of emerald lushness was interrupted by a great, pale-golden mass of sun-reflected brightness, a sprawl of mudbrick and stone that demarcated the vast capital city of Egypt.

"Memphis," Iadmon said, as proudly as if he owned the whole city. "The most beautiful place the gods ever made. Your new home, Doricha."

She stood at her ease beside her master, shielded from the fierce sun by the shadow of the boat's taut red sail. Doricha was quite comfortable now on the water, after several days of sailing south against the strong Nile current. She was comfortable with Iadmon, too. She hadn't been able to forget that she was a slave—property, bought and sold—but at least Iadmon was a respectful master, and even, when his mood was good, a kind one.

He had shown no interest in abusing or molesting Doricha as they'd left Tanis behind. In fact, Iadmon had cared for her quite well, providing her with plenty of nourishing food—bread and beer, smoked fish and tart citrus fruits that made her lips pucker and the corners of her mouth burn in a pleasant way. He had watched her carefully to ensure she ate slowly, too, for (as Aesop, sitting beside her, had explained) a starved belly often revolted when too much food was crammed in, and a sickly little thing like herself might not recover from a bad bout of vomiting. He had seen to it that Doricha was washed and groomed by his female servants, sweet-tempered ladies who had been patient with her wincing and hisses of pain as they combed out the tangles in her red-gold hair. And Iadmon had dressed Doricha in a tunic of soft white linen with a bright-blue belt—simple, yet still much finer than anything she could remember wearing before.

With Memphis in sight, after days of learning Iadmon's temper and habits and his calm, patient ways, Doricha felt sure that her master was the type of man whom she could grow to respect—could even *like*, if a slave might hold any real affection for the person who owned her. Iadmon seemed honest and forthright enough to please anyone, though Doricha held full judgment in reserve. She was insightful enough to realize that at the age of twelve she couldn't quite trust herself to be the keenest observer of men's characters. But she did appreciate Iadmon's direct conversation, which did not seem to hide anything from her, even when the topics they discussed were not altogether pleasant. She appreciated his careful clarity. Every afternoon on their journey, Iadmon had sat with Doricha on cushions beneath the *Samian Wind*'s curtained canopy to discuss the weeks and months ahead. He told her everything he could think to tell about the training she would receive, the ways he planned to shape and mold her until she became the high-class, competitive hetaera he expected her to be. Iadmon never minced a single word, even when his descriptions of the acts she would one day perform made Doricha blush and squirm. "It is best that you be prepared, that you meet your work head-on and undaunted," he had told her. And Doricha agreed.

The *Samian Wind* turned its nose toward a large estate at the city's northern edge. The property was surrounded by a high, white wall; Doricha could see little of what lay within that enclosure, save for the upper edge of a roof-top, flat and expansive and bristling with potted shade palms, their fronts stirring gently in the afternoon breeze. A long stone quay, darkened by age and the river's dampness, reached like a welcoming hand toward them.

"Home," Aesop said, coming up behind Doricha. He leaned on the boat's rail beside her, so she stood between Aesop and Iadmon, between her master and her tutor.

When Iadmon had announced that morning that Aesop was to oversee Doricha in all things—her training, her education, her induction into Memphis society—she had been so delighted she had clapped her hands and hopped in place, the soles of her new sandals tapping on the boat's deck. She had grown to like Aesop even more than she liked Iadmon. On the journey from Tanis, Aesop had often entertained Doricha with riddles, and whenever she would start to sniffle over her family, or gaze wistfully back over the ship's stern toward the distant, vanishing Delta, the short, slightly hunched man would distract her with funny tales about talking animals who played clever tricks on one another. Aesop was not only sharp-witted and wise, but kind enough to see Doricha's pain and offer his stories to relieve her of her wretchedness, even if only for a short while.

Iadmon's crew furled the red sail of the *Samian Wind*. Doricha retreated with Aesop to the boat's mast, watching with fascination as the men worked together to moor the boat at the dark stone quay. They were like the many legs of a spider or a centipede, moving in a perfectly coordinated dance. The *Samian Wind* came to rest gently against its pier. The boat's narrow ramp ran out with a great, ringing clatter.

Iadmon was, of course, the first to descend the ramp. He left Aesop to look after Doricha; she watched as the master in his vibrant yellow *chiton* and perfectly draped, gently rippling *chlamys* strode along the quay toward his home. The white wall of his grand estate featured a towering, double-doored gate, painted the turquoise color Egyptians loved. The gate's two faces were crossed by great, glittering straps of polished bronze. It swung open at Iadmon's distant shout. Beyond lay a garden in full bloom—a riot of colors that blazed enticingly in the sun. Doricha watched Iadmon disappear amid that clamor of brightness. He seemed the very key she needed to unlock a luminous new world, one full of endless possibilities.

But there is still a wall around that world, Doricha thought, squinting at the estate. *Rather a high wall, too.*

"Come." Aesop took Doricha by the hand and led her down the ship's ramp. His skin was warm and soft, as unmarked by labor as Iadmon's. But it would have been a grave mistake to assume that Aesop was idle. By now, Doricha knew that the work Aesop did for their master was not physical, but mental—and no less onerous for that. Iadmon's reliance on Aesop was plain to be seen. So was his courteous treatment of the slave. Aesop seemed satisfied quite with his lot in life, as far as Doricha could tell—and how not? His deformity was mild, yet still it was evident. A person like Aesop could hope for little in life. And here he was, the closest confidante of a very rich man—the most valued member of his household.

Reckon I can rise as high as Aesop someday, Doricha told herself. *Only I won't stay with Iadmon, no matter how kind he treats me. I'll buy my freedom and go back to Thrace as soon as the gods will allow it.*

The plank wavered and bounced beneath their feet; Doricha kept her eyes on the turquoise gate and avoided looking down into the dark green depths of the water below. She could feel a breath of coolness rising up from the surface of the river, brushing the bare skin of her legs with gentle fingers. It was a refreshing sensation—even enticing. But the boat's ramp was narrow and wobbly, and a fall to the river or the quay would be long. She breathed a tiny sigh of relief when she stood on solid ground again. The pier seemed to sway beneath her, rising and falling almost imperceptibly with the remembered rocking of the *Samian Wind*. But all reason told her the quay was as bone-solid as any patch of dry land the gods ever made. It was only a trick her head played on her, to feel the ground move the way the river and the boat had moved.

Aesop's movement was just as strange as the phantom swaying beneath her feet. His gait shambled, no doubt due to the same mild deformity that hunched his shoulders. Doricha had to slow her natural pace so that she could follow him, but that gave her more time to take in the glories of Iadmon's garden. As soon as she and Aesop passed beneath the high, flat-topped arch of the gate, a world of sweet delights unfolded to either side. Symmetrical beds lined the footpath, each one carpeted thickly with black Nile silt and crowned with heaps of flowers. The flowers were like the colored clouds of sunset, come down to rest against welcoming earth. The atmosphere within the walls was peaceful and still, laced with the notes of birdsong and under-scored by the hum of the bees that bobbed from one blossom to the next. Perfumes of lilies and roses hung sweetly in the air, delightful after so many months in Tanis's stinking back district. Doricha walked along leisurely behind her tutor, breathing in the honey-sweet air so deeply that her head was soon quite dizzy.

Presently, Doricha and Aesop left the well-ordered peace of the garden behind. They entered the blue shade of a huge portico, its timber roof held up by a row of pillars. The pillars, like the great house they adorned, were made of pale, prim lime-stone and painted in bands and of bright, angular figures—old Egyptian art that spoke of long tradition and great power. A double door, painted, like the gate, in the bright turquoise-blue of a summer sky, stood open in welcome—but Doricha checked on its threshold.

"What's the matter, child?" Aesop turned back, concern plain on his broad face.

"It's all so fine and beautiful," Doricha said. "I feel as if I don't belong."

He chuckled and grinned at her indulgently. "But of course you belong. You are Iadmon's now—his special investment. You are as much a part of this place as flowers in the garden or the ship standing at the quay."

Aesop held out his hand, but Doricha did not take it right away. She paused a moment longer, staring apprehensively at the high roof of the portico, the bold-painted design of hunters pursuing birds and hippopotamus among river swaying reeds. *Can I truly belong here?* Doricha wondered. She didn't think she truly could, no matter how long Aesop and her master trained and shaped her. But her tutor was waiting. Doricha did not want to make him feel impatient. She slipped her hand into his, and Aesop led her inside.

The portico gave way to a spacious hall, its floor made of limestone so pale and smooth-polished that it shone like silver. Niches lined the entryway, and each one housed a small statue of a god or goddess. Doricha gazed at them in open wonder as she passed. Some of the gods were Egyptian—straight-backed, stern-faced, posed with stiff, proud strides. Many of them had animals' heads on human bodies, a curious feature of Egyptian deity that Doricha had never quite grown used to, despite the two years her family had spent in that country. Other gods were Greek, and more familiar. She recalled them distantly, summoning up memories of visits to the temples in Thrace. She recognized Bacchus with his wide, wild grin and his crown of cascading grapes. And there was Eirene, mistress of peace. There stood Boreas, the North Wind, whose gusty breath made it possible to navigate the River Nile.

Best of all—the most bracing and encouraging sight—was Strymon, Lord of Rivers, with his thick, curly, wind-blown beard and his great vessel raised up to his muscular shoulder, pouring out endless currents of water. True Greeks like Iadmon respected Strymon, of course—for in what land is a river not considered sacred? But Strymon meant more to Doricha than Iadmon or Aesop could have guessed. The river god was the father of Thrace, Doricha's homeland. It gave her a tiny seed of hope to find Strymon here, of all places.

Aesop noted Doricha's fascination with the niches. "They are beautiful statues, aren't they?"

"Oh, ah, yes," she replied. "Every one is so pretty. Why, they're all painted so finely. And look here, this cat goddess has a jeweled collar round her neck!"

"Iadmon demands the finest things in life, and he gets them," Aesop said.

"But does he worship all these gods? There are so many!"

Aesop smiled wryly. "Let us say that our master hedges his bets. He is prudent and careful. Come; there is much more to see."

Beyond the hall of gods lay a room floored with plush carpets and ringed all about with high couches made of ornately carved wood. The couches were strewn with stacks of linen-white pillows; each one had its own small table, too.

"The *andron*," Aesop said, noting the direction of Doricha's awed stare. "It is the men's room. The master and his male guests take their meals there, and enjoy their entertainment there, too."

"Do Egyptian women eat in so fine a place, too?"

"The andron is a Greek custom, not Egyptian. Egyptian women and men mingle in ways that most Greeks find quite shocking, I assure you. Did you not have separate dining rooms at your home in Thrace?"

She blushed, looking down at her toes. They were scrubbed clean now, and seemed very slender and frail in her ornately stitched sandals. "We were poor in Thrace, though not as poor as we were in Egypt. Our home was very small and humble-like."

Aesop smiled gently and answered her original question. "No, Doricha; the women's room—the *gynaeceum*—is not as fine as the andron. But the women's room is prized more for its seclusion and peace than for its richness. The gynaeceum is a comfortable room, though—I can assure you of that. Iadmon's female servants and slaves use it quite happily; it is their retreat from their cares. When his guests bring their wives or daughters, they gather in the gynaeceum, too. You will join them there, now and again. But more often than not, you'll be here in the andron, learning how to pour wine and serve men."

She looked up again, taking in the fine, luxurious room, imagining important men of means reclining on the couches. The thought of being the only female creature in that room, flitting about with a wine jug, made sweat spring up on her back and beneath her arms.

Aesop noted her discomfiture. He drew her away from the andron, further into the depths of Iadmon's home. "You needn't worry about the serving. I will train you carefully, and will be there in the shadows to correct you until you're so skilled at it, anyone would believe you'd been born to the task."

He noted a woman crossing the hall ahead. "Helena, this is Doricha, our new girl. She's to become a hetaera someday. You'll see her settled into her chamber, won't you? I sent word ahead that a chamber should be prepared."

Helena smiled and nodded. She was an older woman, well into her fourth decade, with the honey-brown skin and black hair of a native-born Egyptian. Like Aesop and Doricha, Helena was draped in a loose tunic of white linen, belted with a bright-blue sash. The tunic and sash were the marks of Iadmon's slaves, Doricha realized.

Helena reached out a motherly hand. Doricha went to her, with one wide-eyed glance back at Aesop.

"You needn't worry," Aesop said as Helena led Doricha away. "I'll see you in the morning, first thing. But you are no doubt tired, and need your rest now. Go with Helena; she will take good care of you." With that, Aesop vanished, disappearing down another corridor to tend to some other business of Iadmon's. Doricha turned and followed sedately behind Helena.

The halls of the master's house echoed with the sound of Doricha's footsteps. Helena was quiet and patient, not threatening in the least—yet still Doricha shivered in her company. She had grown to know Aesop over the days of their voyage from Tanis. Without him, she felt hopelessly alone and exposed in a world that was far too grand for an urchin like her.

Helena steered Doricha toward a narrow door. She opened it to reveal a chamber that was nearly as small as the door itself. There was just enough space for a small bed. A pitcher of water and a bowl for washing perched on a narrow wooden stand; a chamber pot rested underneath the stand. A tiny window, hardly more than a slit in the limestone, was recessed into the wall opposite the door. It glowed with afternoon light.

"Not as fine as the rest of the house," Helena said in accented Greek, "but all the slaves have the same sort of room. Simple, yes —but comfortable enough for living."

Doricha stepped inside and looked about, numb with dismay. She was used to small rooms—that didn't bother. But she wasn't used to being alone. Her family's home in Thrace had been small, just as she'd told Aesop, but Doricha had never been lonely inside it. Her mother or her father had always been near, and later Aella and the boys had come along, filling the house with their squalls and their laughter. Doricha had never had a room entirely to herself. Nor had she ever slept alone. She didn't know how to sleep without her sister kicking her or the twins rolling over and pulling the blankets off in the middle of the night.

"It's time for evening meal," Helena said. "Normally we all eat together in the gynaeceum, but I'll bring you a bite here. Just you settle in today; the bed is small, but it's good and soft. There aren't luckier slaves in all of Memphis."

The door closed softly. Doricha was alone with the silence, alone with the single beam of light that spilled in through the narrow window. Specks of dust swirled slowly in the light, glittering like gold, but no shimmer of beauty could trick Doricha's eye. Now, at last, she saw her situation for what it truly was. She crossed the few steps to her window and peered outside. The garden was wide, bursting with color; its sweet breath drifted to Doricha on the breeze. The flowers might have cheered her, if not for the fact that beyond them she could see the wall. Towering, solid—immovable limestone—it hemmed in all Iadmon's possessions with a sweep of its massive, unbreachable arms. Iadmon's estate... everything he owned. She was his property now, as surely as any pretty rose or slender lily in the garden. There was no way to get beyond that wall without her master's permission—without her master's will.

Reckon it'll be a long time before I'm good enough at this business to buy my way free, Doricha mused darkly. *And maybe I never will be good enough, after all.*

As a poor laborer's daughter in Thrace, and even as a street rat in Tanis, Doricha had at least been free to come and go as she pleased. But now even that scanty freedom had met its end.

The blue sash around her waist seemed to constrict like the coils of a hungry snake. Doricha tugged at the sash, trying to loosen it, but it was tied quite firmly. Tears blurred her eyes.

Suppose I ought to be grateful, she thought. *He didn't put rings in my ears or nose, nor tattoo my skin.*

She had seen ringed and tattooed slaves before. Even a collar would have been harder to bear than a mere sash, for only beasts wore collars. She blinked, but the tears would not clear from her sight.

Presently, Helena brought Doricha's supper, a simple but nourishing meal of flat bread, stewed figs, and a cone of soft white cheese, accompanied by strips of something red-brown, dry, and hard. Doricha picked up one of the hard, red bits and examined it. A piece of hide? What good would that do her? After Helena had gone, Doricha sniffed the dry strip and realized it was the preserved flesh of some pungent, oily fish. She dropped it back onto the tray with a clatter.

She had no appetite, not even for the sweet figs. She left the tray untouched beside the pitcher of water and the washing bowl, and crawled up on the bed. There she drew her legs up against her chest and pressed her back against the cold stone wall, just as she had done in Tanis when Iadmon had come for her. The stillness of the room was stifling. She rocked herself gently from side to side and tried to hum a Thracian lullaby. But the tune stuck in her throat and only made her eyes burn all the worse.

Some time later—and hour or two, to judge by the paling of the garden light, the bluish tint of dusk—Helena came back for the tray. The dark-haired woman looked silently at Doricha's untouched supper for a long moment. Then she turned a look of unbearable pity on Doricha herself. Doricha couldn't stand the sight of Helena's eyes, strained at their corners and eloquent with soft-hearted sympathy. She buried her face against her knees and refused to look at the slave woman again, refused to speak.

"Child," Helena said softly, "you must eat your food."

Doricha made no reply. The river wind moved fitfully in the garden outside, and in its breathy whisper she thought she could hear faint murmurs of the Thracian tongue.

"It's not as bad as that," Helena tried again. "Iadmon is a kind and generous master. You'll be treated well here—very well."

The snake-gripping tightness had moved from Doricha's middle to her chest, though her sash was still in its place. She breathed steadily, slowly, trying to dispel the pain that banded her ribcage. Trying not to weep.

After a few more moments Helena went away, leaving the tray of food on the wash stand. Doricha lifted her face from her knees and blinked at the gathering gloom. Her eyes stung terribly, though she hadn't shed a tear. Tears would do her no good now.

There was a soft tap at her door. And then it was pushed open again, before Doricha could give permission to enter—but of course, she was a slave now, and slaves had no right to privacy. She turned sharply at the intrusion, peeved more by her helplessness to prevent it than by the intrusion itself. Then she paused and nearly smiled. For it was not Helena who stood in the doorway, nor Iadmon. Aesop was there, holding the shallow bowl of a stone lamp, a dark curve against his pink palm. The lamp's small flame danced so merrily that it almost seemed to mock Doricha's sorrow. But she liked the way it lit Aesop's face, giving a decidedly friendly glow to his dark eyes, sending shadows to dart and play amid the tight black curls of his beard.

Aesop smiled at her gently. He crossed the room with his shambling gait and set the lamp carefully on the window's narrow ledge.

"May I sit with you?" he asked.

Sniffling, Doricha nodded.

"It's never easy to reconcile ourselves to the great changes that come to our lives. Is it? But they do come to every life, Doricha, whether we will them or no. Upheaval rocks us to our very foundations. But we all experience it, great and small, young and old... master and slave."

Aesop leaned back against the cool stone wall, gazing up into the deep shadows that congregated near the ceiling. "I, too, am a slave. Did you know that?"

Doricha shrugged her thin shoulders. "You have the blue sash, so I thought you must be. Only you don't seem like a slave to me."

"And how do slaves seem?" There was a hint of laughter in his words, but he was not mocking, not unkind.

"Suppose there's a word for it, but I don't know what it is," Doricha said. "Quiet-like, as if they've been walked upon, and were just about ready to give themselves up and become like dust on the ground."

"Subdued," Aesop suggested.

Doricha wiped her nose with the back of her hand. "Suppose that's about right, and all."

"I have met many free men who are subdued—who are ready to give themselves up."

"But a free man can go wherever he pleases."

Aesop nodded slowly. "That is so. We may not go where we please, you and I. Nor can Helena, nor the other slaves of Iadmon's household. But we can choose to bear ourselves with dignity."

Doricha turned a hard frown on him—on her only friend in the world. "I don't see what dignity there is in being owned like a goat or a dog. I won't be happy about it, so don't tell me I ought."

"No, child. I would never tell you that." He touched her cheek gently, brushing away the lone tear she'd allowed to fall. "The thing itself—slavery—is nothing to be glad about. But you can be happy for the sake of your family. You made a great sacrifice for their sake, Doricha. You very likely saved their lives. And that is something to be glad about, don't you think?"

The tears Doricha had held back for so long flooded her burning eyes and spilled down her cheeks. She sobbed raggedly against her knees, wordless with the terrible, mingled force of love and despair. Aesop laid his arm around her shoulders until the worst of her crying had passed.

When she'd subsided into sniffles, he said, "I haven't always lived with Iadmon, you know. He bought me in Samos from a man called Xanthes—a slave-trader like Iadmon, but not as pleasant a person. Far more shrewd and particular about his money, that one was. And I have seen masters who were more unpleasant still."

"Where did you come from?" Doricha asked. "Before Samos, I mean."

"I was born in Kush. Do you know where Kush is?"

She shook her head, watching Aesop intently now. Until this

moment she hadn't thought of him as a man who'd come from anywhere—a man with a past, with a family like her own. A man who had lost what she had lost: freedom, dignity, love.

"Kush is a great, wide kingdom to the south and east of Egypt. The headwaters of the Nile flow from there, and we have other rivers in Kush, too—much like the Nile, but not quite so long or broad."

"Do you remember it well?" Doricha's memories of Thrace were painfully vivid and near, though she hadn't seen her homeland for years. The high, green mountains cloaked in cool shade; the scent of pine on the wind; the roar of sea waves against rocky shores—it seemed the memories were as much a part of her body as her flesh and bones were.

"I do not remember Kush especially," Aesop said. "I know I came from a small village on a hot, dry plain. I know that I was taken from my family by raiders when I was very young—three or four years old. The twist in my spine hadn't shown itself yet, and I suppose the raiders thought I would grow up to be a strong and likely lad. They must have thought to sell me as a mercenary, or perhaps a fighter in the Roman games. But I turned out—" He gestured to his shoulders, the awkward tilt of his head— "As you see me."

"How did you survive?" Caught up now in his story, Doricha leaned toward him, eyes wide and heart pounding. "Didn't they think to kill you, since you couldn't be sold?"

"Ah, but I could be sold—and at great profit, too. I saw the bend in my spine as a blessing, not a curse, for it kept me out of combat. Even with a perfectly fit body, I feel certain I never would have made a good fighter; it's simply not in my nature. But I had talents I could cultivate, Doricha. Even as a slave, I saw that I could give myself great worth and make myself valuable— perhaps even indispensable—to those whom I served.

"I proved my wit and cleverness by telling stories every time I had the chance. I made riddles to amuse those around me—

fellow slaves, and others, too—and I turned the simplest observations of human nature into tales that could charm my masters. Soon I gave my stories a certain polish that looks very much like wisdom, if you see them in the right light. Once my masters began to think of me as a wise man, I rose in their esteem. They gave me access to knowledge no other slaves had. I learned to read and write; I learned numbers and sums. And every new skill I mastered added to my worth."

"Do you mean," Doricha said, "your masters sold you on for a good profit?"

Aesop smiled again. "Yes, that is partly what I mean. But when I say 'worth' I am not only referring to the price each new master paid for me. Even though I was owned—and am owned still—all the seeds I have cultivated within have borne great harvests of fruit. I have worth to *myself*, Doricha, because I have made myself a capable man. However great Iadmon deems my value, he cannot value me more than I do myself."

She sat in thoughtful silence, watching the lamp's flame gutter in the evening breeze. At last, she said, "S'pose that's what you mean by a slave having dignity. But it still seems a hard thing, to feel worthy while I can't even go to the market or the river when I please."

"It is a hard thing; I don't deny it. And, my child, I don't propose that you reap a harvest of worth overnight. Those fruits take time to grow. Like the green things in the field, or out there in the garden, the seeds must first be sown, and then the tender shoots must be nurtured. You are young, with little experience of the world. It takes time and thought, and a great deal of looking within, to find dignity in the face of circumstances like ours. Just remember this, Doricha: Whenever a man builds a house, he must lay the first brick. Yes?"

She smiled in agreement.

"One brick at a time," Aesop said, "you will build your self-worth. And if I know you, by the time you've finished you will be a tower as tall and strong and beautiful as the Great Pyramids."

"What's my first brick to be, then?"

"That's for you to decide," he answered, sliding off the bed and eyeing Doricha's untouched tray of food. "But if you wish to start with pride, then I think you have cause to be proud of the kindness and mercy you showed your family. They will bless your name and sing your praises to the gods—I have no doubt of that."

He picked a fig from the tray and popped it into his mouth, chewing with great relish. Doricha's stomach rumbled loudly; the cramp of hunger pinched hard at her belly.

But she couldn't make herself face her supper yet. She watched Aesop for a long moment, then said cautiously, "Do you remember your family? Out there in Kush?"

Aesop's face went still; his eyes took on a haze of distance, but he didn't seem upset—merely thoughtful. At length, he said, "I was very young when the raiders took me. Sometimes I can remember my mother's face. I catch a fleeting glimpse of her behind my closed eyelids, or I see her in the crowd at the market square, but when I turn to look more closely, she is gone. I remember her voice—not the exact words she said to me, or the lyrics of her songs. But I remember how she sang to me at night, to lull me to sleep. And there was always love in her voice. I will never forget her entirely, Doricha. I will always feel her love for me—here." He laid a hand over his heart.

Doricha drew a deep breath, feeling the ragged beat of her own heart. She slipped off the bed. Her legs ached from the hours she had spent there; they trembled from the weakness of hunger. But when she scooped up cheese with a scrap of bread and put it into her mouth, she felt a little steadier, a little stronger.

"That's a good girl," Aesop said. He helped himself to one more fig, then folded back the blanket on Doricha's bed and thumped her cushion to fluff it. "When you've eaten every bit, you must sleep. Brick by brick, we will build you up, and you'll need plenty of rest for the building."

Doricha nodded, cheeks stuffed with the sweet figs, while Aesop considered the lamp on the window sill.

"If I leave the light here for you," he said, "you won't start a fire with it, will you?"

Doricha shook her head and swallowed the figs.

"Good." Aesop kissed her brow. "Then I'll see you in the morning, child. Sleep well."

When Doricha's belly was full, she climbed into bed and pulled the soft blanket of linen and wool up to her chin. Evening had settled over the garden, a purply-blue dimness pricked here and there by the points of early stars. She had forgotten to blow out the lamp's flame. It went on dancing against the shadows, casting a brave sphere of light out into a cold and darkening world.

Leave it, Doricha told herself. *The light's cheerful and pretty.*

Iadmon was a rich enough man that he would never moan about the wasted oil.

❧ 4 ❧

THE FAVOR OF LUCK

THE SMELL OF PINE WAS SWEET IN THE WARM AUTUMN AIR—PINE and damp leaves, and blue shade beneath the evergreen trees. Doricha closed her eyes, listening to the rushing of the waves, the cry of white birds as they glided over the surf that murmured and foamed somewhere far below, around the rocky feet of the seaside cliffs. She drank in the sounds and smells of her home as if she would never set foot on Thracian soil again. But of course, that was ridiculous. She was home. Where else could she be? The wind caressed her cheek and tangled the ends of her rosy-gold hair. The cool bite of the autumn wind raised a pleasant flush across her skin. Home. Where else could she be?

She heard voices behind her, somewhere up the slope of the hill that led to a little house under a bower of pines. They were children's voices—Aella singing, high and sweet, and the twins, Bolin and Belos, laughing as they conspired in mischief.

Doricha turned toward Aella's song, but she couldn't find her sister among the trees. Nor could she find the path, carpeted with years of dried pine needles, that stretched from the seaside cliffs to the house. They were gone, swallowed in an unrecognizable tangle of branches.

"Aella?" She called.

Only the sea birds answered.

Doricha tried again, shouting louder for her sister. The twins' laughter receded, vanished into the whisper of wind through the trees. And the whisper grew louder, and louder still, increasing to a roar of blood in her ears. The roar pounded like drums, beating in time with her racing heart.

Aella spoke from somewhere nearby, sudden and loud, but still invisible behind the wind-lashed pine boughs, no matter which direction Doricha turned. "You didn't say good-bye."

Doricha bolted upright in her narrow bed. Her heart pounded so hard in her chest that she could practically feel it shaking her thin, fragile frame. She clutched the edge of her blanket, wrinkling the linen in her fists as she strained to hear over the sound of her ragged breathing. She searched the close air of her chamber for the scent of pine.

But there were no sea birds crying, no laughter, no songs. And certainly no Aella in the small chamber of Iadmon's estate. There was only the twittering of small garden birds, drifting in through her narrow garden window along with the first blush of morning light. None of the birds sang with calls she recognized—the birdsongs of Thrace. The air already smelled of heat, though the sun had hardly risen—heat and dry earth and sun-bleached grain. The smells of Egypt.

Fool, Doricha told herself bitterly. *Nothing has changed since last night, and shame come to you for hoping it had.* She was still a slave, still a captive locked up tightly in Iadmon's pretty cage. And she was still in Egypt. Hot, dry, flat and stifling Egypt, where she would remain until the end of her days.

The sheets of her bed were damp with sweat. She had been in Egypt nearly three years but still hadn't grown used to the thick, sticky heat. *Even early in the morning and all, when it decently ought to be cool. S'pose I'll never feel at home here. Not truly.*

Doricha slipped out of bed and wondered what she ought to

do with her belt and tunic. She'd fallen asleep in them; both were rumpled and creased now. She pulled them off and slung them over the foot of her bed, then splashed herself all over with water from her pitcher. The water ran in tiny rivulets along the floor, toward a few drain-holes set along the bottom of the wall, each the width of a finger. Washing up refreshed Doricha somewhat. The water sluiced away the worst of the night's sticky sweat, if not the clinging residue of her dream.

As she returned the water pitcher to its stand, Doricha noticed a fresh white tunic hanging on a peg beside the door. She didn't know whether it had appeared there during the night— delivered, perhaps, by dark-haired Helena—or whether she had simply failed to notice it the night before, wrapped as she was in her misery. Either way, its fortuitous appearance gave her a small stirring of confidence. She pulled the fresh garment on over her head, shook out the worst of the wrinkles from her blue sash, and tied it tightly around her waist. Then she ran her fingers through her hair until she felt no more sleep-tangles, though each time she encountered a knot she winced with the pain of it.

Dressed and as presentable as she could ever hope to be, Doricha stared at the door to her narrow chamber, chewing her lip and wondering what she ought to do. She was a smart enough girl to know that a slave couldn't simply wander about at will. *Reckon that's exactly what it means to be a slave, and all.* But could she leave her room without permission? There was no one present to tell her what she may do—what she *must* do.

Tentatively, she pushed the door open and peered out into the hall beyond. The pale stone corridor was perfectly still and utterly empty. Doricha edged through the door, first one slow, hesitant footstep, a pause, and then another.

All at once, a spry little brown figure sprang up from the floor, so close and sudden that Doricha leaped backward through the doorway, stifling a shriek of fear. She caught herself in the next moment, chiding herself inwardly. It was only a little boy. He must have been crouching on his heels beside the door, waiting for Doricha to awake.

The boy was perhaps six or seven years old, to judge by his size, and he wore the blue sash of Iadmon's property. But he kept his face turned down to the floor as he spoke. His voice was soft, his words barely audible as he muttered toward his sandals.

"What, now?" Doricha said. She tried to sound neither impatient nor intimidating. Doricha knew how shy little ones could be with strangers.

The boy mumbled again, then peered up at her through thick, dark lashes. When Doricha caught sight of his face, she gasped. A split ran through this upper lip, clear to the side of his nose. An unlucky feature. In Thrace, such a child would have been left for the wilderness to claim, in the very hour of its birth.

The boy's cheeks flamed red when he saw Doricha staring. He seemed to draw on some deep well of determination and said slowly, more clearly this time, "You. Are. Wanted."

Now it was Doricha who was flustered. *Aesop is expecting me, and I have kept him waiting. Or worse...* she had inconvenienced Iadmon. It wouldn't do, either way, to keep her master or her tutor waiting.

"Next time you must wake me," she told the boy gently. If she was to build her dignity brick by brick, she must prove to her master that she was reliable. A lazy girl could never be trusted.

The boy shrugged and turned away quickly. Doricha followed him along the wide, empty corridor. They passed the andron where a few slaves were clearing away the remains of a meal and made their way back through the hall of gods. The sacred statues gleamed in the early morning light that spilled in through the open double doors. Doricha imagined she could feel the gods' eyes following her as she passed—the silent judgment of the divine.

Doricha blinked against the sun's glare as she stepped out into the garden. The heat would be especially intense today.

Morning had only just broken, but already the sun raised the scent of drying leaves from the garden beds, a thick, greenish perfume that sat heavy in Doricha's chest. The birds already sounded sleepy from the heat, though a long day of foraging for seeds and flies stretched out before them.

Aesop busied himself in the open air, setting two sturdy mudbricks several paces apart on the garden path. When he had adjusted the bricks' placement, he lifted a long wooden beam and laid it across the bricks like a long, thin bridge.

He looked up from his work, caught sight of Doricha, and nodded, smiling in approval. The little boy, his errand discharged, skittered back into the hall of gods and vanished through the andron.

Aesop gestured to the shaded portico, where a small ebony-wood table waited, laden with food. "There's plenty here to break your fast. Eat, but not until you're overfull. In this heat, a full belly will be a liability, and you have much to learn today."

Iadmon had kept good stores on the *Samian Wind* so that none of his people went hungry on the journey from Tanis to Memphis. Even so, that had been food fit for travel—dried fruit, hard flat bread, and well-aged cheese. This was much fresher fare, of a quality and delicacy Doricha had never seen before in all her young life. There were ducks' eggs, boiled and peeled and coated with red-brown flecks; there were pieces of airy, leavened bread shining with olive oil and sparkling with crusts of salt. The ends of the long, dark-skinned, green melons so loved by Egyptians had been cut and hollowed out, the cup filled with honeyed wine. Instead of the preserved figs Doricha had grown accustomed to, she found fresh ones, as velvety-purple as a twilight sky, cut open to reveal the tender pink, seed-bearing flesh inside. Dishes of pomegranate seeds and tart berries—rondels of cheese, white or wrapped in the leaves of pungent herbs—roasted fish flaking off the bone. There was so much food she didn't know where to begin; Doricha stood staring at the table in delight and astonishment.

"Be quick," Aesop called from the garden path. "There is much to do, and the sooner we begin your lessons, the sooner we'll be finished."

Doricha picked up a wooden bowl and filled it with fig halves and a chunk of the soft, still-warm bread. Then she took two of the ducks' eggs and balanced them carefully atop her heap of food. She sat cross-legged against a pillar and turned to her breakfast with zeal. She was still ravenous, for a few days in Iadmon's care hadn't been enough to sate her long, enduring hunger. The figs were sweeter than she could have imagined, better than a whole comb of honey, and the eggs had been rolled in some intriguing spice, earthy and biting on her tongue. When she bit into the salted bread, she found that beneath its crust it was strewn with rosemary leaves, and the taste reminded her of the pine-covered Thracian hills. She licked salt and olive oil from her fingers slowly, one at a time, savoring the memory.

When she finished, Aesop approached, nodding down at her empty bowl in approval. Then reached a hand down to pull Doricha to her feet.

"It's good to see your appetite returning."

"Oh, the food is so delicious and so nice-made. Iadmon must have the best cooks in Memphis!"

Aesop chuckled. "I don't know about that—I'm sure the Pharaoh's are even better. But Iadmon does have... certain tastes."

A shadow veiled Aesop's face, so briefly that Doricha wasn't sure she could trust her eyes. What had she seen in her tutor, in the tight pressing-together of his lips? Was it doubt? Disapproval? Warily, she laid her bowl aside and followed Aesop out into the sunlight, wondering what could trouble him so. Hadn't Helena said—and Aesop, too—that Iadmon was a good master?

"Keep eating heartily," Aesop said, "and you'll flesh out in no time." They had reached the beam and the bricks. He gestured to the span of wood, longer than two men lying head-to-feet, its surface rough and splintery. It was raised at least three hands' breadths off the ground. "But now that you are here, in your new home, it's time to begin the training that will make you into a woman of elegance and grace."

Doricha glanced at the beam again, uncertain. Surely her knees were far too knobby and her body too thin; a bit of whittled bone like herself had no hope of elegance or grace.

"Balance will be your first lesson," Aesop went on. "You must develop the habit of carrying yourself well, for a proud carriage and a graceful step will be the foundations of all your power."

"My power?" Let Aesop talk all he pleased about bricks and dignity. Even with a wall of dignity as high as the midday sun, Doricha was still a slave. Slaves had no power.

Aesop seemed to read her misgivings on her face. He clicked his tongue in a tutting, mother-goat sort of way. "You may be a slave, Doricha, but recall the plans Iadmon has laid for you. A hetaera has great power—more than any other Greek woman, and more than most Egyptian women, too. Your confidence and your beauty will gain you access to realms where no other woman may tread. That will be your strength, your blessing— and it is a true power, regardless of the sash you wear around your waist. But we cannot allow you to go about knock-kneed and blundering like a newborn colt. You must cultivate womanly movement, womanly poise, just as a flower in the garden is culti- vated for its pleasing qualities."

Doricha was sorely tempted to cast a skeptical stare at Aesop's hunched shoulders, the awkward cant of his neck. What did this man, with his bent posture and shuffling gait, know about grace- ful, pleasing movement? But she had come to trust Aesop completely in the days since she left Tanis. Even more did she trust him now, after the gentle comfort and advice he'd provided when she had been too sorrowful to eat her supper. And so she went obediently to one end of the beam.

"Step up," Aesop said.

She did. The soles of her sandals were thin leather; she could feel the unevenness of the hewn beam as readily as if she'd laid her palm against it. The sensation made her wobble.

Aesop, standing at the beam's other end, called out his commands. "Don't look down. The ground will only disorient you. Head up; that's the way. Now, come to me."

Doricha took a deep breath and stepped out along the beam. At once her balance faltered; her arms shot out by instinct and flapped helplessly as she swayed to and fro, standing precariously on one trembling leg.

"Steady," Aesop said. "Feel with your foot."

Doricha glanced down at the beam, but as Aesop had predicted, it only made the situation worse. Both her feet came down on the beam; she stumbled about and turned until she'd lost sight of Aesop entirely, with both arms circling madly in the air. Then she tipped beyond all hope of righting herself and landed hard on her bottom in the flower bed.

She coughed, waving a cloud of dust and gnats away from her face. Aesop came quickly to her aid and pulled her to her feet once again. She heard soft, masculine laughter, but it took her a few moments to realize it wasn't coming from her teacher. Doricha blinked through the morning glare, into the shadows of the portico.

Iadmon was there, standing beside the breakfast table, leaning one shoulder casually against a pillar. He chuckled as he bit into a fig.

Doricha's face flamed.

"Are you hurt?" Aesop asked.

"Not a bit of it." She swatted at her bottom, scaring the dust away from her white tunic.

"Good. Then back up you go."

"With the master watching? I never could!"

"You can, and you will. He wants to see what you can do already, and what remains for me to teach."

Doricha went sullenly to her end of the beam. "As for what I can do already, reckon it's nothing at all, or near enough."

Aesop smiled as he took his place. "Like most things, balancing is very difficult until you find the trick of it, and then it poses no trouble at all. Now—"

Doricha didn't wait for his command. She stepped up onto the beam again and kept her eyes on her tutor, refusing to glance into the portico where Iadmon waited. She could feel the master's eyes upon her, though, and it made her task no easier, for now her heart pounded and her skin felt flushed with the heat of embarrassment. She still wobbled fearfully, but she kept her arms steady, held out like slim little counter-weights. She would not allow her arms to flap. She swung her foot carefully, felt for the beam's roughness with her sole, and planted one step, steady as she could hope it to be, in front of the other.

"Good," Aesop said.

Doricha took another slow, searching step. Then another. Half a dozen more found her at the midpoint of the beam, where it vibrated and bounced with her every movement, even though her weight was slight. *S'pose even a tiny bird shakes the branch of a tree when it lands.* She crept on for a few more hesitant paces and finally found herself almost face-to-face with Aesop. He grinned and stepped back; Doricha hopped down from the beam with a swell of satisfaction in her chest.

"Well done," Aesop said. "Now do it again."

"Again?"

"Of course. You'll keep on until you can walk the whole beam gracefully, with your arms at your sides, and at a dignified pace."

The banner of Doricha's victory fell. "Reckon I'll be doing it for weeks and weeks, then."

"I doubt it will take quite so long. Now—"

Again Doricha stepped up onto the beam before her tutor

could say another word. But as she took her first hesitant step, Aesop spoke on anyhow.

"This time, Doricha, each time you step forward you will name one of the gods of Egypt."

Doricha paused, wobbling. "But... why, Aesop?"

"When you are a hetaera, you will perform many tasks at once: entertaining, loving, engaging men in conversation—and listening. And you must do it all smoothly, perfectly, without becoming flustered or distracted."

She swallowed hard. It seemed more than an impossible task; it seemed inconceivable.

"Now, then—"

"But I don't know all the gods of Egypt!"

"You will learn. You'll observe, and remember. And little by little—brick by brick, yes?—your knowledge will grow."

She nodded, careful not to upset her precarious balance. "I'll try." What choice did she have, but to try?

Doricha stepped forward. "Horus." She stepped again. "Isis. Osiris. Set."

There she stopped, wavering near the beam's midpoint. "Afraid that's all I know, Aesop."

"Surely you've seen charms and statues in the marketplaces of Tanis. Describe the gods to me."

She stepped forward. "The one what looks like a hippopotamus, with the big dugs and the big fat belly."

Aesop laughed. "Tawaret is her name."

"The one with the head of an ibis-bird."

"Thoth, the god of knowledge."

They went on that way until she reached the far end of the beam—Doricha struggling to recall the faces of gods who were foreign to her, who held no more meaning in her heart than did the gods of Babylon or Kush, and Aesop reciting their names. But when she reached the end of the beam without falling she laughed in delight, turned in place, and re-crossed its length once. This time, she called out the names of all the gods she'd learned, but in reverse order, from the last one Aesop had named to Osiris and Isis and Horus, her final three steps along the beam.

"Very good indeed!" Aesop all but shouted his approval.

"Quick to learn." Iadmon drifted out from beneath the portico's shade, confident and smooth as a great ship cleaving the Nile waters. "What did I tell you, Aesop? I know how to choose the ones with the best potential."

"You do at that, Master."

Doricha glowed under their praise.

"More balancing," Iadmon said. "Let us see just how quickly you've learned."

Doricha obliged. She walked the beam's length quicker than she'd done before—Aesop was right; the task became easier every time—but when she reached the shivery midpoint, Iadmon calmly lifted one of his own feet from the garden path, placed it on the beam, and pressed down.

The change in weight shuddered along the beam; the predictable rhythm of its bouncing changed all at once. It almost felt as if the thing were twisting sideways under Doricha's sandals. She bit back a shriek of surprise and dismay, staggered a few quick steps forward, tipped back on one heel, and in a trice, she found herself facing the opposite direction. She didn't remember turning around, but there she was, facing the wrong way. Her feet were still on the rough, narrow thing—just barely. Momentum carried her back along its course for several fast, dancing steps; she managed to catch herself before she could fall, twirling her arms gracelessly and raising up on the balls of her feet. Doricha rocked back to stand flat in her sandals; then, when she was as steady as she could hope to be, she turned lightly around to face Iadmon and Aesop once more.

Both the men's eyes were wide, their faces still with thoughts Doricha couldn't read. Finally, after a heavy silence, Iadmon narrowed his eyes and tapped one long, graceful finger against his chin, allowing his dark gaze to travel down the length of Doricha's twig-thin body and back up to her face again. He hummed quietly to himself, appraising. Then he lowered his head and said a few quiet words in Aesop's ear.

With that, the master left the garden, moving briskly, not bothering to look back at Doricha who still stood poised on the balance beam. She watched him go, mystified and dismayed. It had been a rotten trick, to rock the board while she'd been walking it. But she had showed him, all right—she wasn't about to topple into the dust, no matter how he tried to sabotage her efforts.

When Iadmon had vanished into the house, Doricha looked pleadingly at her tutor. "What did he say?"

Aesop smiled broadly. "He said you're to be trained as a dancer. And I agree with him; you've plenty of natural grace, and it's clear you're quick on your feet. A dancer—what do you think about that?"

"I... I don't know what to think. I've never danced much before, and then only the village dances in Thrace." She restrained herself from casting a skeptical eye at Aesop's bent and twisted frame. "Will you teach me how it's done?"

He laughed heartily. "Not I! Even if I were sound of body, I'd make a poor tutor in dance. But Iadmon will find the very best teacher; have no fear on that count. He paid dearly for you, Doricha, as you well know. He intends to get his money's worth and then some."

"I'm an investment," Doricha said. "I know. Like a cow or a she-goat, what a farmer expects to bear young to sell at the market, and give milk to make into cheese, and earn back more than what was paid for me."

Aesop cringed at her rustic grammar, but he answered patiently. "That is the way of it, though I doubt Iadmon will want you bearing any young. A hetaera can't work when she is with child."

Doricha stepped down from the beam. "It was only a way of comparing."

"I took your meaning well. It was a clever analogy, my girl. An investment—yes. Assuming we can culture your talents and make a truly great dancer out of you—and I see no reason why we cannot—you should return handsomely on Iadmon's investment. All hetaerae can dance, more or less. But real talent and skill, when honed and practiced, are rare things. Excellent dancers are rare, Doricha, as are the best singers, the best actresses, the best conversationalists. If you can excel at dancing, and do it better than any other hetaera in Memphis, you'll be valuable indeed."

Doricha fidgeted in the hot sun. The sensible side of her knew Aesop was right; she was resigned to the blue sash, the inescapable fact of slavery. Yet still, something inside rebelled at the thought. *An asset, an investment. A cow at the market.* This was her life now, her reality. She couldn't change it, but neither could she make herself enjoy it.

"Assuming," Aesop muttered as he turned away, "Iadmon keeps hold of this asset."

Doricha's breath caught in her throat. Those words had been spoken so quietly, she was certain Aesop hadn't intended her to hear. She knew on the instant that she could not ask him what he'd meant; such a thing would be presumptuous. Uneasily, she squinted through the portico shade to the open doors where Iadmon had disappeared.

He wouldn't sell me on, would he? Not when he's paid so much for me and has yet to see me make any money in return.

No, Doricha decided. Iadmon would not sell her any time soon. Not until he learned whether she could dance. Thoughts of collars and tattoos flashed through her head—images of rings pierced painfully through ears, through noses. She shivered, twisting the ends of her blue sash in fingers that were suddenly cold with dread.

It won't come to that. It can't, *that's all.*

Luck had favored Doricha—as much as it ever favored a slave —by placing her in Iadmon's hands. If she wished to stay here, living in relative comfort and ease, then she must give Iadmon no reason discard her, to pass her along to a master who was less congenial with a house hard and cold.

If Iadmon wanted Doricha to become the greatest dancer in Memphis, then by the gods, she would do it. She couldn't afford to do otherwise. Doricha was determined to allow neither ignorance nor inexperience to hold her back.

5

LESSONS

THE MUSICIANS, GATHERED UNDER IADMON'S PORTICO, PLAYED A tune on their harps and drums that clipped along just a heartbeat or two more lively than Doricha would have preferred. She stepped quickly to the music, elevated on the balls of her feet. She moved in the space between the great, painted pillars with all the grace she could muster, given the quick pace of the music. The long, colorful fringe of her dancing belt swayed around her knees, tickling her skin horribly with every beat of the music, every trained and calculated movement of her limbs.

The tickling added its torment to the subtle, prickly itch of the dried paste that covered her, head to toe. Her naturally pale complexion had proven too tender for Egypt's sun, and whenever she danced outdoors—as she most often did, for there was little space inside Iadmon's house that was suitable for practice —she was required to cover herself from head to food with the protective concoction. It was made of ash, chalk, and a bit of oil. The ash mixture did the job of keeping the worst of the sun's brutal rays from burning her skin, all of which was exposed when she danced, save for the slim beaded belt around her hips with its strip of silk that ran down between her legs and up the other side. The paste made her look frightfully pale—paler than her natural coloring—and as soon as she began to sweat, it streaked and ran down her neck, down her back, and along the sides of her face. She looked ghastly in the stuff, like the spirit of a dead girl, and she never could decide whether it would be better to be scorched by the sun or prickled and itched nearly to death by the crust of ash and oil on her skin.

Doricha did her best to ignore the irritations of fringe and ash... the spider-creep along her legs and arms, and there in the middle of her back, in exactly the one spot she couldn't reach with her hands. She clenched her jaw hard to distract herself from the feeling, and whirled in time to the music, sending the fringe out to spin like a desert whirlwind around her agile legs and her slim, girlish hips.

Aesop, perched upon his folding stool beside the musicians, called out to Doricha as she danced. "What was the name of the Babylonian king who sought to invade Egypt?"

Doricha's brow furrowed, but she didn't falter in her dance. Her arms moved like two snakes, precisely at the right moment, when the music reached a sinuous transition—the flutes taking over where the harps had left off. "Many Babylonian kings have sought to invade," she said.

"In the Pharaoh's fourth hear," Aesop answered.

Doricha bent backward, arching until her palms found the smooth, flat stones of the portico floor. She kicked her feet up and over, and as she turned right-side up again, she replied, "Nebuchadnezzar, the second of his name."

Rap. The sound of Iunet's wooden staff striking the ground cut through the beat of the drums. Doricha looked to her dancing-mistress, wide-eyed and disbelieving.

"Your turn-over was slow!" Iunet barked. "Now you're off the beat."

Iunet raised a hand to cut off the music. Like her once-lovely face, the woman's hand was just beginning to show the wrinkles and spots of age.

Doricha braced her hands against her hips, panting—and trying not to look too desperate for breath while she did it. The back of her throat stung even though the air was thick with moisture, for the season of the river's flood had come, and Egypt was wet and sweet-smelling once more.

"I thought I did well that time," she protested. She looked to Aesop for support, but he only shrugged, glancing away with a sly smile. He always deferred to Iunet's judgment where Doricha's movement and rhythm were concerned.

Iunet advanced across the portico. Her fearful, thin stick waved in her hand like a drover's lash. The old dancer hadn't struck Doricha with that stick—not yet—but she never doubted that hard-eyed Iunet would not hesitate to use it as a weapon if she ever found cause to do so.

"You reached with your hands," Iunet said, "and *there* was your downfall. Do not wait for the floor to come to you, or you will lose the beat. And when you lose the beat—"

"I lose the charm and the magic," Doricha recited.

The dancing-mistress gave a brusque nod. "You must spring from your feet instead, and trust your hands to find the floor when the time is right."

"But what if the time isn't right? What if I misjudge when I ought to spring?"

"Then you'll land on your head, and you'll soon learn better. In any case—" Iunet cut a narrow-eyed glance in Aesop's direction— "your head is so overstuffed now that it will hardly hurt you to land on it a time or two. Now, bend backward."

Doricha did as she was told at once, arching sharply back from the waist. Instinctively, her fingers stretched out, feeling for the floor.

Crack! Iunet's stick sliced through the air and connected with Doricha's palms. Doricha was so contorted that she couldn't even gasp in pain; all she could do was gape, her eyes burning with sudden tears.

"Stop reaching!" the old dancer shrieked. "Spring—now! Without thinking!"

She had no desire to feel the stick again. Doricha pushed off hard with her feet before she could talk herself into greater caution. To her surprise, the floor came up to meet her outstretched hands in exactly the right way; the smooth stone even felt soothing against her stinging palms. The momentum of her leap carried her smoothly through the arc of the turn, fluid and easy.

"Do you see now?" Iunet said. She turned and marched back toward the musicians, but Doricha caught the briefest twinkle of approval in her dancing-mistress's eye.

I am doing well, no matter what she says. Doricha knew it was true; she could feel it. Each time she danced, she felt grace and strength building inside her, and confidence, too—just as Aesop had promised. Now she longed to dance every waking moment of every day, and would have done so, had Aesop and Iadmon not been there to oversee her.

Doricha had more duties, more lessons, than she would have preferred. In the seven months since her arrival in Memphis, she had spent every day at Aesop's side, learning all she could from his great store of knowledge. He had taught her everything he knew about politics, of the ways of kings and common men. And Aesop—as thoughtful and observant as he was clever—was a deep well of knowledge. From him, Doricha had learned all about Egyptian trade—the routes and goods, how wealth worked inside the Pharaoh's empire and outside of it—how trade conferred power upon men and rescinded it, too. She learned histories and gods, riddles and jokes and rhymes. She learned how to speak with culture and care—though she still had not managed to shake all the provincial intonations of backwater Thrace from her tongue. Learning excited her, for she knew that each piece of knowledge she gained was another brick in her hand, another inch gained on her tower of confidence and self-worth. And Aesop was ever a pleasant companion, patient and kind.

But it was dance Doricha loved best. When she lost herself in music, she lost all the substantial cares of her young life, too. It seemed fitting to her that in Egypt dancers went nearly naked, for when the drumbeat rose up around her and the wail of reed flutes shielded her like a screen, Doricha felt as if she were disrobing, shedding all her fears and sorrows, dropping them to the ground like an old, cast-off garment. When she danced, she knew, in the most visceral and unshakable core of herself, that she was strong and good and capable—and free. Truly free, as she never was with the blue sash tied around her waist—free, as she never could be elsewhere in her life. Through dance, she had learned to see herself as someone other than a slave. When she donned her fringed dancing belt, the only master she had to obey was the music.

And Iunet, of course.

Iunet snapped her fingers to cue the musicians. They took up nearly where they had left off, at the transition of harps and flutes. Doricha felt the keening notes of the reeds swell inside her heart, raising a curious flutter in her chest. She shivered her shoulders in time to the beat, shaking those flutters down her arms to the tips of her fingers, making the subtle, serpentine motions of graceful enticement.

"Good," Iunet said shortly.

Aesop, too, picked up where he'd left off. "What is our Pharaoh's name?"

It was such an easy question that Doricha knew it had to be a trick. As she whirled and spun, she guessed at Aesop's true meaning, and meant to surprise him with a trick of her own.

She bent back and sprang into the turn-over exactly in time with the music. "He calls himself Amasis the Second," she said in

Greek. As her feet swung up and over and she turned right-side-up again, she flung herself back into another quick, flashing turnover. This time she said in clear Egyptian, "But those who speak the Old Tongue call him Ahmose."

Doricha had said the words in a sly, teasing tone—a coy nod to the tense currents that ran through Memphis; indeed, through all of Egypt. It was a clever acknowledgment of the way true Egyptians felt about their Pharaoh. The king had done much to regain the country's glory after a dynasty of shameful foreign rule —yet he was so enamored of Greek culture that he seemed to have forgotten he was a native Egyptian.

Iunet, an Egyptian through and through, startled Doricha a raspy laugh of surprise. This time when the mistress's stick cracked against the ground, it was a display of appreciation for her wit—not a correction.

Doricha hadn't missed a beat; she danced on, grinning cheekily at Aesop.

Smiling wryly, Aesop warned, "I wouldn't repeat a jest like that one in uncertain company."

Wise counsel. There was always turmoil between native Egyptians and foreigners, especially those of Greek extraction. Tales had filtered back to Iadmon's household of innocent jests in beer shops and inns, turned in the blink of an eye to drawn knives.

Still, Aesop seemed pleased that Doricha had anticipated his trick and outmaneuvered him. He went on with his questions as she continued her dance, correcting her steps now and then whenever Iunet rapped her stick and barked out another remonstration.

At Aesop's command, Doricha ran through a recitation of the governors of all the nearest *sepats*—the districts up and down the Nile that sent their taxes and tributes to the king in Memphis. As she did so, she executed an intricate, pattering stagger-step across the portico, punctuated by yearning motions of her hands and wrists. Iadmon wandered outside to lean casually against a pillar, watching her double performance of politics and dance.

At sight of her master, Doricha's steps faltered along with her tongue. She stumbled, lowering her hands to her sides. The list of sepat governors trailed off with a graceless "Erm..."

Iunet cut the musicians off with a peeved smack of her stick against a pillar. "What is wrong with you now, girl? You were doing Reed in the Current perfectly, better than I've seen you do it before—and then in the blink of an eye you turn into a lumbering hippopotamus!"

"Sorry," Doricha mumbled. She peered at Iadmon from the corner of her eye, then looked away again quickly, her skin prickling even more than it usually did under the ointment of ash and oil.

In the months since her removal from Tanis, Doricha had seldom encountered her master, for he was often away on business, taking the *Samian Wind* to far-flung cities where he worked diligently at his trade. Although Iadmon was kind—and Doricha's initiation into to the art of dance had been his idea—she was perfectly content to remain apart from him. Doricha had never been able to forget Aesop's darkly muttered words on her first day of training, when she had practiced with the balance beam. On that day, months ago, Aesop had planted the notion in Doricha's mind that Iadmon might one day be rid of her—sell her or trade her, as he might any other asset. She had never felt easy in Iadmon's presence from that moment on.

Doricha bowed hastily, acknowledging the master's presence.

"Your dance is coming along well, Doricha," Iadmon said. "And Aesop has been teaching you well, too, I see. You are even cleverer than I suspected when I first acquired you."

"Thank you, Master."

"But you must lift up your face. A girl as lovely as you should never hide."

Lovely—me? With sweat and ash and oil streaking my skin and the fringe of my dancing-belt tangled? But Doricha did as she was told. She raised her eyes and gazed calmly at Iadmon, pretending her heart wasn't pounding.

"She has all the confidence of a hetaera," Iadmon said to Aesop, though he never once looked away from Doricha. "And twice the beauty of most of them, with that exotic coloring. I fear we may never train that accursed rusticity out of her tongue—she seems determined to retain that habit, in spite of her tutors' efforts—but her beauty and quick wit may be enough to make up for one small shortcoming."

"I agree, Master," Aesop said.

"All we need now is for Hera to touch her, and then her work may begin."

Doricha swallowed hard. Hera was certainly among those goddesses favored in Thrace. She knew what Hera's touch meant: the bleeding that signified a woman's ripeness, her readiness for a man's bed. Although it was her duty and her fate as a hetaera-in-training, still the very thought of it was enough to turn her knees to water.

Iadmon pushed himself away from the pillar and strolled casually toward Doricha. She stood still for his inspection, conscious of his eyes roving over her bare skin. Though he did not touch her, his assessment tickled and itched worse than the belt's fringe or the ointment's dryness. Finally, Iadmon laid a hand on her head, caressing her rose-gold hair, which was braided and pinned tightly about the crown of her head. Doricha's heart gave a painful lurch. For better or worse, Iadmon's household was her place in the world—her *only* place, her only hope, with her family flown back to their homeland. The fear that he might sell her, and send her off to some unknown fate, sent a sickly shiver through her bones.

"You aren't old enough yet to do the work of a true hetaera," Iadmon said, "but you have come quite far with your dance,

Doricha, and you're as sharp and bright as I'd hoped. You are certainly capable of entertaining."

He paused, smiling broadly. It was obvious to Doricha that he expected her to react with delight. She couldn't think why.

She shrugged helplessly. "I... I'm not sure, Master, what you—"

"I am hosting a party tonight—here, in the andron—to celebrate the Flood Season. These Inundation parties are an old Egyptian tradition—quaint, charming. It should be a popular diversion with some of the more powerful men of Memphis. And I will have you there tonight, to serve food and wine in the andron. Perhaps to dance for my guests, too, if the opportunity arises. It will be a debut of sorts for you—your first venture out into the world of men. What do you think of that?"

Doricha's eyes widened; she gave a little gasp of surprise. She forgot her itching skin and even the sting on her palms where Iunet had cracked her. Seven months of training had been leading up to this—her first presentation as an entertainer, the first step of her novice foot into the realm of the glittering, privileged hetaerae. A swell of nervous illness rose in her stomach, but excitement soon quelled it. At last, she would have a chance to prove herself in Iadmon's eyes—to secure her value and her place in his comfortable, easy household, so that he would never feel the need to be rid of her.

She nodded eagerly, relieved that she would finally begin stacking the bricks of her worth. "I like the idea very much, Master. Oh—ever so much indeed!"

6

BLUE SILK

As the afternoon waned, Doricha returned to her small chamber to prepare for the evening to come. Her body was sore, aching with the deep, familiar, satisfying pain of a day spent dancing. Usually, the pleasant soreness of dance cheered her and allowed her to sleep well. But now, the complaints of her muscles and bones only reminded Doricha that she was small and insignificant, and about to step into a world that was far beyond her depth.

In her chamber, Doricha lingered furtively beside the door, staring down at her toes and fidgeting with her feet, as if she were afraid the shadows in the corners of the room might see her discomfiture and mock her for it. A gleam of light caught her eye, forcing her to glance up. The bright glow of afternoon sun shone in a place it shouldn't have been—on the wall just above her wooden stand with its simple, clay-fired pitcher and wide washing bowl.

Doricha approached the stand hesitantly. The flare of sunlight changed as she neared, dimming somewhat, taming its intensity. At last, she could see that it was a mirror. Small, round, made of well-polished bronze, it hung over the pitcher and bowl, casting her reflection back at her. The natural paleness of her features was warmed and livened by the rich color of the metal.

She stared at the mirror—at her face—in frank wonder. Over the past several months, she'd had little occasion to look at herself. She had seen her arms and legs often enough, coated in the white sun-paste when she spent hours outdoors, but seldom had she looked at any of her other features. Doricha examined the face that peered curiously back at her. All traces of the urchin from Tanis were gone. Good feeding had fleshed her out, adding a healthy glow to her cheeks and a certain refinement to her features. She was, much to her surprise, rather pretty. And she was on the verge of womanhood. She could pick out the traces of it here and there—the hint of high, sharp cheekbones yet to come, a loss of softness about the nose and chin as vestiges of her childhood fell away. She stared at her mouth—plump and pink with the natural curve of a half-smile—and saw the lips of a woman, not a girl. Her hair, pinned up in its coiled braid, as usual, might have made her look more childlike if it hung loose, tangled by the wind. But piled up as it was, it made her look older than her true age of almost thirteen years.

She heard a soft tap at the door. Doricha turned to face it, waiting expectantly—she still had no right to give permission to enter, nor any right to tell a person to leave her be. The door creaked open; Aesop entered. He grinned when he saw her standing before the mirror.

"I see you've found your gift."

"Is it from you?"

"From me, and the master. Iadmon is very pleased with your progress, Doricha. He asked me to choose something nice for you at the market today—something to celebrate your achievement."

"And what is my achievement?" She gave a half-hearted laugh, trying to sound light and coy, as Aesop had taught her to sound when she spoke to men—for, as Aesop had often told her, men were put off guard by a girl who giggled and jested, and a man off guard was a man easily read, easily led.

But Doricha knew she had failed at sounding coy. She was a ball of tangled fears, a hopeless knot of anxiety. She had no idea what to expect—what she might encounter that night at Iadmon's party. She couldn't begin to guess what the night may bring, and to her dismay, uncertainty was quite enough to undo all her carefully cultivated poise.

"Your achievement," Aesop said, "is your maturity. You have come far since Tanis."

"Reckon I have," Doricha said, allowing herself to lapse back into quaint Thracian manners. "It was five days' sail at least from Tanis, wouldn't you say? Would have been ever so much farther if I'd walked the distance."

Aesop gave a grunt of appreciation. "Amusing, girl. Truly, though: you've come on in your studies better than either Iadmon or I dared to hope. Do you know, he expected it would be at least five more months until you were ready to entertain for the first time? He thought to train you for a full year before he saw any gain from his investment."

Doricha's face fell. She sank down on the edge of her bed. "But here I am, early. Such a good investment as I am, the master will be certain to turn me all the quicker."

"Turn you?" Aesop's already tilted head tipped further still. "Whatever do you mean?"

"Sell me on." Doricha fought down the lump that rose in her throat. "You said as much yourself, didn't you?"

Aesop came as near to sputtering in shock as Doricha had ever seen him. "By all the gods, girl, what are you talking about?"

Doricha breathed deeply for a few moments, calming herself, trying to order thoughts so that she could choose her words with care. A slave must always choose her words with the greatest care. "I remember when I first arrived. You made mention of

Iadmon's... habits, like. You hinted he's as much bound to get rid of me as he is to hold onto his investment."

"Ah."

Aesop grew quite sober then. He shuffled over and sat beside Doricha, close enough that she could feel the warmth of his skin. She couldn't decide whether she liked his close proximity, a reminder that she wasn't alone in this world—or whether it only made her pain all the worse, for it was certain that whatever household Iadmon sold Doricha along to, there would be no Aesop in it.

"I can tell you that Iadmon has no plans to sell you, Doricha. In fact, I can tell you with all honesty that he intends to keep you in his household for as long as he may. But you must understand something about our master. He is... well..."

Aesop seemed to grope for whatever words would make his point clearly, without giving any appearance of infidelity. Finally, he seemed to find sufficient expression for his difficult thoughts. He cleared his throat and said, "Iadmon is a man, after all—just a man. And as you know—I've taught you, yes?—all men have their flaws."

Doricha swallowed the tears that trembled in the back of her throat. "What flaws? What do you mean, Aesop? Can't you tell me plain, so I don't have to fret about it anymore?"

"The gods have given us many pleasures, but they are best taken in moderation. When we fling moderation to the wind, we can lose our mastery over ourselves, and become a captive to those same pleasures. Then our joys may imprison us, you see. We fall under their power, and they control us, so that they are no longer joys at all, but torments."

The air in the chamber seemed to go very still. The silence in the garden outside was dense and stifling.

"What pleasure has made a captive of Iadmon?" Doricha asked.

Aesop seemed about to reply, but the chamber door opened.

Both of them jumped guiltily; Doricha hadn't noticed until that moment how tense the mood was between them, how dangerous was their conversation.

But it was only Helena. She beamed at Doricha—never before had Doricha seen the Egyptian slave looking so excited—and pulled a wisp of floating silk out from behind her back. The silk was a lovely, blue-green shade, like the Nile below a clear morning sky.

"Iadmon has sent me," Helena said. "You're to wear *this* to the party! And I'm to help you prepare." She sounded as pleased as a Thracian farmer's daughter, gloating over her first harvest festival.

Doricha slipped off her bed, approaching the silk hesitantly. She lifted it and allowed it to slide through her fingers. It flowed just like water—it was as cool and soothing as the river. She turned back to stare at Aesop, wide-eyed, speechless with awe.

Aesop rose and offered the two women a polite half-bow. "I will leave you to your preparations."

Doricha found her tongue at last. She dropped the silk like a hot coal; Helena tutted and caught it up before it could fall to the floor. "Aesop, whatever will I do? I've never served men yet—except for you, and that was only in practice. Will you be there, too? Will you show me how—"

He chuckled, shaking his head. "You don't need my help, dear girl. You know how it's done. You need only imagine all the men at the feast are me—just the way we've practiced all those many times in the past, yes?"

She nodded miserably, tears stinging her eyes. "But you won't be there?"

"No; I haven't been asked to attend the master." He noted her tears and came to her, holding her by both shoulders and giving her a tiny, bracing shake. "But I won't be far away; that I can promise you. I'll watch you from afar, and afterward, I'll tell you everything you did right."

"And everything I did wrong."

"I expect your list of wrongs will be very short. You are ready for this, Doricha. You're an intelligent, capable girl. New experiences are only frightening the first time. After that, they aren't new anymore, and so there's no fear left in them. And once the heat of your fear bakes those new experiences solid, what are you left with?"

Doricha smiled, and was glad to find she didn't need to force it. "A brick."

"That's right. Another brick for your tower. Now—"

As ever, Aesop didn't need to follow that word with any further instruction. Doricha turned away from him, as steady as she would ever be, and faced Helena squarely. Uncertainty still warred within her, but after all, Aesop had spoken the truth. *What's new can only frighten me once.*

Helena said, "Off with your tunic and sash. And look, you still have some of that ash stuff on your arms. We must wash you, head to toe, before you put on such a fine and pretty silk."

Doricha removed her slave's garb as Aesop left, shutting the chamber door behind him. She tossed the tunic and blue sash aside. Helena had more than just the silk; a small basket was slung by its straps over one shoulder. She deposited it on the bed and began sorting through its contents while Doricha washed away the last streaks of her sun cream.

"Turn about so I can check you," Helena said.

Naked, Doricha did as she was told. Helena raised one dark brow. "Good enough. What you truly need for an occasion like this is a real Egyptian bath. Do you know how we do it here in Egypt? The baths are sunk right down into the floor, so you can submerge your whole body. And the water is warm and perfumed with oils. It lifts all your dirt and cares right away from your skin, so they flow away from you like the Nile's current... ahh! But we must use what we have, I suppose. Here, now; let me scent you before the silk goes on."

Helena picked up a small vial, enameled in red and blue. She pulled out its stopper and sniffed the contents, closing her eyes in a transport of luxury. "Roses and myrrh," she said with a deep, heady sigh. "The best combination."

SHE HELD the stopper out so that Doricha could smell it, too. The perfume oil was so decadent, so spicy-sweet, that it made her feel dizzy.

Helena poured a few drops into her palms, then rubbed Doricha with the perfume, massaging her tense, tired muscles until they relaxed and the oil sank into her skin.

"I feel just like an Egyptian princess," Doricha said.

Helena laughed. "You'd wear a wig if you were a princess. A big, heavy, beaded one that would look like a laden grain sack draped over the top of your head." She returned to her basket and pulled out a few more pots, then unrolled a curious scroll of leather across the bed. The leather scroll, once opened, revealed a collection of tiny brushes. "But I will paint your face like to look like a princess," Helena said. "Come."

Doricha stood before Helen, who sat cross-legged atop the bed, carefully dabbing her little brushes along Doricha's eyelids, cheeks, and lips. The paints smelled strongly of thick oils, and the red color Helena painted on Doricha's lips tasted bitter, but she held herself perfectly still while the woman did her work.

When she was done, Doricha tried to go to her mirror, eager to see what she looked like, all painted and adorned like a true hetaera. But Helena wouldn't hear of it. "Not until I've arranged your hair and dressed you. Then you can see how pretty you are."

The blue-green silk came next. Helena draped it over Doricha's shoulder, stood back to squint critically at its fall and flow, then re-draped it several times before she was satisfied. She secured its shape with a few knots, then cinched it around Doricha's waist with an embroidered sash. The sash was tied in the old Egyptian style, wrapped tightly around Doricha's bottom, with a square, low-hanging knot in front, framing the tops of her thighs.

Doricha's hair was the final touch. Helena undid the old braids, then combed the dust and sweat from Doricha's long, red-gold tresses. She worked more of the dizzy-smelling oil into her hair, combing through from roots to ends until her hair glittered in the narrow shaft of sunlight. Helena wove a new braid, fearfully intricate; Doricha could feel the woman's fingers moving deftly against her scalp, pulling strands into several different weaves, then plaiting those smaller braids together.

"It's fortunate the gods blessed you with so much hair," Helena said as she worked. "If you hadn't enough, I would have been obliged to braid more right in, but there's no one in all Egypt with hair of this color. I could never have matched it. You would have looked bi-colored, like those flop-eared goats at the marketplace."

She secured the braids with a thick bone needle and some twists of gossamer yarn, a ruddy orange color close enough to Doricha's shade that the stitches would remain mostly unnoticed. Then Helena piled the thick braid into a tall coil at the crown of Doricha's head and stitched that in place, too.

With the coiled braid rising high above her, Doricha's head felt too big for her body. It seemed to wobble precariously on her neck; the weight and height of her hair felt utterly unnatural. She moved with ostentatious care, turning her head this way and that, testing the security of Helena's stitches.

"Harder," Helena said.

Doricha shook her head as roughly as she dared.

Helena nodded. "It will hold." Then, grinning, she pulled Doricha by the hand and positioned her proudly in front of the little round mirror.

For a moment, Doricha thought she was looking at Helena's reflection in the bronze. The face that stared back at her was far too grown-up, too womanly and refined, to be her own. Even through the golden discoloration of the metal, Doricha noted the bright green powder that accented her eyes, the pink blossoms of her cheeks, the bold lines of her half-smiling mouth. Her eyes seemed twice as wide as they had been before, and they had a mysterious, enchanting air, like the sun peering through drifts of temple smoke. And her hair...! Coiled and wound back upon itself, the braid-of-braids rose to a high mound, peaked at the top and fragrant with the oil of roses and myrrh.

"Long ago," Helena said, "great Egyptian ladies wore pointed crowns of wax to rich men's parties. As the night wore on, the wax melted and dripped down into their hair. It left the scented oil behind."

Doricha saw at once what Helena had done. "Why, it's like a cone of wax that will never melt. Helena, how clever!"

Helena smiled shyly, gazing down at the floor. "I expect the master will be pleased. He told me to make you look like an old-fashioned Egyptian lady, so his guests will be properly amused."

Doricha held out the skirt of her silken gown and twirled. There was no bothersome tickling, as with her fringed dancing-belt. "I feel as rich and beautiful as one of the Pharaoh's wives."

Then she stopped spinning and let the skirt fall from her hands. Her misgivings had returned—each one with a vengeance. "Oh, but Helena! I'm ever so afraid. What if I forget something I oughtn't to, or spill wine all over one of the men?"

"You won't," Helena said with conviction. "You're too smart for that, little Doricha."

Doricha wished she could feel so confident in her abilities. Aesop hadn't had time to tell her about Iadmon's fatal flaw, his mortal failing. Until she knew what it was, she knew she would never feel entirely comfortable in his presence.

S'pose I must take special care with everything I do, even down to pouring the wine, and hope I don't give Iadmon any reason to be rid of me.

Helena eyed the slant of light at the garden window. "Now it's time you were off to the andron," she said. "The master's guests will be arriving soon."

Doricha squeezed her hand gratefully. "Thank you, Helena. I'll do my best tonight."

And pray to the gods that my best is good enough.

7

IADMON'S FLOWER

DORICHA GLANCED DOWN NERVOUSLY INTO THE PITCHER. THE purple-black circle of wine reflected her face almost as clearly as her mirror had done; the strain of fear was plain to read on her features.

You must be charming and light. Doricha could hear Aesop's words, his oft-repeated instructions, repeating in her mind. *A happy, frivolous girl is no threat to a man, and so any man, even the greatest, will let down his guard if you smile and laugh and play the flirt.* She didn't feel like bringing down any man's guard now; she didn't see what good such a feat would do her. The only thing Doricha wanted in all the world was to retreat to her tiny chamber, close the door, and pull her linen blanket up over her head, and shut out Iadmon's feast... the night... indeed, the whole world.

The andron was still empty, awaiting the arrival of the first guests. Each long wicker couch had been dressed with fresh pillows of pure-white linen and draped with colorful cloths—festive in their brightness, and useful for cleaning hands and mouths throughout the feast. Flower petals had been strewn over the cushions, too, a salute to the riotous colors and sweet perfumes the flood season brought to Egypt. Beyond the heavy draperies that separated the andron from the halls of Iadmon's house, Doricha could hear the distant murmurs of his household servants and slaves. But the voices were faint, far-off; the distant whispers only emphasized Doricha's isolation and uncertainty.

One familiar voice did seem to draw closer, though, growing more distinct all the time. If Doricha had been a hound, she would have pricked up her ears eagerly as Aesop approached. One of the curtains at the other end of the room stirred; Aesop drew it aside and led in the first of Iadmon's guests. They did not enter by the great turquoise double-doors—those that opened into the garden and gave access to the quay beyond; the ones by which Doricha had entered upon her arrival. Instead, the guests came in by the formal entry, a walled courtyard that connected Iadmon's estate to the busy streets of Memphis.

As the first two men stepped inside the andron, Doricha's spine straightened all on its own. Her eyes fastened on Aesop, widening in an unspoken question, seeking his support, his approval. He gave Doricha the tiniest nod—barely an acknowledgment—but the mere fact that he acknowledged Doricha cheered her. He knew where she was, saw that she was dressed and ready. And now she didn't feel quite so alone.

Aesop led each man to his couch; they reclined on their left sides, adjusting their cushions to support their upper bodies. Doricha both men carefully as they settled in. One was a sandy-haired fellow, his skin deeply tanned from long exposure to the Egyptian sun. The other was darker, with an olive complexion like Iadmon's. His hair was dark like Iadmon's, too, but there the similarities ended. Where Iadmon was lean and elegant, the darker man was big and broad. His shoulders were as wide and imposing as the beam of a warship. He had a fleshy face, with dark eyes, narrowly set; they glittered with innate shrewdness. His hair was artificially curled, arranged in neat rows that spoke of perfectionism. Such fastidiousness was in startling contrast to his big, bullish frame. He gave Aesop a crooked smile as he settled on his couch—more of a mocking leer, Doricha thought with a prickle of dread.

"My good man Xanthes, is there anything I may bring you before the meal begins?" Aesop asked politely.

"Nothing, old fellow." Xanthes made a dismissive gesture, a curt brushing-away.

Accordingly, Aesop turned to his other duties. But Xanthes called out to him before he could leave the andron. "I say, Aesop. Is this all your doing?" He made a wide sweep with his hand, taking in the andron with its neat couches, the white hall beyond with its niches of gleaming gods, the turquoise doors—and the garden outside, too, no doubt; the whole estate, with its private quay where the *Samian Wind* bobbed at its moorings. The grand spectacle of Iadmon's life.

Aesop hesitated. From across the room, Doricha could read the barest hint of annoyance in her tutor's posture and face. "My good man?"

"Iadmon never contrived to build all this for himself. I've known the man for years. It must have been the work of some intelligent servant. And who is more intelligent than you?"

Wisely, Aesop gave an evasive answer. "If you think to buy me back from Master Iadmon, then you'd best speak to him about it, good man. Though I doubt very much that he'll part with me. He finds me quite... *indispensable.*"

Aesop ducked his head in a perfect display of polite excuse, then turned on his heel and vanished from the room. Xanthes cast a peeved look at his sandy-haired companion and muttered something under his breath.

Doricha bit her lip at the tension that filled the room, but she recalled the work Helena had done painting her face, and forced herself to open her jaw. She didn't want to smear the red paint on her lips. So, this Xanthes fellow was the very one who had once owned Aesop! More startling still, Doricha had discerned the truth in Aesop's evasive answer. He would have given Xanthes a straight reply—*No, sir, I had nothing to do with Iadmon's success; he is a self-made man and quite capable of building his own riches*—if it had been the truth.

Aesop had all but made Iadmon, then. The bent-backed slave was clever enough to push a man up into the highest ranks of society. How in the name of all the gods had Xanthes let a treasure like Aesop slip through his fingers? And now that he saw what Aesop was capable of, would he try to steal him back? Or buy him and reinstate Aesop in his household?

While Doricha wrestled with her surprise, Xanthes and the other man talked quietly together, laughing over Aesop's elegant evasion. She lifted the wine pitcher carefully, testing its weight, practicing a properly elegant, fluid movement with the full pitcher in her hands. It wasn't an easy task. The vessel itself was heavier than it looked; the wine added considerably to its weight. Doricha tried a few surreptitious steps with the pitcher in her hands; some of the wine splashed over its rim and ran in a purple line down her knuckles.

"Come here, girl," Xanthes snapped. "Bring that wine."

Doricha looked up quickly. Xanthes was leaning eagerly from his couch, his smile wide and anticipatory. But his eyes were searching, darting. They seemed almost cautious. She did as she was told, stepping carefully around the empty couches as she crossed the andron, trying to drift like a cloud in a Thracian sky, hoping the strain of carrying the heavy pitcher didn't show on her face or in the trembling of her arms. Xanthes held up a cup made of polished horn, its mottled sides banded with silver. Doricha poured carefully, and was pleased when she didn't spill, but Xanthes tutted at sight of the wine that had already splashed onto her hand. He gestured to his table, and Doricha, hesitating, set the pitcher down.

Xanthes man took her hand gently and wiped away the wine with one of his linen napkins. "Aren't you a pretty thing," he said, looking up at her with a crooked half-smile. His gaze tied a knot of caution in her stomach. "Such delicate beauty, and yet... how would you describe her, Nikandros?"

The blond-haired man eyed Doricha for a moment, too, then said with a dismissive toss of his head, "Rustic."

"Yes. A rustic charm peeks through the trappings of refinement. Whatever polish Iadmon hopes to put on her, this one is still a naïve little country girl, isn't she?"

Doricha's heart beat loudly in her ears. Xanthes still clung to her hand, though now his thumb moved slowly where the cloth had before, lightly brushing her skin. She didn't like his touch, but she knew what duties awaited her once she became a hetaera. She schooled herself to stillness and did not pull her hand out of Xanthes' grip, no matter how she longed to rid herself of his touch.

Xanthes nodded toward Iadmon's couch. It had been strewn with more flower petals than the rest; the best, softest cloths draped its length. "Fill the master's cup," Xanthes said.

Doricha turned to retrieve her pitcher, but Xanthes kept her hand captured tightly in his own. Caught between the man and his command, she stared at him wide-eyed, frightened and out of her depth. She saw how his broad, heavy body had already crushed the petals on his couch, bruising their tender edges.

Xanthes tugged her back toward him, roughly, making her stagger on unsteady feet. For a moment, Doricha thought he would pull her down on the couch, and the blood roared in her ears, for she didn't know what she would do—or could do—if Xanthes tried to overpower her. But he released her hand with a roar of laughter, amused by her discomfiture. Doricha stepped back, out of his reach, struggling to keep anger and fear from showing on her face. She was losing that battle, and quickly, too. She could feel her cheeks and forehead beginning to heat as Xanthes threw back his head, shaking his neat black curls as he laughed.

Doricha took her pitcher and filled Iadmon's cup as quickly as she could manage.

"Be sure to fill it well," Xanthes said.

"Full, then fuller still," Nikandros added. "Just the way Iadmon likes it."

"There's nothing your master loves more than wine—unless it's innocent little flowers like you."

"Or a game of chance," said Nikandros, chuckling into his empty cup.

Doricha filled Nikandros' cup, then retreated to her place beside the serving table, grateful to be well away from the men. She set the pitcher down with a graceless clunk and stood with her back to the andron, trying to slow her heartbeat, praying that the trembling in her arms would cease. As she stood shivering, Aesop led in another group of guests—these had all arrived together, it seemed, and were already in a festival mood, clapping Xanthes and Nikandros on the shoulders, shouting out jests and offering loud, half-drunken acclaims to Iadmon and his hospitality.

Once Aesop saw the guests settled in their places, he passed a subtly questioning glance to Doricha. By then, however, her training had asserted itself, breaking through her fear. She was in control once more, poised and calm. She smiled at Aesop briefly, coolly, as if to say, *There's not a thing to worry about.* The flush of mortification had left her face.

"My good men," Aesop said to the room at large.

The guests quieted their boisterous talk, more or less, and Aesop drew aside the heavy red curtain to reveal Iadmon, standing proud and dignified in a flowing chlamys of vivid green. His hair was neatly oiled, held back from his brow with a beaded circlet reminiscent of the old Egyptian style. A wide collar of carnelian and lapis beads rested on his strong shoulders.

"Ah!" Xanthes said with a chuckle. "One would think the Pharaoh himself had come among us."

Iadmon lifted his hands, a gesture of welcome. "My friends! The river is high and the fields have gone to sleep beneath the waters. In days of old, Egypt celebrated the flood with feasting, good drink, song, and dance. We may not be Egyptians—not exactly—but tonight, let us do the same!"

The guests cheered raucously, raising their cups in salute. Doricha seized the opportunity to dart among the couches, pouring here and there, ensuring no cup remained empty for long.

Helena emerged from behind one of the red draperies. Her arms were draped with chains of lotus flowers. The waxy blooms with their spiky petals gave off a heady aroma as she wove through the andron, draping each guest's neck with a garland. The lotuses were symbols of Egypt—appropriate for a celebration of the flood, yet Doricha couldn't help but wonder what Helena, a true Egyptian through and through, thought of Iadmon's party and the rather frivolous use he made of the sacred flowers. Doricha tried to catch Helena's eye, but the woman kept her face turned down. She had a resolute smile fixed to her face. It did not waver, no matter what any of Iadmon's guests said to her.

One of the men sniffed ostentatiously at his lotus garland as Doricha filled his cup. "Quaint," he said. "Why, I feel as if I've stepped back in time a hundred years, and am attending a feast at one of the old Pharaohs' palaces."

"Gods preserve us," another said from nearby. "The last thing we need is to push Egypt backward a hundred years."

Doricha moved on, tending to their cups as if the wine vessel were her only care in the world. But she listened intently as the men joked and laughed.

"Our good King Amasis," a man called, raising his cup in salute. "Let the native Egyptians curse his name! Let them throw his effigy to the crocodiles! The best thing he ever did for Egypt was to turn it into Greece. See how we prosper now!"

"Careful," Xanthes said, sipping casually at his wine. "That sort of talk is all well and good among Greek merchants at a private feast, but woe to you if you say such a thing where a true Egyptian can hear you."

Doricha burned to look at Helena, but she kept her eyes on the cup she was filling.

Nikandros said, "Woe to you? What can the Egyptians do, except mutter and give you dark looks? What *will* they do, beyond that? I'll tell you what: nothing. You know how fanatical they are about their Pharaoh. Even when they despise him, they still uphold his rule."

Iadmon broke smoothly into the conversation. "How not? They believe he is the very mouthpiece of the gods. To native Egyptians, his word is holy; his whims are to be obeyed. Even, it seems, when his whims cut against the grain of everything Egypt has ever stood for."

"Don't be so sure the natives will never resist the will of their Pharaoh," Xanthes said darkly. "I believe that even Egyptians have their limits, and good King Amasis might soon push them to the brink."

"Oh?" Iadmon raised one dark brow.

"Only yesterday, near one of my warehouses, an Egyptian man was killed. He attacked a Greek—a big, strong fellow who works as a guard at another warehouse. Why this Egyptian thought it wise to throw himself upon a man of Timon's stature is anybody's guess, but he was shouting out his hatred for all Greeks as he did it. Pulled a knife on Timon—stabbed him a few times, too, though Timon isn't seriously injured. It would take more than a knife to bring that fellow down."

"How did it all end?" Nikandros asked, suddenly sober. "I've seen Timon at the warehouses many a time. I wouldn't fancy tangling with him. He looks like a warehouse himself, huge and blocky and solid."

"It ended with the Egyptian's neck broken," Xanthes said

bluntly. "Though not before a few more Egyptians joined the fray, and some more of Timon's fellows, too. It was an outright brawl, I tell you. Could have erupted into a riot, if Timon hadn't killed his attacker almost at once."

Nikandros gave a low whistle. "Dangerous days."

"Still," Xanthes went on comfortably, "I'd rather be a Greek under Pharaoh Amasis' rule than an Egyptian. At least we are favored by the man in charge, while his own Egyptians... well..." He trailed off, finishing the thought with an eloquent shrug that shifted his garland of lotuses against his burly chest.

Nikandros raised his cup. "To being Greek! To our good King Amasis!"

The andron fairly rattled with cheers. Doricha looked up from her work in time to see Helena hurrying out of the room, her face dark and her eyes narrowed to slits.

By the time the men had settled back into their conversation, the first courses of the meal arrived, accompanied by a small group of musicians. Soon the andron filled with traditional songs of old Egypt. Doricha took Iadmon's bowl, filled it with the best portions of each dish the cooks had prepared, then returned to the master's couch, offering his supper with a graceful bow. When she straightened, it was to find Iadmon smiling at her with great satisfaction.

Shrewd-eyed Xanthes didn't miss the exchange. He said, "Tell me, Iadmon: where did you find this little delicacy? Her copper hair is very charming."

"Thrace, by way of Tanis. Her family was stranded there, as so many are these days."

"And so," Nikandros chuckled approvingly, "you made a fortune out of others' misfortune."

The glance Iadmon gave Doricha was quick, but not unsympathetic. "Doricha, go and get me a little pot of that fish sauce I like. The cooks should have some on one of their trays."

She set off across the room, flushed and furious—though

whether she was angry over Nikandros' unfeeling mirth or her dismissal, Doricha couldn't have said. But she kept herself attuned to Iadmon's voice as she crossed the andron, filtering his smooth words out of the buzz of conversation around her.

She heard Xanthes say, "You can't find looks like that in Egypt. Of course, I figured she must have come from the north."

"I hope her exotic appearance will pay well." That was Iadmon, forthright and elegant as always.

"I should think a woman of her sort *will* pay well. As the Egyptians grow more desperate, I come across more pornae of the local type—dark and dusky and rather plain. A porna with a fresh, unexpected look will be a rare treat for all her customers."

"Ah," Iadmon said smoothly. "This girl will not be a common porna. I mean to set her up as a hetaera. Xanthes, my good fellow, I hope you won't find me too intimidating as a competitor for your business."

Both men laughed in a brotherly way, but a tingle of foreboding raced up Doricha's spine. She hurried back with Iadmon's fish sauce and deposited it on his table. Just as she tried to dart back to her serving table, Xanthes caught her by the hand again. She resisted the instinct to jerk her fingers out of his grip.

"Little hetaera-to-be," Xanthes purred, "your master's wine cup has gone dry."

It was true; the master's cup was empty. *I only just filled it. He must have a terrible thirst.* She fetched the wine pitcher. One of the cooks had refilled it while she'd lingered beside Iadmon and Xanthes, and now it was heavier than ever. She filled Iadmon's cup carefully, but almost as soon as it was full, he lifted it and swallowed a long draft.

"All the way to the rim," Xanthes said to Doricha in a low, slinking voice. "You mustn't let the master go thirsty."

Doricha topped up the cup once more, then hurried off to other corners of the andron, before Xanthes could speak to her again. Each time he looked at her, there was a glimmer of speculation in his dark eyes. Doricha didn't like it. And whenever he spoke, there was a subtle note of taunting in his voice, though Doricha couldn't have said whether his quiet needling was meant for her, or for Iadmon. She made the rounds of the couches, filling cups and smiling complacently whenever a man spoke to her. But by the time she returned to Iadmon's table, she could see that his cup was nearly empty again. When he called out gleefully to one of his guests, his voice had lost some of its usual, smooth control.

Doricha shifted uncomfortably from one foot to the other.

"Go on," Xanthes said. "Fill your master's cup."

"I..." She swallowed hard. Was she even supposed to speak to the guests, let alone answer them back with a refusal? "I don't think I ought to, my good man."

Xanthes chuckled indulgently. He patted the edge of his couch. "Come here, girl. Sit."

Still she hesitated, fear fluttering in her belly.

"Hasn't Iadmon taught you how to obey?" Xanthes said, annoyance edging his words.

Doricha set the wine pitcher on the floor and shuffled reluctantly to Xanthes' couch. He took her by the hand and pulled her down beside him, stroking her bare shoulder, twisting in his fingers the wispy, stray curls that had escaped her braid.

She stared at Iadmon, pleading with wide eyes and trembling lips. It seemed to take the master an eternity to recognize, through the haze of his wine, exactly what he was seeing.

Iadmon cleared his throat. "Xanthes, my dear friend," he said thickly. "I'm afraid little Doricha is not ready for that sort of work yet."

"Oh, isn't she?" He ran one finger along her collarbone.

Doricha curled her toes in her sandals, resisting the urge to spring up and flee.

"How I hate to disappoint you," Iadmon said. "But she is still in training, and I won't have a girl of such magnificent potential spoiled by too-early use. Surely you understand, as you are the very best purveyor of hetaerae in all Egypt." Iadmon was slurring his words now, but his eyes had sharpened, and he held Xanthes with a firm, challenging stare.

Xanthes' hand fell away, and Doricha stood, forcing herself to move with casual grace, as if she were not in the least disturbed by the man's pawing, and in no hurry to remove herself from his reach.

Xanthes peered up at her, making no attempt now to hide his speculation. "Potential, you say? She looks rather young to be considered accomplished at anything."

"She is an excellent dancer. One of the best I've yet seen."

Doricha flushed. She lifted the wine pitcher from the floor, holding it tight against her chest as if it were a shield or a soldier's armor. Iadmon was drunk; there was no truth in his words. How could she extricate herself from this situation without utterly humiliating herself and her master? She edged back toward the serving table, but Xanthes pounced on Iadmon's proclamation like a cat on a wounded bird.

"A dancer! What better entertainment for this quaint festivity? Come now, men! Who doesn't love to see a pretty girl dance?"

Several men around the andron raised their voices, and their cups, too. "Yes, a dance! Let's have a dance!"

Trembling and queasy, Doricha looked helplessly around the room, searching for someone—anyone—who might help her. She avoided Iadmon's eye, frightened he would seize the moment and issue and outright command. Then there would be no hope of evasion.

Doricha caught sight of Aesop, barely visible across the andron, peering out from behind the curtain. She pleaded with him silently, hoping he could read her distress from that distance. But if he did note her uncertainty, he remained unmoved. He nodded in what was surely meant to be an encouraging way; to Doricha, it felt like the command she had dreaded receiving. If her tutor would not save her, then there was nothing for it but to dance—and pray she didn't embarrass her master in front of all his guests.

She set the wine pitcher aside, stiff with anger. Then she returned to stand ready in front of Iadmon. She hadn't even a dance belt; surely the master wasn't so drunk that he would miss that important detail. She couldn't be expected to dance in the fine blue silk.

But Iadmon was apparently unaware of Doricha's predicament—unaware, or uncaring, shrouded as he was by the haze of wine. He called out to his musicians. "Give us another tune in the old style; something truly Egyptian."

At this, the guests cheered, and Doricha felt a current of dread race through her blood. The old, traditional dances were not the strongest in her repertoire, though Iunet had taught her plenty of steps. She would have preferred something more modern and familiar, something Thracian or Greek. But the men were invested in the party's theme; nothing but the charming steps of a bygone era would satisfy them now.

Doricha found Aesop again. He watched her levelly, his eyes shining with simple, confident expectation. As she held his gaze, the words of one of his lessons came back to her, quiet and insistent in her mind. *Look closely, girl, and trust your own eyes. Blind yourself to hopes and fears, and see what is honestly before you.*

While the musicians consulted quietly in the corner, deciding on which traditional tune they might play, Doricha narrowed her eyes and peered more shrewdly around the andron. Every face she saw was flushed, every eye rather glassy. Iadmon wasn't the only man who'd gone deep into his cup, though he was perhaps the farthest along. Only Xanthes seemed to be firmly in control of himself, yet Doricha knew, from the way he'd held and stroked her hand, that she could do no wrong in his eyes tonight.

They're all too drunk to know whether I put on a real Egyptian show or not.

The music began: a short and lively marching beat, with high, piercing trills of a flute. It brought to Doricha's mind the songs of springtime birds. Springtime in Thrace—where the seasons were distinct and true, unlike the oppressive, year-round heat of Egypt.

Quickly, Doricha loosened her belt, pulled up the skirt of her blue silk gown until it hung high above her ankles, and re-tied the sash. If the gods were good, that would be enough to keep her from tripping and floundering about the andron like a cow in a mire. She whirled into one of the lively ring dances performed by girls at Thracian harvest festivals. The ring dances were supposed to be the work of a dozen girls or more, with arms linked and feet stamping in unison. Together, the girls worked themselves into intricate, interweaving lines. But Doricha could recall the steps of her favorite ring dance even without other village girls surrounding her.

The music carried her around the room; she followed naturally where it guided her, responding to its cheery refrains with smiles that were forced in the first few moments of her dance, but that yielded to genuine pleasure as the music overtook her fears. As she passed the guests one by one, she paused to charm each man in turn. She bent back to grin at one man upside-down, and batted her eyes shyly at another. She dipped down to sit for one beat of the drums on the next man's couch, then leaped up and spun away with a mischievous grin the moment he reached out to touch her. She whirled, making the silk of her skirt trail enticingly along a man's arm or the back of his hand. She stamped and clapped and linked her arms with invisible Thracian girls, glorying so completely in the music that the men began to clap along with her, caught up in her honest pleasure. Soon the andron reverberated with the rhythm of one great, shared joy.

The music sped, rising in pitch, racing toward its climax. Doricha took one brief moment to set her path, eyeing a narrow passage between tables and couches. Then she bent backward and pushed off with her feet, flipping sandals-over-hands down the length of the andron, just as Iunet had taught her. She ended with a bounce on her toes, her arms flung up in victory, right between Iadmon and Xanthes.

The music ended on a boisterous, upsloping note. The silence that followed couldn't have lasted longer than a few heartbeats, but in that brief time, fear flooded Doricha again. Had the men discerned, after tall, that the dance was not Egyptian? Would they chastise her—would Iadmon be disappointed, disgusted with her disobedience? Then, with one great roar, the men shouted her acclaim, raising cups and calling out for another dance. It seemed the very walls of Iadmon's estate quaked with approval.

Doricha flushed, allowing pleasure and relief to wash over her in a wave. She lowered her eyes demurely to the floor.

"I would say this girl has potential after all," Xanthes said over the cheering of the crowd. "What do you call her, Iadmon?"

"Her name is Doricha."

Xanthes pushed himself, sitting on the edge of his couch. He leaned closer to Doricha. "And you say she is to be a hetaera."

Young as she was, Doricha's skill at reading men went only so far. There was a peculiar light in Xanthes' eyes, but she couldn't determine what it meant, what he was feeling. It was akin to hunger, or lust... and yet it was more calculated than that, less visceral.

She tried to think of some response to Xanthes' statement. Was she expected to respond at all?

"See how she blushes," Xanthes said to the room. "Skin as pale as alabaster, yet her cheeks are red as roses. Did you ever see a girl so charming? Won't we all be lucky fellows when she makes her debut as a hetaera?" He plucked one of the flowers from the garland around his neck, then slid the blossom into Doricha's hair. "To Iadmon's white lotus!"

The men repeated the cheer, and Iadmon, with his barely-focused eyes and wide grin, seemed as pleased as if they had saluted him personally.

"I do believe, little lotus," said Xanthes softly, leaning closer to Doricha's ear, "that your master needs more wine."

Doricha bit her lip. "My good man, I don't want my master to have a sour head in the morning."

"Such a conscientious slave," Xanthes said. His voice was amused, but his emphasis on that last word frightened Doricha. She hurried to fetch her wine pitcher. As she ran, the light sweat her dance had raised chilled her skin and made her shiver.

Iadmon drank down half his cup of wine as soon as Doricha filled it.

"What a night!" Xanthes exclaimed. "You do know how to celebrate, Iadmon, my old friend. Good food, excellent wine, a beautiful girl to dance for us... only one thing could make this night more enjoyable."

"And what is that?" said Iadmon, slurring.

"Why, a gamble, of course! Who doesn't enjoy games of chance?"

The men of the andron agreed with hearty cheers.

"Dice?" Iadmon suggested. There was a thick eagerness in his voice that made Doricha feel cautious and small. Iadmon never sounded so boyish, so... coarse. He was a man of refinement, of self-control. He didn't stoop to frivolous amusements like dicing.

"I'll play you at dice," Xanthes said.

"Excellent!" Iadmon summoned one of his household servants and sent for dice. When they arrived, he rattled them enthusiastically in their cup. "What shall we wager?"

Xanthes turned to Doricha, raking her head to foot with a speculative, almost predatory air. She couldn't stifle a gasp, nor could she stop her knees from buckling. Without being told to sit, she sank down on the edge of Iadmon's couch.

The master laid a soothing hand on her shoulder. "Not her, Xanthes." Some of the drunkenness seemed to flee his voice, if only for a moment. "She is too precious to me."

Xanthes relented immediately, with no display of ill humor.

"That collar of yours, then. I could use an authentic Egyptian piece myself, for when I'm feeling nostalgic for the old days."

"Very well!" Iadmon had some trouble with the clasp of his beaded collar. Doricha moved to help him, but was almost as useless as he had been. Her fingers trembled badly, and she could feel Xanthes' greedy stare upon her.

೨.

THE NIGHT WAS deep and old by the time Doricha returned to her room. She slipped inside, weak with relief, and leaned hard against the door, as if her small, frail body was strong enough to stop the world from entering.

The party had dragged on for hours; Iadmon had grown morose as the night wore on. He seemed to feel the loss of his Egyptian necklace keenly.

The more despondent Iadmon became, the greater seemed Xanthes' self-satisfaction. The bull-broad man had lounged on his couch with an air of victory that made Doricha's skin creep every time she passed with the wine pitcher. She could feel Xanthes' eyes upon her everywhere she went—could sense all too clearly the slow, careful nature of his speculation.

Helena had left a small basket of supplies on Doricha's bed: a vial of oil and a soft linen cloth to remove the paint from her face, and a tiny iron scissor with sharp blades. Doricha stood before her mirror and delved into her high crown of hair with her fingers, searching until she found the knot of wool that held together the elaborate braid. She pulled the thread out to expose it and raised the scissor; she was just about to squeeze the flexible curve of thin iron and snip the thread, when she heard two male voices, soft and low, very close to her narrow window.

She set the scissors aside and crept to the window. There was no mistaking the voices now: Aesop and Iadmon. The master was still quite drunk. His speech was thick and stumbling, but even through the wine-haze, Doricha could hear his despair. "That necklace, Aesop! It was priceless."

"It wasn't priceless, Master. I have your account books in my chamber; I can tell you exactly what it cost. You can always buy another." He sounded patient and long-suffering, a parent comforting a squalling child.

"It's not the price, after all," Iadmon moaned. Doricha had never known him to sound so undignified. "It's the *principle*."

"The principle, Master?"

Iadmon sighed deeply. "You know what I mean, Aesop. You know what I mean."

There was a pause, a hesitation. Doricha found herself holding her breath, tingling with anxiety, wondering whether her tutor would speak frankly.

He did, though his tone was obsequious. "Your fondness for drinking and games of chance will get you into worse trouble someday, I fear. The wise philosophers all counsel moderation, Master."

"Moderation," Iadmon said with an energy of disgust.

"Master, I fear your propensity for strong drink is too well-known among your enemies."

"My enemies! Who is my enemy?"

"Xanthes, for one."

"Bah." Iadmon hawked and spat, and Doricha flinched at the sound of such unexpected coarseness. "Xanthes is a fellow after my own heart. We work toward the same ends."

"You certainly do now—now that you are training a hetaera of your own." Aesop's spoke quietly, but the caution in his words was obvious.

Doricha trembled, glancing nervously at her bed. She should be in that bed now, drifting off to sleep—not listening in on these men, not frightening herself with things she could never hope to control. But she remained rooted to the spot, held fast by a perverse need to know more.

Aesop continued, "When you were a peddler of mere *pornae*, Xanthes could afford to see you as a friend. But now... now you are his competition. And he has seen Doricha for himself; he knows what a treasure she is. You mustn't give him the opportunity to best you, Master. He will ruin you if he can. I know Xanthes better than you do; he is the most ruthless man the gods ever made."

Doricha backed away from the window until she collided with her wash stand. She turned in time to stop the half-empty pitcher from falling to the ground. The scissors still lay beside the washing bowl. She cut the thread that bound her hair and let it fall, shaking out the braid, massaging her scalp until the ache of her tight-pulled hair dissipated. Then she cleaned the paint from her face and stood staring into the mirror, eyes wide, features stilled by the dull, throbbing shock.

She didn't look like a hetaera now. She looked like a girl—just a girl, as ordinary as any other. Yet now this common girl—this slave—knew she was a bargaining chip in the hands of two of the most powerful men in Memphis. Couldn't they see she was only a plain, everyday thing?

With a searing pain in her chest, she remembered the first conversation she'd ever had with Iadmon. He had asked her, *Are you brave enough to make a good attempt? Brave enough to learn the ways of a hetaera?* And she had answered, *Do I have a choice, but to try?*

Now, staring hopelessly at her face, Doricha thought, *I don't want to be a hetaera, if this is what it means. Put up for the trade, tossed into the kit on a drunkard's gamble.*

But she had no choice—none at all. That was what it meant, to be a slave.

Holding back useless tears, Doricha pulled off the blue-green silk and hung it on the peg beside her door. Helena would come for it in the morning.

8

THE MASTER ACCEPTS

THE FLOOD RECEDED FROM THE FARMS AND FIELDS THAT surrounded the sprawling metropolis of Egypt's capital city. Memphis had been like an island during the long, wet season of the Inundation, ringed all about with water that had glittered in the sun. But as the months turned and the waters abated, the city rejoined the rich, black land, and native Egyptians who had left with their homes to build monuments for the Pharaoh returned now to Memphis. In the lush farmlands north and south of the city, the Egyptian workers sowed crops of barley and emmer, of onions and squash, melons and greens, all planted in the rich black mud that the shrinking river had left behind.

When the early crops had grown to their full height and the year's first harvest was approaching, Doricha knew her thirteenth year had come. Aesop had taught her how to read the Egyptian calendar, how to watch the moon's phases and count the days between the appearance of each new constellation on the horizon. Doricha had never known the exact date of her birth, but she knew that a year had passed since she'd left her family in Tanis and stepped into Iadmon's world.

Every day, she examined herself carefully in the little round mirror, searching for signs that she would soon leave girlhood behind. The changes were slight, but she was observant and could discern them with little trouble. Her breasts had begun to grow more prominent; her face had shed the soft blur of immaturity, that round, snub-nosed sameness common to all children. Now her features had begun to define themselves, taking on the sharpness, the angularity that would define her grown-up appearance.

Doricha could tell her maturity was approaching by the changing way men looked at her, too—and she fond herself often in the company of men. Iadmon was very fond of parties and feasts. There was little to do during the flood season anyhow, except to entertain—and Iadmon never missed an opportunity. His trade had done quite well over the preceding year; thanks to the wise advice of Aesop, the master's prosperity had steadily increased, and he was eager to show his peers how his star was rising.

Doricha's training had grown in step with Iadmon's fortune. The master had devoted ever more time and care to Doricha's dancing; he cultivated her carefully, almost obsessively, as an orchid is trimmed and watered and pampered under glass. For hours each day, Doricha drilled under Iunet's stern gaze—and she danced again almost every night, for whenever her master didn't host a lavish supper or an afternoon boating party, he offered small, intimate gatherings to his closest friends. Doricha looked forward to the parties, whether big or small, for now she could see how her dancing skills increased with every performance. As her talent grew, so too did her confidence and self-worth.

It was well that Doricha's dance progressed well, for her other lessons presented more of a hazard. Young as she was, the finer points of sophisticated conversation were still beyond her—and neither Aesop nor any other tutor had succeeded in erasing the inflection of rural Thrace from her voice. But she had a charming habit of self-deprecation that Iadmon's guests seemed to like. Doricha was quick-witted enough to realize that most men were flattered by her displays of simplicity and girlishness. By playing the country bumpkin, she allowed the men she entertained to adopt the role of wise and sophisticated lords of Memphis— people of real importance and power. She played along gamely, giggling and joking, batting her kohl-darkened lashes, and allowing every man she encountered to believe that she was nothing more than a pretty little bauble, an ornament hanging from Iadmon's neck.

But Doricha was no mere ornament. She was more intelligent, more subtly observant than Iadmon's friends suspected. In fact, she was even brighter than Iadmon knew her to be. She flitted around the andron, giving every impression that she was nothing more than a butterfly—pretty, enchanting, and ultimately mindless. But her jewel-studded ears heard every whisper that passed from couch to couch, and those exotic green eyes may hide behind a screen of fluttering lashes, but still, Doricha noted every glance, every frown, every secret gesture that passed from one man to another. The only man under Iadmon's roof who knew Doricha's real strengths—her burgeoning potential—was Aesop. For it was he who had taught Doricha what powers might come to an observant, discerning slave—he who had refined her and trained her with assiduous care.

Despite her growth, her quiet successes as an observer of men —despite even the great joy she took in dance—the months since Doricha's first party had not been entirely pleasant. The shocking realization that she could be traded off without a moment's notice had sharpened something in Doricha's spirit. The fear that she might be sent to live with some other master often plagued her. She had grown accustomed to this life—indeed, it was a far better life than any she had known before, even if she was a slave.

Doricha didn't know how she could hope to secure her place in Iadmon's household, other than to make herself so remarkable, so valuable, that Iadmon would never be able to justify her loss. And so Doricha became as keen as a hungry hound, intent on her quarry, racing on to close with her fate, to subdue and conquer it. Day by day, she strove toward her goal with a focus that impressed even herself. She *would* become a hetaera, and not because Iadmon had left her with no other choice. She *wanted* to be a hetaera. That single, shining goal had become her sustaining passion, her inner fire. It was, as the Egyptians said, her ankh: the breath of her spirit, the force that made her live. For when she achieved the power and latitude all hetaerae enjoyed, then she would be all but impervious to Iadmon's drunken whims. When she was a hetaera, Doricha would have her crowd of admirers—high-status men whose wealth and patronage would keep her safe against any sudden shifts in the winds of fate.

Of course, Doricha now knew that some hetaerae earned enough money to free themselves from their masters, and continue their work independently—or take up a new life, as a wife and mother, if they wished. That possibility had only heightened Doricha's ambition. The more she had seen of Memphis—its parties, its grand estates, the lives of the wealthy and powerful —the less she could understand why any hetaera would give up access to all that beauty, that wealth and glory. Surely a quiet marriage and a brood of children couldn't compete with Memphis society.

By the time the flood season had ended, Doricha's reputation as a dancer and a charmer had spread far enough that Iadmon had begun receiving requests for the loan of his slave girl with the rose-gold hair. She was asked to entertain at other men's parties so often that Iadmon employed an extra scribe, whose only task was to write polite but firm refusals to all Doricha's invitations.

"You won't be ready to entertain on your own until you have become a woman," Aesop had told Doricha, one afternoon when she had complained about all those missed opportunities. "And believe me," he added drily, "Iadmon's stance on this issue is to your benefit. You are still very young, my girl."

"But I've had ever so much experience with men now!"

Aesop had smiled rather grimly at that. "Men tend to behave themselves when they're guests in another man's home. Especially when they're guests in Iadmon's home, for his reputation as a sophisticate is well known. It would be a different tale altogether if another man were at the helm of a night's entertainments."

Iadmon's ruling on the decision was not open for debate. Doricha could do nothing but pray fervently that her first blood would flow, so that she would finally have some hope of making her fortune—of building her bulwark against fate.

Soon the flood season was poised to come again. Days before the rising of the Dog Star—herald of the new year in Egypt— Doricha worked beneath the garden portico with Iunet, rehearsing an exuberant new dance the sour-faced old mistress had taught her. The steps were difficult, even intricate, for the music followed a strange, asymmetrical rhythm that put Doricha in mind of a person limping along on a lame foot. She struggled to land each light, crisscrossing step in time with the faltering beat, and was rather afraid that she looked lame herself. But the way Iunet leaned against a pillar with arms folded, watching her pupil in silence, told Doricha that she was dancing well enough after all. She had come to understand Iunet's moods and subtle expressions. The woman's tight, still mouth might look like she'd bitten an unripe plum; her dark eyes may narrow in a critical squint. But Iunet's switch hung limply from one hand, so Doricha knew she hadn't disappointed her teacher yet. Iunet seldom found a reason to use the switch anymore, enthusiastic and gifted as her pupil was.

Iunet and Doricha were not alone beneath the portico. They seldom were; most days, several of Iadmon's household staff—as many as could be spared from duty—gathered in the shade to see their little dancing-girl put through her paces. Doricha's rehearsals always brought pleasure to Iadmon's people. Her love of dance was so much a part of her that she couldn't restrain her happiness; her simple joy in music and movement spilled over and spread to others until they, too, were smiling and tapping their toes. And Doricha, for her part, used those crowds of servants to further her skill, fluttering her lashes at them as if they were men in the andron, challenging herself to raise a genuine smile from every watcher before her dance was finished.

She knew every face in Iadmon's household well. But on this day, when she whirled close to the edge of the crowd, leaning and reaching as if she longed to touch the nearest man but couldn't quite overcome her shyness—Doricha locked eyes with one youth whom she had never seen before. His light skin and sand-colored hair marked him out as Northern Greek. His blue eyes fixed on her, tracking her movements with an intensity that nearly made her stumble. She managed to save herself at the last moment, turning that momentary hesitation into another coy display of feigned shyness that fit in perfectly with the tone of her dance. But in her surprise, she failed to keep the smile on her face. It slid from her like melted oil. As Doricha spun away from the crowd again, she hoped neither Iunet nor Iadmon had noticed her discomfiture.

The musicians brought their piece to its close with a high skirl of notes, and Doricha struck her final pose, holding the position like a marble statue while Iadmon's people stamped their feet and shouted praise. Doricha's chest heaved from the effort of her dance, but otherwise, she remained serene, masking her surprise at the newcomer's presence until the shouts had died away. Then she relaxed, waiting for Iadmon or Iunet to issue another command.

In the momentary silence, the strange man stepped forward and bowed deferentially toward Iadmon.

"Master, your peer Xanthes has sent me with a message."

Doricha's stomach turned a sudden, queasy flip. She had never forgotten Xanthes' hungry stares on the night of the Flood feast. Nor had she forgotten the threat he posed. True, he had made no attempt to touch her—nor even to speak to her—in all the long months since that party, even though Doricha had seen him at plenty of feasts and festivals since. Still, the sudden appearance of his messenger set Doricha's nerves ringing with caution.

Iadmon waved the man forward; the Greek approached the master of the estate and bowed again, this time with more extravagance.

"Xanthes plans to host the greatest New Year party Memphis has ever seen," the messenger said. "He begs your indulgence and hopes you will attend, for it would not be a true celebration without his dear friend Iadmon. Those are the words he instructed me to say, Good Man."

Iadmon's smile was cool, amused. "Good old Xanthes. Of course, I cannot disappoint such a close friend. I will certainly attend his party."

"Xanthes makes one more request, Good Man."

"Oh? What is it?"

"He asks that you bring your magnificent dancing girl with you. After seeing her myself, I can understand why my master was so insistent on this point. She is young, but I believe I have never seen a finer dancer in all of Memphis."

Had any other man paid Doricha such a compliment, she would have been pleased, would have felt surer than ever in her future as a hetaera. But this stranger spoke for Xanthes. *Doesn't that make it same 's if Xanthes said the words himself?* Doricha couldn't forget Xanthes' assessing stare, the possessive feel of his hand as it had stroked her shoulder. Her heart beat loud in her ears; she lowered her eyes as the messenger smiled at her. *So Xanthes hasn't forgotten me, even if he has taken to avoiding me like I'm plague-struck.*

Doricha glanced up just in time to see Iadmon's smile broaden. She knew her master well enough to understand that he was susceptible to flattery, as all men were—and that his greatest source of pride was his wealth and his taste. Doricha's popularity flattered Iadmon, reinforced his high opinion of himself as a man of exquisite taste, of unmatched refinement.

"Of course I shall bring my dancer." He turned to Doricha. "What do you think of that, my girl?"

What could Doricha say? She was no freed hetaera yet. She was only a slave.

Doricha stood as tall as she could manage, lifting her chin with a confident air. "Reckon I'll be very glad to dance for Good Man Xanthes, Master. So long 's it pleases you."

9

IN THE CROCODILE'S POOL

IADMON'S LITTER MOVED THROUGH THE STREETS OF MEMPHIS AS smoothly as a boat gliding downstream. Doricha, seated on a soft cushion at her master's left hand, peeked through the loose-woven veil of the litter's curtains, watching city life bustle all around her. It was the longest day of the year, and although the supper hour had passed, Memphis still hummed with activity. A market square rang with the shouts of merchants, enticing passers-by to taste their honey wine, their smoked fish, their winter melons, still firm and sweet six months after the harvest. Odors of cinnamon and coriander mingled with the dusty smell of dissipating heat. A boy stood on the corner of two broad avenues, holding up his painted duck-feather fans for passing ladies to see. In a narrow alley, a pack of children shrieked with laughter as they played with a straw-stuffed leather ball, while on the rooftop high above, their mothers beat rugs and sleeping mats to rid them of dust and fleas. From a railed balcony, a painted porna leaned, pulling down the neck of her gown to show her full, round breasts. And somewhere in the distance, mingling with the low, plaintive calls of animals being led out for their nightly drink, a woman's voice sang soft and sweet, *My slip-*

per, my shoe; who has a stitch to fix me? I cannot cross the desert sand alone. Night's hour had arrived, but not night's darkness. The whole of the city still glowed, golden-red, with the long, lingering sunset of the New Year, while low in the sky, with a flash of fire like an African opal, the Dog Star had returned to coax the Nile to its fullness.

"It is beautiful, isn't it?" Iadmon said quietly.

Doricha turned away from the curtain with a guilty blush, but the master seemed disinclined toward scolding her for the unseemly gawking. Iadmon was watching the city, too, with a wistful warmth in his eyes. "I have always loved the New Year. Not only the long day, which is enjoyable enough by itself—but the reminder that everything starts anew, that we always have the chance to try again, to do better, to right our wrongs."

Doricha didn't know what to say. She wasn't confident that Iadmon expected a response; she couldn't even be sure he was aware of having spoken his thoughts aloud. She smiled at him rather timidly and laced her fingers together, the better to resist pawing at her hair. It was mounded atop her head in a pile of red-gold curls, sewn firmly in place—another of Helena's intricate constructions of braids, back-combing, ringlets and ribbons. Helena always stitched Doricha's hairstyles firmly enough that they held through her most exuberant dances, but although Helena's creations had never given way, still Doricha had never grown used to the feel of a tower of hair on her crown.

"I like the light, Master," Doricha said. "The sunset is so pretty this time of year."

"Golden light." Iadmon spoke slowly, with a drawn-out sigh. "Gold, gold... what a color, what a substance. The things men do for gold."

Doricha's cheeks still burned with the embarrassment of confusion. What ought she to say? How could a slave respond to her master's bleak musings? She stared straight ahead, over the heads of the litter carriers, and did not look at Iadmon. He seemed captive to his own thoughts; Doricha feared that later, if Iadmon realized he had betrayed some subtle weakness to his slave, he might grow angry with her. The elegant man was not one to beat his slaves, but Doricha's secret fear that Iadmon might get rid of her still curdled in her stomach, sour as ever before.

"Do you know," Iadmon said conversationally, "they used to believe that Egypt was made of gold. Other people believed it, I mean... people who were not Egyptians. The Hittites, the Greeks, the Canaanites—everyone. They believed that in Egypt, gold was everywhere. Lying all around, sparkling in every crack in the floor, getting into your eyes like sand. They believed it blew about on the wind in great, shimmering clouds. Can you imagine such a thing?" He emitted a small, distracted chuckle.

This was not the first time Doricha had dealt with a man in a dark mood. She turned to Iadmon with a bright smile and giggled like a bubbling Thracian stream. "What a silly thing to think! Some men haven't the sense of a donkey. If Egypt ever had golden sand storms, then why did a great cloud of gold never blow off to Canaan or Mitanni? 'Less they think the gods can change gold into dust, while it's blowing about on the wind. But if the gods could do such a thing, then they must be cruel indeed, to stop all that gold from piling up in drifts in every Hittite city. What's a person to think about his gods, if they don't let Egyptian gold blow in? Why, it would just about be enough to make me renounce the gods of my land entirely, and worship Isis and Osiris instead, for at least they appreciate a good storm of golden sand."

Iadmon's laugh was neither dark nor distracted this time. He seemed genuinely amused by Doricha's observation. "You're right, of course. I'd never thought about it that way before. Imagine the gods working frantically to change gold to ordinary dust as it blew across Egypt's borders. It is a silly notion... and of course, there's not a bit of truth to it. But men will believe what they want to believe, not what common sense tells them. That's especially true where gold is concerned. Gold and women."

"Reckon it's not hard to see where the rumor started, Master," Doricha said. "When you look out there at the city, with the sun still lingering, like, down low in the sky, everything looks like it's covered in gold. Why, it's the prettiest thing I've ever seen; even prettier than a good necklace or a fine dress, because it's all *alive*, isn't it, Master? Look at those oxen there. Going down to the river to have a drink. They're just ordinary oxen in the daytime, and at night, too. But now, just for this hour, when the sun's at just the right angle... see how they shine! And the little drover boy. He's ordinary, too, but in this light, with his skin all a-glowing, he could almost pass for one of the gods of old Egypt himself."

Iadmon turned to her with a smile as lingering and warm as the sunset. He gazed at her for so long that Doricha lowered her eyes to her lap, suddenly nervous under the master's scrutiny.

"You clever thing," Iadmon said. "I was right about you. You've made a herd of cattle and a dusty drover boy seem like magic, conjured up out of a sorcerer's fire. And you've lifted my spirits, no doubt. Oh, my Doricha... there's nothing ordinary about *you*, is there, in daylight or in darkness? When you become a hetaera, you'll set Memphis reeling."

"But why should the great Iadmon's spirits be low?" Doricha said playfully. "Doesn't he have the finest riverfront estate in the city? Isn't he the very best at his trade? And—" she made a little flourish where she sat, twisting her arms and hands dramatically, raising a cheerful jingle from the bracelets on her wrists— "doesn't the great Iadmon have the best dancer in all of Memphis?"

"The best dancer in all of Egypt, I dare say."

"No, Master. All of Egypt? Not I."

"You are still young, but... one day. One day your name will be known up and down the length of the Nile. And as for why my spirits are low... well. I couldn't refuse an invitation to Xanthes' party, now could I? Everyone would think me uncouth. But I don't like the man; I never have. I don't believe he's ever forgiven me for buying Aesop. But Xanthes hardly has good cause to blame me for his blindness. He wasn't quick enough to see what a treasure he had in Aesop, and by the time he realized he'd made a grave mistake in selling him, it was too late. I wasn't about to give Aesop up again—I won't still, not for any price. Oh, I know Xanthes makes a good show of being a jolly, trustworthy friend, but he has always been the type of man to carry a grudge for eternity. He's waiting for his chance, Doricha: mark my words. He will ruin me if he can. I know a crocodile when I see one."

"Oh... I beg you not to think about it now, Master," Doricha said. She was already anxious enough about being in Xanthes' presence again. She could still feel the revolting sensation of his rough, greedy fingers sliding along the soft skin of her collarbone. She didn't need the threat of Iadmon's ruin hanging over her, too. "Not on the first day of the new year. It's bad luck to have grim thoughts now. If you think such terrible things, then the whole year will go poorly for you. That's what we always said in Thrace, any rate, when the new year came."

The litter turned off the road and passed beneath a tall, vine-wrapped gate. The gate was set into a white stone wall, its top spilling over with twining vines that opened fragrant pink blossoms, a sweet offering to the approaching night.

"Here we are, at any rate," Iadmon said. "Xanthes' estate. We descend into the crocodile's pool. I shall do my best to enjoy it. At least I will get to see you dance, and at one of the grandest parties of the season, too—so the night won't be a total loss. This party is a good opportunity for you, Doricha. You'll meet plenty of wealthy men, all of whom will be eager to make your closer acquaintance once we debut you as a fully-fledged hetaera."

The litter sank gently to the ground in a crescent-shaped courtyard. A servant in the dark blue of Xanthes' household came forward to draw back the curtains and help Iadmon and his young dancer to their feet. Doricha gazed in wonder at the estate. The pale curve of the yard was set off by a heavy fringe of lush green foliage, dotted liberally with sweet-smelling blooms. A thriving flower garden was an extravagance now, at the tail end of the harvest season when the river was at its lowest. Xanthes' house was tall and broad, its walls coated in pure-white plaster that picked up the rosy glow of the sunset. Three or four young girls, their heads crowned with circlets of woven emmer, moved about the courtyard with water skins slung across their bodies. The girls used twig whisks to scatter droplets of water on the bare earth, damping down the late-summer dust. Musicians had already begun to play inside the great house; a bright and optimistic tune drifted out through the windows, and from the red-painted door, which was held open in welcome by another male slave robed in deep, luxuriant blue.

"This way, if you please, Good Man," the slave said. He bowed with one arm extended, welcoming Iadmon to the party. Iadmon nodded with brisk resolve—a man making up his mind to go unflinching toward danger—and strode toward the door. Doricha hurried after them, careful to remain the proper two paces behind her master's shoulder.

Xanthes' house was magnificent—even finer than Iadmon's, for it was more spacious and more richly adorned. Doricha stared in frank awe at the polished ebony furniture, strewn with silk cushions; the intricate detail of the friezes carved on every limestone wall; the astonishingly vibrant hues of the rugs beneath her feet. The ceilings and arched doorways reached up so high, they may as well have been stone skies stretching overhead. The air was perfumed with roses, and everywhere—inlaid into tables, woven thread by thread into the carpets, leafing the delicate art of the friezes—the opulent glint of gold flashed and danced as blue-robed servants lit the evening lamps.

Reckon Xanthes is one of those men Iadmon spoke of, Doricha mused, *one of those who would do anything in the world for gold. It's all so pretty, but I dare say his tastes aren't as sophisticated as Iadmon's. It's all a show, like. It matters very much to him, that people see exactly how rich he is, and no mistake about it.*

Presently, they reached the andron. The room was almost twice as large as Iadmon's, with a curving rear wall. A pair of doors stood open to a view of the shadowy garden and the dark, sunken line of the depleted river beyond. Dozens of lamps glowed, illuminating the pillars and arches of the andron, shining brightly on the faces of Xanthes' laughing guests, sending fingers of light to trace the gold adornments of the dining couches. The musicians gathered beside the garden door. Two pipers bobbed and swayed beside a double-ribbed harp, which was so tall the harpist couldn't hold it upright himself; a youth with lean, muscular arms braced the harp on its painted wooden stand while the player a tumbling melody from its strings. Three women wielded an assortment of tambours and bronze bells, while an old man strummed rich chords from a lyre made of the spiraling black horns of a white-striped antelope.

"Your couch, Good Man." The blue-robed slave directed Iadmon to his place, a couch placed very near Xanthes' own, covered in scarlet cushions.

But the couch was not empty. A young woman, not much older than Doricha, lounged across its foot, leaning back on her hands and swinging her gold-laced sandals to the music. Her black hair was combed through with a shiny oil, redolent of rich spices. The oil was applied so thickly that it made each long, curled lock hang in a distinct and perfect ringlet. The girl was dressed in the old Egyptian style, with a topless gown of berry-red held up by a turquoise-beaded strap around her ribcage. Another strap ran up between her bare breasts and over one soft-brown shoulder. The linen of her gown was so finely woven that it was quite transparent, concealing nothing from the eye. Yet she had pushed the hem of her dress up anyway, exposing her smooth thighs well above the knee, as if she couldn't countenance that any part of her should be veiled from public view. The dark-haired girl cast a long, rather arrogant stare at Iadmon, then turned her attention back to the musicians without even offering a bow. Her heavy-lidded eyes were thickly lined with kohl, which only served to emphasize their startling blue color. Those pale eyes in an otherwise Egyptian face spoke of some northern, perhaps even Greek, blood.

"Good Man Iadmon." A familiar voice cut across the room, deep and booming. Doricha's spine prickled, but she turned when her master did to greet Xanthes, a smile fixed to her face. The host, still as bullish as ever, was making his way across the andron, turning sideways to slip between tables, bending toward his guests with quick apologies and excuses as he went. When he reached Iadmon, he offered his forearm to clasp in friendship; Iadmon did not hesitate to take it, though Doricha could feel her master bristle subtly beside her. She kept her eyes lowered to the floor, hoping she would have some respite, some time to get her bearings in this new house before she was thrust into the furnace of Xanthes' attention.

"I told them off especially to seat you near my own couch," Xanthes said, "so that we may talk. It has been too long since we've had a good conversation, eh?"

"Indeed," Iadmon replied smoothly. "You were most gracious to invite me. It looks to be a fine gathering already."

Xanthes' huge, too-warm hands closed suddenly on Doricha's shoulders. She stifled a squeak of surprise and looked up into his broad, fleshy face.

"This night will be all the more enjoyable when we get to see this one dance. Your pale little flower, Iadmon—how glad I am you've brought her. You honor me with the gesture; I know you've refused her loan to many a man's party before now. But enough for the moment; there'll be time enough later to watch the white lotus dance. I am hungry—aren't you? Let's have something to eat!"

Xanthes gestured to his household staff, standing at attention along the curved walls of the andron. As he and Iadmon settled on their couches, the first courses were carried in. The dark-haired girl in the red dress rose gracefully, making room for Iadmon, but as soon as he had arranged himself comfortably, she perched lightly beside him once more. Doricha, slave as she was, remained standing near the head of her master's couch so that she might serve him as needed. She couldn't help staring at the girl in the red dress. Who was she? And why was she sitting with Iadmon?

Xanthes nodded toward the girl. "Do you like this one?" he asked Iadmon. "She's not the newest of my hetaerae—a few are more recently acquired—but she is the youngest."

The dark-haired girl glanced back over her shoulder, showing Xanthes one dimple of a half-smile. Her blue eyes nearly closed in an expression that might have been sleepy, if it hadn't seemed so mocking.

Doricha's own eyes widened at the girl's display of cheek. She expected Xanthes to shout at the girl, to punish her. Instead, he laughed.

"Archidike," Xanthes said, by way of introduction. "The youngest in my stable, but by far the most adventuresome. You'll like her, Iadmon."

"She is a lovely woman." Iadmon's comment may have been for Xanthes, but he looked directly into Archidike's blue eyes as he spoke, bending his neck urbanely.

Doricha curled her toes in her sandals to distract herself from her surprise. She had never seen Iadmon bow to a woman before. But of course, this Archidike wasn't just any woman—she was a hetaera. She had achieved the great goal; she had become what Doricha most wanted to be, and *would* be, if the gods were good.

Iadmon and Xanthes tasted the evening's first dish and fell deep into conversation, while Doricha peered around the room. It seemed as if Xanthes had provided a special entertainer not only for Iadmon, but for every one of his guests. Each supper couch in the andron was bejeweled by a woman. Some stretched languidly beside their male partners, joining them as they nibbled at the first course. Some had seated themselves demurely on the couches, sipping wine while they talked with the men. Doricha stared at each woman in turn, hungrily searching their faces, their bodies, their every manner and gesture for a sign of what she must do to join them. Every hetaera was beautiful, glittering with gems at wrist and throat, wrapped in a sheen of silk or displayed, as Archidike was, in finely woven linen. They moved with the grace of river reeds swaying in the wind. Many of them were of an age with Archidike—little more than girls, still shy of their twentieth year. But plenty of the women had sailed gracefully beyond their youth. Those older hetaerae, so deliberate and practiced in every movement, in every smile and melodious laugh, shone with a patina of refinement that was even more alluring than the fresh charm of the youngest.

How can I ever hope to be like them? Doricha watched as one of the women, an Egyptian beauty with a slender, almost boyish figure, took her place in the center of a group of couches. Lamplight sparkled in the golden combs that held her black hair; it caused the draped white silk of her gown to glow like the Dog Star in the evening sky. The woman sang a few lines of some sweet, lilting song in the Egyptian tongue, in perfect harmony with the chords the musicians strummed. Doricha did not understand the lyrics, but she felt the delicious ache and wistful longing conveyed by the singer's voice. The men who watched her raised their cups in salute, and she accepted their praise with a confident nod of her jeweled head. *I'll never look so fine, never command the attention of a whole room that way.* Doricha's thoughts were dismal. *She makes it look easy as falling down, but I know better. Reckon Iadmon made a mistake in buying me, after all.*

A few lines of her master's conversation pulled her abruptly from that morose reverie. "Won't you have some wine?" Xanthes said to Iadmon.

Doricha's face flushed hot; she flicked her eyes back toward her master, watching and waiting tensely. Xanthes was gesturing to a passing slave, who bore a wine pitcher glazed in the bright, reflective blue-green of Egyptian faience. Doricha swallowed the sudden lump in her throat, wondering if she ought to speak up—and how she might safely deflect Iadmon from his host's offer.

But to her relief, Iadmon turned Xanthes aside with a self-deprecating chuckle. "I must disappoint you by asking for watered wine, my friend. Your feast promises to be such a fine affair; I want to keep my head clear well into the night, so I may enjoy every moment."

Xanthes' smile was all good-natured acquiescence, but his narrow-set eyes gleamed in a way that made Doricha feel wary. "Surely, Good Man Iadmon, that makes you the wisest man in attendance." He snapped his fingers, summoning a different slave, who carried a less potent drink in her pitcher.

As the paler red of the watered wine flowed into Iadmon's cup, Doricha allowed herself to relax—but did so little by little, loosening one knotted muscle at a time, so Xanthes would never notice her shift in mood. It wouldn't do to let him see how the prospect of Iadmon in his cups had worried her. That might give him some unfair advantage over Iadmon, and Xanthes was shrewd enough to spot such an advantage and act on it at once. Iadmon's show of good sense was a comfort to her. It seemed the master had taken Aesop's advice to heart; he was mindful of his wine now and would make an effort to maintain a clear head, rather than letting the spirit of festivity carry him beyond his depth. She would keep a keen eye on his wine cup, and would do whatever she could to prevent Xanthes the crocodile from interfering with Iadmon's composure and good sense.

The host's servants carried the next course of the meal into the andron: roasted geese, artfully presented on wooden platters lined with fresh grape leaves, which had been cut to resemble feathers. Balls of soft cheese rolled to the size of goose eggs completed the theme. Xanthes exclaimed over the cleverness of his cooks, then took the choicest portion of the roast goose. He spooned a thick plum sauce over the meat steaming in his supper bowl.

"Brought down by my fowlers last week," he said, gesturing with his knife toward the goose. "Aged to perfection in my kitchen. I swear the Pharaoh himself can't have better cooks than my own. You must try the goose, Iadmon."

"Certainly. I'm a man who appreciates a well-roasted fowl. We ought to go out hunting someday, Xanthes, you and I."

As he spoke, Iadmon lifted his shallow supper bowl and extended it toward the servers, but Archidike sprang up from the couch and took the dish from his hands. "There, now," she said briskly to the servers. "A slice from the breast, from the other side. Plenty of skin, just like the piece you served to Master Xanthes. Good Man Iadmon is our most esteemed guest." Her voice crackled with a rough, gravelly edge, yet somehow it still managed to be feminine—just high enough to border on sweetness. "Come on, plenty of sauce. It's the best part, isn't it?"

Doricha wavered uncomfortably on her feet, torn between remaining where she was—for Iadmon had given her no orders—and serving her master with her own hands. Wasn't *she* his slave, not Archidike? Was it a breach of etiquette, to allow another person to serve her master, when he had brought her, Doricha, especially to this feast? As she hesitated, her quick mind sorted frantically through all the lessons on service and propriety Aesop had ever taught her, but she could find no answer to her questions. All she could do was stand there, blushing and flustered, caught between duty and a strange new social climate she did not yet understand.

Archidike turned away from the servers and presented the filled bowl to Iadmon. She set it on his table with exaggerated care. Her small, firm breasts only seemed to grow rounder and more appealing as she bent over. Then she lifted one finger, red with plum sauce, and slowly sucked it clean.

Iadmon smiled tightly at the hetaera, but did not otherwise respond to her bold advance.

Too bold, Doricha thought sourly. *Guess she's just as young as Xanthes says. None of the older women would be so forward. It isn't— well, it isn't dignified, like. A man can get that kind of thing from any common porna. A woman as privileged as a hetaera ought to be more refined.*

As the men resumed their conversation, Doricha watched Archidike as surreptitiously as she could manage. She was at once fascinated by the young hetaera and repelled by her— intrigued by her coarse, raw, unapologetic sexuality, and faintly offended—on behalf of all hetaerae and hetaerae-to-be—by Archidike's complete disregard for propriety. The other women in the room moved with grace and dignity, holding their heads high with the certainty of their value. But Archidike lolled and shrugged, and cast invasively direct stares about the room, using those strange blue eyes like weapons. She seemed drawn to everything at once, like a child set loose in a room full of toys. She reacted to everything that entered the wide orbit of her interest— passing servants, a shift in the music, the conversations of men at some other group of couches. She laughed at jokes neither Iadmon nor Xanthes made, turning away from the men she was supposed to be entertaining as if they mattered to her not one bit. She shouted a greeting across the room to one of her friends, then licked her thumb and trailed it along the linen-clad buttock of a slave as he walked past. As Xanthes and Iadmon talked sedately, she heaved a sighed in a sudden show of boredom, then flopped back to lie flat along on Iadmon's couch. There she lay, moaning—and Doricha couldn't decide whether the sound was one of annoyance, or some barely restrained passion. Archidike resembled nothing so much as a spoiled house-cat: slinking and cunning, spoiled and petted, thinking and acting only for herself, and no one else.

No, not a cat, Doricha decided. She watched as the prone Archidike arched her back, thrusting up her naked breasts with a beset-upon, horribly fascinating groan. *If the other hetaerae are jewels, then Archidike is a little piece of broken pottery. You find it in the mud, and it's all caked with dirt and foulness. But you can see where it was painted with a scene of a man and a woman together, doing what they do—and even though it's not worth a thing anymore, still you can't keep yourself from looking at it.*

Course after course, the extravagant supper was served, and as each new platter arrived at the master's couch, Archidike rose to serve Iadmon from her own hands. She kept his cup full, too—with the watered wine, relieved Doricha noted. She noted, too, how hard Archidike worked to find some path into Iadmon's affections. The hetaera was observant enough to understand that her initial, more brazen displays had not suited Iadmon's taste. But every new dish she presented gave Archidike another opportunity to refine her approach. By the time the sweet rose-water biscuits were offered to Xanthes and his most distinguished guest, Archidike had hit upon the right way to tickle Iadmon's fancy. She knelt gracefully beside the couch, proffering the biscuits up to her patron-for-the-night with a soft, feminine smile and an air of gentle promise. At last, Iadmon seemed to take real notice of her. He lifted his hand to sample a biscuit, but then he paused with the delicacy halfway to his lips. His eyes roamed over Archidike's face, taking in her undeniable beauty and the faint shimmer of mischief behind the pleasant, very proper smile. His free hand lifted slowly, as if under an enchantment, and drifted to her bare shoulder. He stroked her gently, then caressed her smooth face.

Archidike now seemed satisfied—assured of her patron, confident in her approach. She resumed her place on the couch, pressing close beside Iadmon, who seemed to welcome the contact now. He was still engaged politely in his conversation with Xanthes. But his left hand moved in a slow, insistent rhythm up and down the length of Archidike's thigh.

The hetaera grinned up at Doricha. "So this," she said in that oddly growling voice, "is the very Doricha in the flesh, the famed dancing slave-girl of Good Man Iadmon."

Doricha was at a loss for words. She wasn't even certain she ought to speak to a hetaera. It was permissible for a slave to speak to men inside the andron, of course, if she were there as entertainment or to serve food or drink. But Doricha had never been so close to a hetaera before. She had never encountered one in this way—lying beside her master, and talking to her... actually *talking* directly to her! Was Archidike mocking her, or was her interest in Doricha real? She bit her lip and hesitated, not knowing what she should do—what she *could* do, given the circumstances.

The hetaera continued smiling up from Iadmon's couch, never taking her eyes from Doricha's face. Doricha thought perhaps the older girl's attention should be interpreted as encouraging, perhaps even friendly. Having finally succeeded in attracting Iadmon's attention, perhaps Archidike was more inclined toward fellowship with the girls around her, even if the nearest girl was a slave. What other reason could she have for acknowledging Doricha now, more than an hour into the feast?

"Can't you speak, dancer?" Archidike said—teasing, not unkindly. "Or doesn't your master allow it?"

"'Course he does. It's just that I never spoke to a hetaera before."

"We don't bite." She paused, considering. A dimple appeared in her cheek again as she half-smiled. "Not unless the men pay us to, anyhow. Do you think your master likes it that way?" She snapped her small, sharp teeth together. "Of course, you don't know anything about *that*. Not yet. The pristine condition of

Iadmon's precious, red-haired lotus-flower is legendary. I do believe he guards you more watchfully than he guards his silver."

Doricha felt hot all over with some wild emotion she couldn't identify. Was it shame? Anger? Before she could think of a rejoinder, Archidike sat up suddenly and called out to a group of men and their languid hetaerae, gathered on the nearest couches.

"Hekabe, Iola! And you, Good Man Teris. Who do you think we have here? Look—it's the dancing-girl Doricha!"

"Isn't she a pretty little thing," one of the women said warmly to Doricha.

"That hair," the other agreed. "If you ever lose your wits and decide to sell it, dear, let me know. I'd pay a fortune for a rose-gold wig."

The men laughed good-naturedly. "You can give up that dream now, Hekabe," one of the men said. "Iadmon will never permit you to shear his favorite slave."

"But don't you think her hair would look dazzling with my complexion?"

Doricha's hands flew instinctively to her mound of neatly styled hair. Her cheeks burned.

"What a little sweet-cake you are," the other hetaera said fondly. "The way your cheeks color—you can't hide a single thought, can you? It's terribly charming."

Hekabe's laugh was musical. "Look lively, Iadmon. Iola wants to steal away your slave-girl and raise her like her daughter. Mother Hen, always fluffing up her feathers!"

"I'll peck you hard if you try to cut off my little darling's hair," Iola said. "A wig, indeed!"

Archidike called out again—louder this time, so that all across the andron men and their hetaerae looked up expectantly from their supper and their conversations. "Iadmon won't let you have his favorite slave's hair, Hekabe, but he might let us all have a dance."

"Yes, yes!" someone shouted. "A dance!"

Soon the andron rang with shouts of "A dance! A dance from Iadmon's famous girl!"

Doricha burned with mingled embarrassment and eagerness, so hot she felt she could rival the flames of the oil lamps. The hetaerae nearest to Doricha encouraged her with applause and with their glittering wine cups, raised up in their jewel-covered hands.

Archidike leaned close to Iadmon, murmuring in his ear, "Won't you please agree, Good Man? We would all so love to see your girl perform."

Doricha glanced nervously at Iadmon. She had done nothing to serve him all evening long, yet now the idea of leaving his side sent an inexplicable fear creeping into her gut. Archidike noted her anxious look and said, "Don't worry; I'll take good care of your master while you're away."

Iadmon sat up and gazed around the room. His smile was indulgent. Doricha could see how the acclaim affected him— seduced him. He was a good and kind master, but he was a man like any other, susceptible to flattery and desirous of approval. To have the attention of Xanthes' guests—to have his excellent taste recognized in Xanthes' andron—was a temptation Iadmon found impossible to resist. He savored the shouts for a long moment, then rose from his couch with his usual cultured grace. Iadmon turned slowly, holding up his hands to restore quiet to the room.

"I would be a poor guest," he said, loud enough for everyone to hear, "and would dishonor our generous host, if I refused to let my girl dance for you. I shall be very pleased and gratified to present to you... Doricha!"

He swept an arm toward her. For half a heartbeat, Doricha didn't know what to do. She only blinked at her master, mute and helpless. But in the next moment, her many long months of training rose to the surface of her mind. The eyes of an audience were upon her; she felt their hopeful waiting, their collectively indrawn breath, like a feather's brush across her skin. She responded to her audience's expectation like an animal attuned to the subtlest cues of its trainer, moving with a practiced confidence akin to instinct. She stepped forward, lifting her arms in a dancer's pose, beaming as if she'd never felt a greater joy in all her young life. The andron rippled with the anticipatory murmurs of her audience.

Iadmon gave Doricha a quick, reassuring nod.

"Master," she whispered, "what should I do—what dance? And who will tell the musicians what to play?"

"Any dance you please," Iadmon said. "I know you will choose your best. And as for the musicians, you may tell them yourself."

Doricha turned to consider the musicians. Such an elegant, refined group of people. They were, if anything, even finer than many of the hetaerae at the party... certainly they were more dignified than Archidike. After so long a slave, subject to every whim of her master and tutors, the prospect of choosing anything for herself was precarious and disorienting to Doricha—never mind telling those magnificent players what she wanted of them. How could she even speak to them, let alone command their great talents? Yet they were watching her, waiting for the dancer to name the tune.

It's just got to be done, and nothing else for it. The party was, as Iadmon had told her, a great opportunity, a chance to find admirers and build her friendships now, before she had even arrived at her golden fate as a hetaera. She must be brave, must be excellent, for her future depended on it. *If that chit Archidike can make it as a hetaera, then I can do just as well, if not better.*

With a deep breath to strengthen her spine, Doricha went resolutely toward the players. Behind the musicians' backs, the doors were still open wide on Xanthes' garden. Darkness had finally come; the black cloak of night was thick and velvety, the air lush with the spicy scent of well-watered flower beds, with that first hint of crispness, the harbinger of the Nile's coming flood. The cool air coming in from the garden cut through

Doricha's dazed sense of unreality, sharpening her wits and firming her resolve.

"I'm to dance for the guests, Good Man," Doricha said to the eldest musician, the one with the horn-framed lyre. "Do you know 'The Maiden of the Reeds'?"

"Indeed we do, my girl. But it's a difficult one, and long."

"I'm up to the work." Doricha flashed her most beguiling smile.

"A moment, please." The lyrist turned to the other members of his troop. They consulted quietly, murmuring among themselves, each player in turn casting a doubtful glance at Doricha.

The lyrist returned to Doricha. With a kindly smile, he said, "Wouldn't you rather we played 'Stork on the Wing' or 'The Cattle Drover's Love Song'? They're simpler and shorter, but they always please Good Man Xanthes. We've never seen any but the most experienced hetaerae dance 'Maiden of the Reeds.'"

Doricha had no doubt that Xanthes, with his coarse manners and bullish spirit, enjoyed the simple, inelegant pieces the lyrist had suggested. Xanthes put on a great show of wealth, yet his very ostentation proved that he had little in the way of taste. 'The Maiden of the Reeds' was a far more subtle, expressive dance, full of sweetness and longing—nothing like the clap-and-stamp gaiety of the music Xanthes preferred. And that was exactly why Doricha would settle for nothing else. She had no care for pleasing Xanthes that evening. It was his guests she sought to win over—every great, influential man in the andron. This was her chance, her night to reveal the true depth of her skill to the largest possible group of future patrons. She would not squander the moment on one of Good Man Xanthes' vulgar favorites.

She beamed sweetly at the old musician. "You needn't worry about me. I've been learning the steps for ever so long. And if I make a mistake, why, they'll all think it's terribly charming, won't they—a girl young as I?"

The lyrist chuckled softly. "Perhaps you're right, at that. Very well, young madam. We are yours to command."

Doricha struck the opening pose, raised on the ball of one foot with the other leg lifted high, both arms held straight up, over her head. It was a difficult pose to hold without any graceless wobbling. The muscles in her legs and back strained with the effort of keeping still as she waited for the music to begin. Had she chosen the wrong piece after all? "Maiden of the Reeds" was ambitious... perhaps, as the lyrist had suggested, Doricha was reaching too far. She ought to call it off, choose another song before she made a fool of herself...

But in the next moment, the first unmistakable, softly falling notes of "Maiden of the Reeds" whispered around the andron. The room filled with wondering murmurs as Xanthes' guests recognized the tune. Doricha was committed now; there was no going back, no changing her mind.

Nothing for it now but to dance.

Doricha stepped into the first movements of "The Maiden of the Reeds" with some relief; the strain on her leg and back eased. As she danced the opening strain, the music brought the story to life around her. Such was their skill that Doricha could almost see the small Egyptian village, the lush riverbank flourishing in the first waters of the flood, and her place in that conjured setting, a girl left behind by her first love, summoned off to fight in the Pharaoh's war. She turned and flowed with the music, arching her spine, describing with her hands the ripple of the Nile waters, the swaying of the tall reeds around her, the movement of the wading birds half-hidden in the riverside foliage. Harp and lyre sang together of a tender, wistful longing, and Doricha responded, shading her eyes to peer north along the river, to the place where her lover had vanished on the last boat departed from the quay.

Distantly, she was aware of the stillness that had come over her audience. She held them rapt; they were invested wholly in the story of her dance, even though it was a tale most of them had seen performed many times before. Men paused with their wine cups half-raised to their lips; hetaerae ceased their whispering and leaned toward her, intent on her every move. But awareness of the audience's response barely pierced through the veil of Doricha's fantasy. The musicians were better than she'd hoped, better than she'd realized as she had half-listened throughout the hours of the supper party. They seemed to cradle her every move with miraculously responsive sound, shaping their notes and chords to her every movement, bending the song to fit neatly within a world of her making. Doricha reached out with one searching foot, feeling along the silt of the river's shallows, and the music stretched and extended with her. She spread her arms wide, as if to tell the indifferent water how terribly her heart ached, and the chords swelled in response to her music. She began to work her way around the andron, and the music moved with her, perfectly attuned to her steps, so that Doricha could no longer tell whether she was following the music or the players were following her.

The tenderness of their playing, their gentle caress of every chord, struck Doricha deeply in her heart. A swell of forgotten longing raised in her chest, bringing a mist of tears to her eyes. But it wasn't the soldier of the story, gone off to fight in the Pharaoh's army, that Doricha yearned for now. It was her family, her home—the dark-green hills of Thrace, so far away, but no less dear to her, no matter how much time may pass. She turned and bent and stepped within each cluster of couches, one after another. She met the eye of every guest, man and woman alike, conveying with her every gesture the loss she felt, the longing, the desperation to hold close once more what cruel fate had taken away. Now and then, when the music demanded it, Doricha delivered a coy smile or a girlish flutter of her lashes—but those expressions of maidenly shyness were all the more memorable for the shimmer of tears in her eyes.

Doricha connected, however briefly, with each man and woman in turn. But she did not truly see Xanthes' guests—or if she did, they registered only as shadows, half-formed figures and blurred faces seen through a veil of her true desires. She saw before her everything she wanted but could not have—freedom and security, confidence and strength—and most of all, the prestige and glory that could only belong to a hetaera. She reached for those desires with all the earnest longing of her heart... but like the lover gone off to war, she never could touch them, and the agony of denial showed itself plainly on her face. Long before the song had reached its midpoint, Doricha noted more than a few hetaerae dabbing at their eyes with linen kerchiefs; the faces of even the drunkest, coarsest men had fallen into thoughtful frowns. The copper-haired girl, small and slender as a reed herself, made them all believe the fantasy of her dance.

At last, Doricha had circled the entire andron. She found herself where she'd begun; the music swelled toward its final crescendo. She spun, hands covering her face in the last display of the Reed Maiden's grief, then wilted gracefully to the floor. As the river's current took her, ready to drift her lifeless body north to her lover's ship, Doricha arched herself in the most provocative pose she could manage. The music pattered into its last, wistful chord. But the moment it stopped, when Doricha had hoped to hear her audience's shouts and applause, the andron was so still that she had to hold her breath to keep her ragged panting from filling the room. She was tired from the long, demanding dance; her muscles cried out for air. But to gasp and wheeze now would spoil the heart-rending effect of the Reed Maiden's tragic death. The breath burned in her lungs, but she kept her face perfectly calm, refusing to show any discomfort.

What had gone wrong? Had she displeased Xanthes' guests? Perhaps she should have danced some drover's tune after all. But just when she could stand the suspense no longer, a great crash of applause thundered through the andron. Doricha let out her pent-up breath with an explosive and grateful sigh.

She rolled over and pushed herself up from the floor, moving with slow, careful grace to disguise the trembling of her limbs. She faced the audience and posed again, arms up and one leg out, accepting their acclaim. Then, a slave once more, she lowered her eyes properly and returned to Iadmon's couch.

Iadmon looked up at her with a foolish smile. Gone was his usual air of cultivated control; he peered at Doricha with bleary eyes, his face flushed and his forehead beaded with sweat. "That's my favorite," he said thickly. "My favorite, my famous dancing girl."

Doricha's heart pounded, and not from the exertion of her dance. She looked at Iadmon's cup. Only the smallest pool of wine remained, but it was dark, full-bodied—not the watered stuff he had restricted himself to all night long. *But how can he be so addled up already?* The dance had been a lengthy one, but not long enough for Iadmon to quaff five or six cups of strong wine. It would have taken that many at least to bring him to his present state.

"Master," Doricha said faintly, "are you well? You seem—"

Iadmon flicked the back of his hand at Doricha, brushing away her concern. "More wine!" he called.

Archidike, lounging on the couch beside Iadmon, picked unconcernedly at a cuticle and smiled.

Xanthes' servants were quick to respond to Iadmon's request. Doricha stepped in front of them. "Please, no," she told them quietly. She wanted to preserve her master's dignity—she must; it was her duty. But his sudden state of intoxication frightened her. Something was amiss; the waters of the crocodile pool were rising rapidly around her.

"Your dancing was magnificent," the man with the wine said. But he did not listen to her plea; he stepped around Doricha and refilled Iadmon's cup.

"Please, you mustn't," Doricha said helplessly, clinging to the servant's sleeve. "You can't!"

"What a night," Xanthes boomed. "And Iadmon, what a friend you are. What could make this party better? Ah, I know. Why don't we dice?"

No. Gods have mercy, it's just like the night with the necklace... just like that night...

"Yes!" Iadmon said at once. "Yes, let's have a gamble. I'm feeling lucky tonight, Xanthes. You had better beware."

Xanthes laughed heartily. He clapped his hands to be heard over the hum of conversation and sent one of his slaves to fetch his dicing cups. Other blue-robed servants cleared the table between Xanthes' and Iadmon's couches, making ready for their game. Doricha could do nothing but stand beside her master's couch, watching the dreaded event unfold with a growing sense of unreality. Minutes before, she had earned the highest acclaim with her dance. Minutes before, she had almost been the mistress of her fate. Her skill had taken her to the edge of greatness, and she could see a better future before her—just beyond her grasp, but not for much longer. Now, she was as helpless as a mouse in a hawk's talons.

"Dicing is never any fun without a wager," Xanthes said.

"You are so right," Iadmon slurred. "What shall we wager? For I tell you, I can't lose tonight, my good man."

Doricha knew what Xanthes would say. How long had he waited for this chance? How long had he planned? Like a spider, he had carefully woven this plot, laying a trap to undo Iadmon, whose only slights against Xanthes had been cleverness and a good head for business. Doricha hung her head, avoiding Xanthes' narrow, calculating eyes. But she couldn't shut her ears to the cold triumph in his voice.

"Since you are agreed, Iadmon, and since it is the New Year—a time of great luck, you will agree—then I propose high stakes. Whoever has the best throw will keep your dancing girl."

"Ah!" some of the nearby guests exclaimed. It was a bold proposition, after the whole room had witnessed Doricha's dancing, and seen what a great treasure she was.

"Very well," Iadmon said.

"You heard him," Xanthes called out good-naturedly to his friends. "The bet is on; whoever has the luckiest throw will keep the girl."

Grinning, Iadmon scooped the ivory dice into his cup, but nearly fumbled and dropped them. His movements were slow, clumsy. Doricha chewed her lip as she watched him. Clearly, something more sinister than mere wine was affecting him. Had Xanthes slipped a drug into his cup? *No, not Xanthes...* Archidike lolled and purred beside Iadmon as he shook his cup in the air and spilled out his throw on the table. Three of his dice bounced to the floor—out of bounds, by the rules of the game, and ineligible toward his score. Doricha narrowed her eyes at the hetaera. Archidike seemed to sense her accusation. She looked up at Doricha, dimpling innocently, shrugging as if to say, *You know how men are. So weak and silly when they've had too much to drink.*

The game was over with brutal swiftness. Xanthes threw his dice carefully and well; not a single one fell, and his score was more than enough to handily defeat his opponent. Xanthes clapped again, and his servants hurried in to clear away the dice and the table.

Iadmon sat in silence for a long moment, staring at the place where the table had been—at the place where his fate had turned.

Say something, Doricha silently begged. *There must be something you can do, something you can say to change this. Master, please!*

When Iadmon finally raised his face, he stared at Xanthes with hard, hate-filled eyes. The loss had sobered him up, but it was too late now to take back the wager. Far too many men had witnessed it; the bet was as good as a bond. And Iadmon had lost.

Desperation wracked Doricha's body, chilling her like a blast of Thracian wind. She shuddered, and, ignoring all propriety, wedged herself between Archidike and Iadmon. She clung to her master's arm, drawing his sad, regretful, entirely bemused gaze.

"Master, send for Aesop," Doricha said quietly. "He's clever enough to find some way to make this all right again."

Iadmon did not speak. He only shook his head slowly.

"Aesop will know what to do," Doricha said. "He'll know how to—"

Iadmon stood abruptly. He shook Doricha's grip from his arm. Refusing to look at her or Xanthes, he strode stiffly from the andron.

"Master!" Doricha cried. She hurried after him, ignoring Xanthes' guests as they shouted praise for her dancing. Most of the had not seen the gamble; they didn't know that Iadmon's foolishness had just wasted Doricha's hopes for her future.

As soon as she had caught up to Iadmon, in the dimly lit hall beyond the andron, Doricha seized his arm again. She clung harder this time, wrinkling the silk of his sleeve in both her fists. She dragged at him, weeping desperately, not caring that the hot tears were making a mess of her paint.

"Please, please, Master! Don't leave me here, I beg you! Don't leave me to Xanthes. You know what he wants to do to me!"

Iadmon kept on doggedly toward the door. He did not look at Doricha, did not react to her words. It was as if the gods had struck him deaf—and had turned his heart to stone. He dragged her down the halls and out into the curved front courtyard of Xanthes' estate. There stood his litter, waiting to bear him home —offering its comforting curtains to screen him from the eyes of Memphis, to hide his shame.

Doricha tried once more to appeal to his heart. "Master, haven't I been a good and loyal slave? Haven't I learned well, and all to make you proud of me? Please, Master. You promised me once that you wouldn't waste your money on me if I didn't waste your time. Think of the cost, if nothing else! Don't throw away the cost, Master!"

Iadmon paused. He still did not look at her, only stared into the distance with a grim, fixed expression—but at least he had stopped. With trembling hope, Doricha loosed her hold on his sleeve and waited, looking up at him through the blue shadows of night.

Sobriety had returned to Iadmon. No doubt it was the shock of his loss that had brought him back to his senses, combined with the great shame of being bested by Xanthes before so many witnesses. Now he understood the full weight of what he'd done —what his weakness had cost him. Doricha could see the truth of that in his strained, tragic expression.

Silently, Iadmon turned to Doricha and looked down at her for a long moment. In the faint starlight, she could see a rhythmic twitch at the side of his face as he clenched his jaw again and again. Soon, Doricha knew, soon he would find his words, and would speak to her. Soon he would send his men for Aesop, who would outwit Xanthes and set everything right again. Soon the terrible trajectory of fate would be corrected, and Doricha would go on as before toward a hopeful future.

She reached out and took his arm, gently this time. "Please, Master—"

Iadmon struck her across the face, so hard and fast that at first she couldn't breathe, couldn't understand what had happened to her. All she could do was release his arm and stare blankly into the darkness of Xanthes' garden. By the time Doricha gasped and lifted her hand to her cheek, pressing her palm against her burning face, Iadmon was already halfway across the courtyard. He barked a few words to his litter-bearers, then stooped to enter his litter. But he paused just before hiding himself within the litter's curtains.

"I'm sorry, Doricha," Iadmon said calmly. "But none of this is my fault. You are what you are—a slave—and I am... well, I am also what I am, no more than that. We must both live the fates the gods have made for us."

With that, Iadmon slunk inside his litter. The curtain fell, hiding him from Doricha's view. The bearers lifted the litter swiftly to their shoulders, carried it through the vine-covered gate... and Iadmon was gone.

Doricha stood alone in the courtyard. She shivered; the night felt far too cold for summer, and the taste in the back of her throat, the churning in her stomach, was far too bitter for life. She had imagined every possible way Iadmon might be rid of her, every disappointment she might bring him, every way she might inadvertently anger him and seal her fate. But she had never imagined this. The worst of it was, she wouldn't even have a chance to say her farewells to Aesop.

THE HETAERA'S KNIFE

DORICHA WAS LEFT ALONE IN THE COURTYARD, SAVE FOR XANTHES' household servants in their dark-blue robes. The servants lingered near the row of empty litters, doing their best to fade into the shadows. Surely they wanted to distance themselves from Doricha's obvious distress—and the shame her foolish weeping and pleading had brought upon herself and her master.

Her *former* master. Reality sunk its claws painfully into her flesh; she shuddered and hugged her body tightly, a useless shield against the agony of knowing what lay before her now. She was Xanthes' property, gambled away in a drunken game. There was nothing she could do to change that fact. The last threads of her fragile hope snapped inside her; she covered her face with her hands and wept bitterly, loudly, keening out sorrow and fear, shame and horror as she had never done before, not even when she had first become a slave.

What would happen to her now? The distant memory of Xanthes stroking her in Iadmon's andron, pawing at her skin, came back with revolting force. She could feel his hands on her even now; she flinched but could not escape the sensation. Dread choked her; she coughed, fighting nausea that surged in her stomach.

And then Doricha felt real hands against her body. It was not her imagination, not a curdling memory of Xanthes' greed. But the two hands that rested on her shoulders were gentle and sympathetic—not rough or commanding, as Xanthes' touch would be. Before she even looked up, Doricha knew the touch was feminine. She swallowed and sniffed, quieting her noisy sobs with a great effort, then peered between her fingers to see who had come to offer her comfort.

To Doricha's surprise, Archidike stood before her in the darkness. The light of the Dog Star shone on the hetaera's face, sparkling in the scented oil that saturated her heavy black curls. All the lazy, impudent arrogance Archidike had displayed in the andron was gone now. She looked at Doricha with such obvious fellow-feeling that Doricha began to weep all over again, hiccupping loudly as she struggled to control herself.

"Hush now," Archidike said, rubbing Doricha's back. "Hush, little flower—hush. It does no good to cry. Believe me; I know."

Doricha's cheek still burned where Iadmon had struck her. *He never would have done it, never would have done a bit of it, not even the gambling, if it wasn't for her—Archidike. He would have kept his wits about him, and I would still be his.*

She jerked away from Archidike's touch. "You put something in my master's cup. You made him drunk—worse than drunk! You addled his mind in some way, didn't you? Drugged his wine, and all so he'd forget himself and make the wager."

Archidike sighed, but she didn't deny the accusation. It would have been foolish to try. No one but she had had access to Iadmon's cup. No one but Archidike—who had worked all night to ingratiate herself with Iadmon, like a worm burrowing into the heart of an apple.

"Xanthes knows," Doricha said coldly. "He knows, doesn't he, where Iadmon is weak, what he's likely to do when he loses his wits? He has always known about Iadmon. Xanthes knows, and you did his bidding."

"Yes," Archidike shot back, losing all her patience now. "And what was I to do? I haven't bought my freedom yet. I'm still Xanthes' property, still owned goods, just like you are. If Iadmon had ordered you to do the same to Xanthes, you would have obeyed him in the twinkling of an eye, and put the drug into *his* wine. Don't pretend you wouldn't." Her expression softened. "You'd have been welcome, too, I'm sure. Xanthes is an eel's anus. Drugging him would only improve on what the gods have made."

Archidike reached into the turquoise-beaded band of her dress. It was snuggled tight beneath her exposed breasts; Doricha was surprised to see the older girl pull out a crumpled linen kerchief.

"Where'd that come from, then?" Doricha said, letting her icy disdain slip.

"No one ever knows exactly what I've got hidden about my person." She gave Doricha a sly grin. "Even when I'm naked. You may think you see the whole of Archidike, but you never do. Here, now; let me clean you up. It won't do to go back inside with your face smeared all to Hades."

"I never could go back," Doricha said miserably. "I can't belong to Xanthes now—I simply can't!"

Archidike took Doricha's chin in her hand, fixing her with a serious stare. Those blue eyes leaped at her from the darkness, piercing through Doricha's shroud of misery. "My dear, you haven't any choice in the matter. You'd best get that straight right now, or life will go hard for you. I'd heard before that Iadmon is too free and permissive with his slaves. Now I see that's true. Or have you somehow managed to forget that you're a slave?"

Doricha shook her head. She lowered her eyes to the ground in shame.

"Sensible girl," Archidike said. She released her grip on Doricha's chin. "You must never forget who you are—*what* you are. Soft little duckling like you... haven't got a chance in this game, unless you think sharp and keep your wits about you. And never step out of your place, do you hear?" She began to dab at Doricha's face with the kerchief, cleaning away all evidence of her tears. "You can't afford to forget—what's your name, again? Doricha, is it?—you can't afford to forget that you are a slave, bought and paid. We are both owned goods, you and I... at least, I am for a little while longer. If you're to survive as a slave, you've got to be tough and smart, and aware, duckling, do you see? You've got to know where your boundaries lie—the edges of a slave's territory. You can't make any mistake about that territory. If you get careless and blunder across the boundary, it won't matter that you did it in ignorance. There are knives out there in the world, Doricha—"

Swiftly and suddenly, something sharp stabbed at Doricha's rib. She gasped and tried to twist away, fearful that Archidike had pulled a knife from somewhere unseen, as easily as she'd produced the handkerchief, and had pressed its point into Doricha's flesh. She looked down, fearful that she would see a dark stain of blood soaking through the silk of her dress... but it was only Archidike's finger thrust against her side. The hetaera's long, lacquered nail bit into her skin.

Slowly, with a lazy smile, Archidike withdrew her finger and resumed cleaning Doricha's face. "As long as you know your place, and keep to it, it's really not so bad, living here. Xanthes does have the very best reputation for making hetaerae. There's no one better in all Egypt—or in all the world, I suppose—to set you up properly, get you to the top of the heap. And Xanthes is honorable, in his way. He will free you if you can come up with enough money. I've seen it done myself, so I know it's true."

Doricha sniffled. She didn't want Xanthes, didn't want his

help building her career. She wanted Aesop—her only friend in all the world, the only person she could confide in.

"Reckon I wouldn't feel so bad if I had a friend here," Doricha admitted. She knew it would have been wiser to keep that weakness to herself, but in the face of such unexpected tenderness—from Archidike, of all people—she couldn't stop the words from coming out.

"Friend?" Archidike dabbed the last of the mess from Doricha's face and tucked the soiled kerchief back into her gown. "Make no mistake, Doricha: no one here will be your friend. We're all competing for the same prizes: the men who buy our affections. The money in their purses. The freedom their coin can buy us, but only if we're the best, the most beautiful, the most charming—the most popular. No one in Xanthes' house will be cruel to you, for you're far more valuable whole and unbroken than ruined and abused. But no one will be your friend, either." Archidike held up her finger, the very one she had pressed into Doricha's ribs. The nail shone in the light of the Dog Star. "And always remember, little lotus: hetaerae have the sharpest knives of all."

She turned briskly toward the house. "Come along, now. The feast is nearly over; the men will soon start drifting off to private rooms, or out into the garden with their girls. My patron has run off home with his tail tucked between his legs, so there's no reason for me or you to go back to the andron. I'll take you to the women's quarters instead."

Doricha curled her toes in her sandals, rooted to the spot. Archidike may have been kind to her, but she wasn't her friend. She had just said as much. Doricha had no reason to trust her. "I won't go with you. You deceived me and my master."

The hetaera brushed her black curls from one shoulder. Archidike watched Doricha with a stubborn levelness that sent a prickle of dread up her spine. "Xanthes told me to bring you to the women's quarters," Archidike said quietly. "I always do what my master says. Do you doubt it?"

"No," Doricha answered meekly.

"Then don't make me prove it's true. You won't like it if my hand is forced."

She turned away again, sauntering off toward the house, no bothering to glance over her shoulder to see whether Doricha was following. Doricha lifted the hem of her skirt and hurried after. She fell in step behind Archidike, and as they made their way through the gaudy corridors of Xanthes' house, Doricha recalled Iadmon's warning on that first day, when she had stood with him beside the Samian Wind at the docks in Tanis.

If you are not strong enough to face the other hetaerae, to fight for the wealth that could be yours, you may find yourself knocked down to the status of a common porna. Or worse, you may end up in the river, dead at the hands of some rival who is fiercer and cleverer than you.

The stars peered in through every window Doricha passed, glittering cold and hard as the points of knives.

❧

XANTHES KEPT a whole wing of his house dedicated to the hetaerae who worked for him—a dozen or so beautiful and talented young women—and the staff that tended exclusively to their needs. The hetaerae themselves referred to the wing as the Stable, half joking, half grim. The Stable was connected to the main estate by a long corridor, yet it stood well apart from the great rooms where Xanthes dwelt, where he conducted his business and entertained his guests, and where the remainder of his servants and slaves lived. The hall that led to the Stable was quiet, dimly lit by the amber-yellow flames of a few guttering oil lamps. The light flickered in a monotonous rhythm along the painted walls; the murals of women entertaining men—in every conceivable way—seemed to dance lazily as Doricha passed.

Archidike threw open the door at the end of the hallway, revealing the place Doricha must now call her home. The room was as empty as the hall had been, and nearly as long as the corridor outside. Its mudbrick walls were brightly painted, too— although here, the images were more serene than in the corridor. Plenty of freshly lit lamps illuminated the murals: gardens and lily pools bloomed along the walls, while goddesses both Egyptian and Greek looked down benevolently from the skies.

Recessed alcoves were set deeply into the walls, spaced evenly down the length of the room. Each alcove had a curtain across its mouth. A few curtains had been left open; Doricha could see that the alcoves were just wide enough to hold a bed and a couple of shallow shelves. Women's personal effects lay scattered on some of those shelves: combs and hair pins, bottles of perfume, the faded twist of a dried bouquet.

Large and grand as the room itself was, the stuffy, dark alcoves made Doricha's heart sink. Her room at Iadmon's house was small and plain, but at least it had been private. These curtained holes brought back hard memories of Tanis, and promised no opportunity for seclusion, for time alone with her thoughts. Doricha wished for her home—Iadmon's estate—with a sudden, painful wrench of longing. There was no chance here that fresh breezes would find their way in from the garden. The air of the Stable was heavy, close with the reek of perfume and hair oil. And there was certainly no Aesop here to visit Doricha— to cheer and encourage her.

"Come along, Duckling," Archidike said.

She led Doricha briskly down the length of the Stable, to an alcove near the rearmost wall. Its curtain was pulled back to reveal a space emptied of all personal items. The bed was of the old Egyptian type: a wooden platform raised up on four simple legs, with a slight slope that ran from head to foot. It was topped by a thin mattress of coarse, unbleached Kushite cotton, stuffed with flax stems that crackled faintly when Doricha poked the mattress experimentally. Linen sheets, reasonably soft-looking, were neatly folded and stacked on the foot of the bed. A silk cushion lay atop the sheets. The two narrow shelves that jutted from the alcove's wall were entirely bare; they didn't hold so much as a speck of dust.

"Your bed," Archidike said. "This one used to be Semat's, but she left us a few months ago—bought her way out, the lucky bitch. I hear she's set herself up in Mendes. Of course, there can't be a lot of patrons in a town like Mendes—it's so small and unimportant. But there can't be many hetaerae there, either, so no doubt Semat has no competition. It's hard to keep ahead in Memphis, with so many other girls vying for your men."

The Stable door banged open. Doricha peeked out from her alcove to see a few hetaerae wander in. They were talking among themselves, yawning and stretching as they went. A few were already untying the laces of their gowns and pulling the jeweled combs from their hair, long before they'd reached their beds.

"I always get stuck with the oldest men," one of them complained as she loosened the neck of her vibrant orange dress. "They leave early—before any of the real fun starts."

"Xanthes' parties are boring, anyway," another girl said, stifling a yawn. "You aren't missing a thing."

"It's true," said a third as she slid golden bracelets from her wrists. "Believe me; I've seen enough of his feasts to know. Besides, you should be glad you're always paired up with the old men. They rarely want to tup you with their tired old cocks, but they still pay just as handsomely."

The first—the one in the orange dress—agreed. "Some of the money I've had from the white-haired grandfathers, you'd think they'd ridden me all night long. But I never had to do anything more than smile at their jokes and bat my eyes."

The girls giggled. One of them tossed something high; it winked and flashed as it rotated in the air. It was a hedj coin,

Doricha realized. The hetaera who'd thrown it caught it and flipped it again, grinning up at her pay as it sparkled in the air.

"Careful," Archidike called. "Persephone will steal your pay right out of the sky. She has quick fingers."

"Not as quick as yours," said Persephone of the orange dress. She flashed a rude gesture at Archidike—the first two fingers of her hand waggling in a suggestive way—and the group of hetaerae laughed again.

"Look there," said the one with the silver coin. She caught the coin, tucked it into the bodice of her dress, and drifted closer. "It's the dancing girl. Come to be a filly in Xanthes' Stable, have you?"

The hetaera was clearly joking, but when she saw fresh tears spring to Doricha's eyes, the mocking smile slid from her face. She clucked in sympathy.

"Xanthes won her in a wager," Archidike said airily, as if she'd had nothing to do with it.

"No doubt he did. After the way you danced, girl, I'm sure Xanthes would have done anything to get you."

"It really was a marvelous dance," one of the other girls added. "I don't mind telling you so. You've got real talent, especially considering you're so young. But don't ever let Bastet think you know how good you are. She fancies herself the only real dancer in the Stable; she'll claw your eyes out if she thinks you aim to steal her praise."

"Bastet," Persephone agreed darkly. She hissed, curling her fingers like claws, giving a good impression of the Egyptian cat goddess from whom the jealous hetaera had evidently taken her name.

"Thank you for warning me," Doricha muttered. It only intensified her pain, to think that dancing—her only joy in the world —had inspired Xanthes to take her away from Iadmon. Doricha had done her best to impress Xanthes' guests, but now she felt as if the dance had betrayed her.

"Keep dancing like that," one of the girls said, "and you'll buy your freedom before you know it."

Doricha glanced up at the hetaera. "What does it cost, anyway? To buy my freedom?"

"What, leaving so soon?" Persephone asked slyly. "You only just got here."

"Is Iadmon's white lotus too chaste for this kind of work?" said the one who had warned her about Bastet. "Mother Isis here will be a virgin until she dies!"

"Leave off, Callisto," Archidike said wearily. But she raised one dark brow as she eyed Doricha skeptically. "Surely you're not a virgin, Duckling. Iadmon had you plenty of times, I'd wager."

Callisto snorted. "If you're going to wager, best to do it with Iadmon. You'd be sure to win a nice, fat prize." She mimed tipping a cup to her lips again and again, while the other girls laughed.

"Never mind if you are untouched," Archidike said to Doricha. "Xanthes will soon cure you of *that*. Now come along; we need to find you some robes. That dress of yours is pretty, but it's only suited to a feast, and anyway, it'll go into the dresser's closet now, for anybody to use. That's the way we do it here. If you want something to be yours and yours alone, you've got to buy it with your own coin. But who'd waste hedj on pretty dresses when she could save all her silver for freedom?"

Archidike opened the big, green-painted door at the rear of the Stable. Lamplight spilled inside, revealing a room packed with cedar chests, standing wardrobes, and jewelry casks on countless shelves.

"The dresser's closet," Archidike said. "Don't ever try to steal anything from it. Amenia is the official dresser, and she knows every damned stitch and thread in this collection. She'll ruin your life if you cross her—absolutely *ruin* it."

"Amenia's got a wasp up her cleft," Callisto said dismissively.

"You're just dying to reach in and pull the wasp out,"

Archidike retorted. She turned back to Doricha. "This wardrobe here holds all the everyday clothes. You can wear anything you like from this chest, without having to ask Amenia first. But be sure you keep on her good side; she'll tell you which clothes you can wear from the other chests, and which you can't—jewels, too. Once you're working as a hetaera, your appearance will either make your career or destroy it. Best to be sure Amenia is your closest friend."

"What did you do to cross her, then?" Persephone muttered at Archidike. "You look like a cheap porna in that dress."

"Better a cheap porna than a dockside slut who gives it away for nothing," Archidike replied. She worked as she spoke, gathering supplies from Amenia's wardrobe and dropping them in a small basket at her feet.

Doricha shrank from the venom in the two girls' voices. A hard edge of mistrust, even of hatred, was plain to be felt within the Stable. Xanthes' hetaerae might put on a good show of camaraderie when they were among their patrons, but now it was plain to see that their friendships were brittle and shallow.

But that makes sense, and all, Doricha thought. *Don't their futures depend on finding men to pamper and keep them? They've got to stand out in a crowd of beautiful women. And now,* she realized with a shiver, *so do I.*

Even in a city as grand as Memphis, there were only so many rich men to go around. She twisted her fingers together to keep her hands from shaking, doing her best to smile at the other women—to make herself as unthreatening as possible—while they laughed and joked and slung their casual barbs back and forth. Now Doricha saw clearly that every one of those girls—indeed, all the women in Xanthes' Stable—was her enemy. Each was already a fierce competitor in a game Doricha had not yet begun to play... but must now somehow win. She hadn't yet reached her fourteenth year, and already she was far beyond her depth. But there could be no going back—not now, not ever.

Only way through is forward, she thought. *Right into the thick and the mess of it, gods have mercy.*

Doricha figured she had better start playing the part now. If she could convince these hard, world-wise hetaerae that she belonged with them, then she could convince anybody of anything. She turned to Persephone, bracing her hands on her hips, and said brusquely, "Tell me what it'll cost to get myself free. Don't try to put me off, now; I want to know."

Persephone blinked at Doricha, startled by her sudden boldness. Archidike laughed. Doricha couldn't decide whether the laugh sounded cruel or amused.

"It all depends on what Xanthes thinks you're worth," Archidike said. She threw an arm around Doricha's shoulders. "And he already thinks you're worth plenty, or he wouldn't have risked Iadmon's anger."

Archidike picked up the basket and left the dresser's closet, kicking the door closed behind her. She led Doricha back to the alcove. There, she plucked item after item from the basket, laying them out on the bed.

"Tunics," Archidike said, pointing, "ten hedj each."

"Ten! They're never worth that much."

"They are if you ask Xanthes. Belt and rags for your monthly flow, whenever that finally comes—another ten hedj. Sandals, twenty. Hair oil—ten for now, but Xanthes and Amenia will want you in better stuff, something that smells much sweeter. Fifty? Sixty? Possibly more. Paints for your face, and the brushes to apply them: at least a hundred."

Doricha gasped.

"Believe it," Archidike said. "The paints are of such high quality that they might actually be worth that much, too—the only honest cost Xanthes charges. And there will be more expenses." Archidike ticked them off on her fingers. "Food to keep you alive, oils for your baths, the hairdresser's fees, the fees for the musicians who will accompany your dances. I could go on; there are more costs I haven't named yet—costs I've entirely forgotten. And all that's on top of the value Xanthes sees in you—what he must get back if he ever hopes to replace you with a girl who's just as talented and pretty."

"Oh," Callisto called languidly as she undressed in her alcove, "and don't forget the three-quarters. You'll give three-quarters of everything you earn to the master."

Doricha swallowed hard, fighting back the burn of fresh tears.

"That's how he makes his fortune," Archidike said. "By skimming off nearly everything we earn."

Doricha looked down at the folded tunics and the basket of cosmetics lying on her bed. She struggled against a rising tide of despair; its dragging current threatened to suck her under and rip the breath from her lungs. She knew—Aesop had told her—that the younger a hetaera freed herself and struck out on her own, the more successful she would be, and the longer her career would last. *But how will I ever get out of this place while I'm still young? How can I hope to make my way in the world, with such a debt already hanging over me?*

"I'm for bed now," Callisto announced. "Don't keep me awake with your chatter, any of you, or I'll scratch your eyes out faster than Bastet could."

"We should all go to sleep," Archidike said quietly. "It's always wise to get some rest when you've got the opportunity. In this line of work, only the gods know when the chance will come again. Oh, I know it seems grim now, Duckling. But you're a very fine dancer—one of the best I've ever seen. Certainly, you're better than Persephone over there, and if you want to know the truth, Bastet dances like a cow wallowing in a marsh; she's nothing to worry about. Don't tell her I said so, but it's true. Good as you are, you'll earn your way out from under Xanthes' heel before you know it. Just wait and see if you don't."

Archidike gave Doricha an encouraging smile, then pulled her curtain shut. The lamp light was mostly blotted out, leaving only soft, greenish gloom in the alcove where a weak glow seeped past the edges of the curtain. Doricha transferred her things—the shackles that would keep her chained to Xanthes—on the lowest shelf, then spread her sheets over the bed and climbed numbly onto the mattress. Her breath was ragged and stunned in the small space of her alcove. She lay with her covers pulled up to her chin, willing herself not to cry. Her eyes remained dry until at last, the gods took mercy on her, and she drifted away to sleep.

11

THE NEEDLE

A VIOLENT CLATTER RIPPED DORICHA FROM SLEEP. SHE GASPED AS she lurched up in her bed, half convinced she was still sleeping and was caught in the grip of a nightmare—for a woman's hard, angry face hung inches from her own, glowering and severe. Doricha jerked the covers up to her chin, her teeth chattering with fright. But even in her shock, Doricha's careful training in observation—that crucial skill which Aesop had so patiently instilled—rose to the fore. She looked carefully around. The furious woman had knocked aside Doricha's curtain—that accounted for the startling sound. The sleeping alcove was still cloaked in gloom, but the quality of its dimness had changed. There was a warmer cast to it now: the sun was entering the great chamber of the Stable, probably via the long stone shafts of the wind-catchers, and gently suffusing the whole room with its light. Morning had come.

Doricha decided that she was not dreaming after all; the angry woman was all too real. She scrambled from the bed, naked and shivering in the cool air. The woman seized her by the arm and dragged her roughly from of the alcove. She heaved

Doricha across the room. Doricha stumbled and flailed, crossing the whole of the chamber with a terrifying momentum. Archidike caught Doricha in her arms, just in time to prevent her from sprawling across the floor.

Archidike righted Doricha, then turned her about to stand beside her, facing the wrath of the pinch-faced older woman. Only then did Doricha notice that Archidike's curtain was tucked neatly back, revealing her perfectly made-up bed and her orderly shelves. The older girl was already dressed in one of the white tunics from the dressing closet, which, though plain, was soft and well-woven. Archidike's long, black hair had been brushed out and was now pulled back with a wooden comb. The curls she had worn at the previous night's party now hung in loose waves down her back.

The woman stalked toward Doricha and Archidike. "Sleeping the morning away like a cat in a patch of sunlight," she boomed. Her voice filled the whole chamber—startling, from a woman as thin and wiry as she.

Doricha risked a quick glance down the length of the Stable. The other girls were up, too, dressed in white tunics with their hair combed out, like Archidike. Each of them stood beside an open alcove; the beds inside were neatly made.

"That won't be tolerated a second time," the woman said. She was not shouting, exactly—yet Doricha was sure that every word could be heard throughout the chamber and beyond—in the corridor outside, in the farthest reaches of Xanthes' estate— across the whole city of Memphis. "You will be up with the sun each morning, dressed and presentable, unless you are nearly dead from illness. Or unless you would like the strap. Am I understood?"

Archidike dug her elbow into Doricha's ribs. "Yes," Doricha said at once. "Yes, er... Mistress."

The woman narrowed her eyes at Doricha and leaned in

closer. "Your skill as a dancer is laudable enough, I'll grant you, and well known by now. But you have much more to learn if you're to do Xanthes' name any credit."

For a moment, Doricha wondered what else there could be for her to learn. But then Archidike gave a quiet snicker, and Doricha understood. She knew, of course, what hetaerae did with men—what their true function was, beyond the singing and dancing and artful conversation. Aesop had prepared her well for the path that had lain ahead, telling her in frank but gentle terms everything she would need to know to work successfully as a hetaera. But she was on a different path now. Xanthes was not Iadmon—and he was nothing like Aesop.

Her mouth went dry at the thought. She said meekly, "I'm not a woman yet, Mistress."

The glowering woman—quite tall for her sex and angular as a spearhead—reached quickly for Doricha. She thought the woman might strike her for talking back, and flinched away. But instead of hitting her, she pinched one of Doricha's small breasts —like a cook assessing the fatness of a calf, determining whether it was ripe for the slaughter.

"You'll be a woman soon enough, if these are any indication. It's best if you begin learning the trade now. Archidike has an engagement later this morning. Tell me who you're to see, Archidike."

She wasn't asking out of any lack of knowing; Doricha understood that at once. She was testing Archidike's responsiveness.

"Old Nikostratos," Archidike answered. She leaned toward Doricha and added, "He's a regular. Funny old creature: likes it in the morning instead of at night."

The mistress gave a single sharp nod. "The very one. Our new girl here will accompany you. I know Nikostratos won't mind. Doricha, you will wear the green girdle, and *do not take it off*, no matter what may happen or who may implore you—or who may *command* you. The green girdle marks you as untouchable—not a worker yet. You will attend this engagement so that you may observe and learn. But you will only observe. Am I understood?"

"Yes, Mistress," Doricha said hastily.

The tall, thin woman moved back down the chamber toward its exit, inspecting each hetaera she passed, issuing orders and snapping out corrections along the way. Not once did she offer a kind word; not once did she praise any of Xanthes' girls.

"Her name's Zona," Archidike whispered, "but we call her Vélona." The name meant *needle*. Doricha thought it very apt. "But you should call her 'Mistress,'" Archidike advised, "and do everything she says. If you're obedient and don't cause her any bother, she'll leave you well enough alone."

"But who is she? I thought we belonged to Xanthes. Why do we call her Mistress, if Xanthes is the one who owns us?"

"Ah, so he does. But you can't expect Xanthes to run things himself, can you? With all the important business he has to conduct—all the big, dreadfully dull parties he has to throw? He leaves management of his Stable to the Needle, and I've no doubt he pays her very well. She used to be a hetaera herself, you know, but only the gods can say how she ever made a living at it. Probably, that's why she works for Xanthes now—can you imagine any man wanting to tup that hard old piece of fish-leather?"

Vélona shouted out a few final orders and swept from the room. The moment the door closed, the Stable swarmed with activity. The dressing closet door swung open from the inside, revealing a plump woman with a pursed mouth and a critical eye, whom Doricha took to be Amenia, keeper of the wardrobes. A few of the girls gathered towels, combs, and jars of oil, then headed toward the bath—but the majority hurried toward the dressing closet, shoving and pulling at one another in an attempt to get there first.

"Come along," Archidike said. She took Doricha by the hand

and rushed her toward the closet. "Let's get ready. We'll need to leave soon after the first meal; Nikostratos will be waiting."

Because their alcoves were so close to the closet, Archidike and Doricha were the first to arrive. The other girls queued up behind them, muttering impatiently. Archidike ignored them.

"I've got a very particular client," she said to Amenia. "I'll need to look like a young, fashionable, high-society wife."

"The old man again?" Amenia said, amused. "I've got just the thing. Easy to get in and out of, too; you'll like it, Archidike."

The plump dresser retrieved a sky-blue robe from one of her chests, then chose a beaded white sash to complete it.

"These are pearls on the sash," Archidike said. "My thanks— good old Amenia! Nikos will like it, I'm sure."

"All the newly married ladies in Memphis are covering themselves with pearls. If he wants you to look like a fresh bride, this is just the thing." Amenia turned to Doricha, fondling her chin thoughtfully. "But you... Ah, yes; I know just the right look for you."

Amenia went to another wardrobe and produced a flowing, silky dress in an innocent blossom-pink. She held it up beside Doricha's face, squinting critically at the color. "It will go nicely with your hair. And here, I have a girdle in the right shade of green to complement that robe nicely. Archidike, you'll have to show her how to put the girdle on. Be sure you tie it tightly."

Archidike led Doricha back to her alcove and showed her the proper way to don the pink robe.

"Now the sash," Archidike said. "Wrap it tightly. No, tighter. *Tighter*, you mouse! You've got to leave enough of a loose end, so you can shape the knot just so. And then the knot is stitched with matching thread, to be sure nobody breaks into the precious vault. Tie the knot this way; Vélona is very particular about the look."

Archidike wasn't satisfied with the green sash until it wrapped

Doricha from just below her breasts to the tops of her hip-bones. Its snugness made it nigh impossible to bend or slouch, but once Archidike had stitched the knot in place, the sash did feel rather defensive and fortifying, like a soldier's armor. Doricha supposed she would soon grow used to the thing.

"Now sit here, on this stool," Archidike said. "Right up close beside the lamp. Hold my mirror up so you can see your face; I'm going teach you how to paint yourself like a real, high-class hetaera."

Doricha pressed her lips together, smothering a smirk. Archidike was the last girl in the Stable with any claim on class. But she was grateful for the help and had no desire to alienate her only friend in this dangerous new world.

"I had another slave's help with the paints, back at Iadmon's place. With my hair, too."

"You'll get a helper here... eventually. But no new girl ever has help with her paints. You've got to earn that kind of attention from the master—and from Vélona. We all share the hair dressers, though, even the new girls like you. And Vélona only hires the best, believe me. Hair is too easy to get wrong, and takes too long to fix if you make a mess of it. The hair dressers will be along shortly. You'll see; they're marvelous at their art."

Archidike led Doricha through the ritual of lining her eyes, darkening her lashes, and brushing her lids with bright colors. The older girl was skilled with paints and the thin antelope-hair brushes, but the lovelier Doricha looked, the lower her spirits fell.

"What's the matter with you?" Archidike said, taking the mirror from Doricha's hands. "Can't you cheer up, even a little? It's me has to work today, not you."

"All I can think of is how long it'll take me to pay for these things," Doricha said. "The kohl and the lip-color and all the rest. And use of this robe, and the hair dresser, and... oh, it seems to me I'll never get free."

Despite her natural hardness, Archidike did seem to have a soft, sympathetic side. She patted Doricha on the shoulder, then gave her a bracing squeeze. "Once you have patrons of your own, you'll be amazed at how quickly your money adds up. You'll learn what each man likes, and you'll learn how to present yourself in the way that pleases each patron best. That's the way to get the most money: make yourself over for each patron especially; be the living embodiment of his fantasies. Any pretty girl can pass for a hetaera, if she can talk without sounding too foolish. And if she can fall on her back at the right time. But if you can transform yourself for your patrons—if you can become the secret fruit they hardly even knew they were craving—then you'll be one of the great ones." She winked, flashing her dimples. "You can trust my word on that count. I'm very close to buying my freedom already."

"Are you?" Doricha said, surprised. "But you can't be old enough. How old are you, anyhow?"

"I'll be seventeen soon. Been a working hetaera for three years." She raised her voice, so all the girls in the Stable could hear her boast. "But I'm one of the best there is—not only in Xanthes' Stable, but in all of Memphis."

Callisto answered with a doubtful snort. Archidike's fist tightened on the handle of her mirror; she held it stiffly at her side as if it were a sword, staring around the room, silently challenging the other girls to deny her claim. No one spoke against her, though several of the girls snickered or cast peevish looks in Archidike's direction.

Archidike tossed her head. She returned to Doricha and dabbed another touch of red paint on her lips. "Success at this age is rare," she said coolly, "but it can be done. I'm living proof—or I will be, with a bit more silver saved. You'll get there, too, Doricha. Just follow my lead, and be glad you have the chance to learn from the best."

❧

AFTER THE HAIR dresser had finished with them, the two girls hurried to the gynaeceum and made quick work of their breakfast, a light meal of emmer porridge and fruit. Then Archidike presented herself to Vélona, so the mistress might approve her looks.

"You'll do," Vélona said, which Doricha took to be the highest praise one might expect from a woman of her sort. "Off you go, then. The gate guards will expect you back by the time the sun is high."

"Why aren't we sent off in a litter?" Doricha asked Archidike as they strolled out through the vine-wrapped gate. Doricha was made to carry an ostrich-feather fan on a long pole, which was meant to keep the sun from burning her skin and ruining her tender complexion. She fussed with it as they walked, trying to find a comfortable way to hold it. "Seems to me a litter would be safer."

"If we had a long way to go, or if the weather were bad, we would certainly go by litter. But Xanthes and Vélona know I'm a girl who can be trusted. They're pleased to let me walk, if my patrons are nearby. And I'm glad for it; litter-bearers don't work for free, you know. Every hedj I can save is another piece of silver to buy my freedom. Besides, walking is pleasant, don't you think? It's nice to get some fresh air after the Stable's stink—all that perfume and oil in one place, not to mention the way some girls come home reeking of sex. I'd much rather smell the garden and the breezes off the river. Walking keeps you from growing too plump, as well."

"But what's to stop either one of us from running off?"

"You'd be a fool to try it," Archidike said. "Xanthes' girls are well known, all throughout Memphis. Some of us have reputations that reach beyond Memphis, too. You will certainly be well known in the city, with your dancing. You'd be caught straight away and brought back to Xanthes. He'd probably have you maimed in punishment."

Doricha shivered.

"What would you do then?" Archidike went on. "You'd never work as a hetaera with your beauty spoiled, that's for certain. No, escape is right out—too risky. Earning your way out is the only sensible thing. But why would you want to get out, anyhow? It's the easiest life there is, Duckling. Oh, I know the Stable and Vélona are horrid, but they won't last forever—not for a couple of likely girls like us. What would you rather do, except be a hetaera? Go take up as the wife of some goat-herd out there in the western hills, and whelp a litter of screaming brats in the mud? I don't think so."

Doricha laughed comfortably. What Archidike said was true enough. She was still mourning the loss of the easy life she'd enjoyed in Iadmon's house, but even so, Doricha knew she hadn't fallen so far that she couldn't pull herself back up again. The crisp, damp air rolling off the Nile did seem to refresh her spirits. She smiled up at the sun dazzling on the roof-tops of Memphis as she and Archidike moved south along the river, and waved gaily to the group of young men who shouted greetings as they passed. Memphis was beautiful in the morning light, blushing like a maiden, the white-plastered houses and merchants' shops picking up the rose-petal tint of the sky. Doricha had lived in the city for more than a year, but she had never been allowed to wander freely. Now she understood why Iadmon had always proclaimed Memphis was the grandest city in the world. Its quiet, dignified beauty stirred Doricha's heart with pride; the shops and inns she passed thrilled her with their intriguing combination of old Egyptian and new Greek styles.

As she followed Archidike across a market square—just beginning to fill with the peddlers who would soon noisily hawk their wares—Doricha noticed the square, high roof-tops of a distant building peeking above even the tallest estates.

"Look," she said, pointing, "what's that place, there? That big building rising over the rest?"

"Don't you know? It's the Pharaoh's palace, for Hathor's sake!"

"Never saw it before, that's all," Doricha said rather sulkily. "Or if I did, I never noticed it much. But oh, it looks so pretty with the light running all along the top of it, like melted honey. It's the biggest house I ever saw."

"It's even bigger than it looks from here. King Amasis lives in high style, I can tell you."

"How do you know? Have you been inside his palace?"

"No," Archidike admitted. She sounded resentful. "Not yet. The Pharaoh doesn't have much use for hetaerae, does he? He's got wives and concubines by the dozen. As for how I know... he's the Pharaoh, Doricha. The richest, most powerful man in all the world. How else would he live, except in the very highest of styles?

Doricha shrugged.

"I would like to see the king's palace someday, though," Archidike mused. "I'd wager the whole place is leafed in gold, and even the privies smell like myrrh. It seems half the men I know think King Amasis is a proper fool who's forgotten how to be Egyptian, but a Pharaoh can't be that bad, can he? Otherwise, the gods would be rid of him. They'd replace him with a better man. And anyhow, I don't see why it's so much better to be Egyptian than Greek. I'm half of each, and I do all right."

They came upon a lane that curved toward the riverfront; the air was dense with the rich smell of water warming in the ever-strengthening sun. Doricha could see the dark, damp stone quays ahead, and the flat expanse of the Nile winking and glinting between them.

"Why are we going to the river?" she asked.

"It's Nikostratos' preference. Remember, I said every man has a secret fantasy, and the best hetaerae play up those fantasies to make their living."

"I remember."

"Well, Nikostratos likes to pretend I'm a newly married woman who's meeting him for a tryst. So naturally, we carry out our transactions in secret, out-of-the-way places. It's not at all necessary—Nikostratos' wife is dead in her grave, and even if she weren't, nobody would bat an eye at a man as rich as Nikos carrying on with a hetaera. But all the sneaking about makes his cock harder than anything else. And the old fellow needs all the help he can get in that regard."

They left the narrow lane, stepping out into the sun-struck barrenness of the quays. Archidike scanned the docks until she found her patron's boat, a small, blue-hulled vessel bobbing gently in its loose mooring. Archidike headed toward the boat the moment she'd spotted it. Evidently, this wasn't the first time she'd met Nikostratos at the riverfront.

"There he is," Archidike said. "The white-haired fellow standing beside the boat's ramp. Now watch me closely. The great act begins now, long before I'm stripped down naked. This is how you make your patron happy."

Archidike drew herself up; her face opened, softened, shed its habitually carnal leer. She transformed before Doricha's startled gaze—so subtly, Doricha couldn't have described precisely how the change took place, yet there was no denying that an entirely new woman stood beside her. Where before Archidike had been rough and brazen, now she fluttered like a delicate blossom tossed by harsh winds. She batted her eyes, sighing as if the world were all too much for one girl to bear—as if she needed a man to protect her. She clutched anxiously at the neck of her sky-blue robe and headed toward her patron's boat, darting glances this way and that. Doricha followed as closely as she dared.

Nikostratos was nearing the end of his sixties, if he had not already surpassed them. Despite his advanced age, he was tall and broad-shouldered; the hint of a stoop and a nearly unde-tectable limp were his only physical concessions to age. His hair was still passably thick, but it had gone as white as the walls of Memphis. He had a kindly smile that put Doricha at ease.

"Ah, my little honey-cake," Nikostratos said when Archidike reached him. "So you decided to come after all."

"Oh," Archidike said in a high, breathy voice, all her usual gravel and grit smoothed away, "I barely got away without my husband noticing. He's so jealous, you know; he watches me like a hawk watches a mouse. Oh, Nikos... I've only been married to that beast for three weeks. How can I *bear* a whole *lifetime* as his wife? He's cruel and cold-hearted... not like you."

Nikostratos glanced at Doricha. His bushy white brows raised. "And who is this, my darling?"

"Erm..." Archidike though quickly. "My maidservant. I told my husband's men that I was going to the market, so naturally, they required me to take my maid with me. But she's mute—" with a sharp, meaningful look at Doricha— "so don't worry. She won't say a word about us. She can't. And if she ever finds some way to tell my husband, I'll stick a knife in her."

A chill raced up Doricha's back. Was Archidike's threat only part of the game? Or did Doricha sense a hint of real malice in her words?

"I see she's untouchable," Nikos said, letting the mask of their play-acting slip.

"Yes. I've got to train her. Mistress's orders." The high, teasing lilt returned to her voice. "You don't mind, do you, Nikos? She won't interfere with us. She'll be a good little thing, I promise."

"Of course I don't mind," Nikos said. He stepped forward and wrapped Archidike in his arms, planting a series of wet-sounding kisses along her neck.

"Oh, I shouldn't," Archidike said. "It's so bad, so wrong. The gods see me! What will I do if my husband finds out?"

"My honey-cake," Nikostratos said thickly, pulling Archidike toward the boat's ramp. "You know you're safe with me. At least until I get you into my bed."

Archidike giggled, and Nikostratos growled with the force of his appetites. Doricha, suppressing a sigh, followed them both up the ramp and onto the boat, which had already begun to rock wildly against its lines. She could only pray that Archidike's assignment would conclude quickly. She had never felt more reluctant or embarrassed in all her life.

THE MASTER'S MONEY

THE GODS DID NOT SEE FIT TO ANSWER DORICHA'S PRAYERS. BY THE time Archidike and Nikostratos had finally finished their transaction, the sun was near its peak, and the streets of Memphis were unbearably hot. Archidike collected her silver from her patron, tucked it safely away, and headed briskly back toward Xanthes' estate.

Doricha trudged along beside her. Her head pounded in the heat. She was sweaty beneath the green girdle; there was grit in her eyes and mouth from the dusty streets, tasting of the faint, oily fishiness of the Nile waters. She was thoroughly worn out from her long ordeal of embarrassment, for she had sat upon on a stool in the corner of the boat's cabin while Archidike had gone about her business, trying to look anywhere but at Nikostratos and Archidike, wishing she could stop up her ears to shut out the mortifying sounds of what was transpiring, too.

Doricha had noticed, though, that the older girl seemed to genuinely enjoy her work—not because Nikos brought her any real pleasure, but because to Archidike it was all one amusing lark. She had played the role of the shy but unfaithful wife so well that even Doricha had begun to believe the narrative, and would have bought into the fantasy entirely, had Archidike not reminded her of the truth now and then. Whenever she was sure Nikos was distracted, Archidike would catch Doricha's eye and comically yawn, or cross her eyes and roll her head on her neck, in a mockery of being ridden so hard that she was losing her wits. More than once, Doricha had come dangerously close to laughing.

But the scene had dragged out for what seemed an eternity. In spite of his advanced age, Nikostratos was as vigorous as a he-goat. Now, as they made their way home through the noon heat, Doricha could hardly countenance Archidike's energy. Wasn't she worn out from the work? Doricha certainly was, and she'd done nothing but perch on a stool, trying to pretend she was somewhere else.

Archidike seemed more energized than ever before. She fairly bounced down the street, calling out to friends and acquaintances as she passed. "Why, there's Phobos, back on his feet. Is your broken leg all healed? Call for me at Xanthes' place—I'll break it for you again!" And later, "Djedi, how's business today? Made enough hedj to come and see me yet? Too bad—next month for sure." She kissed her hand to the admirers who shouted her name from across streets and market squares, and accepted a flower from a man in an old-style Egyptian kilt, who ran to catch her as she stood in the shade of a shop's awning, waiting for a train of donkey-drawn carts to pass by. Archidike squealed in delight over the flower, tucked it coyly into her hair, and then, when the man had showered her with compliments and gone on his way, she had rolled her eyes dramatically.

"That was Seth," she said. "Used to be a man of some means, and saw me as often as he could, but he fell on hard times and lost all his fortune. I think he's quite in love with me," Archidike added lightly, and continued across the street.

"It was sweet of him to give you a flower," Doricha said. "It's good he remembers you."

"I'd like him to go on remembering me, in case he ever comes into money again. But sweetness is all poor Seth has to offer now. That sort of thing's all right if you're a wife, but a hetaera can't pay her debts with flowers and gentle words. It's silver I'm after. Jewels also gladly accepted, as are goldwork pieces, half-share in profitable businesses, and scripts of ownership to estates and farms."

"You never got paid with anything of that sort," Doricha said, laughing despite the pounding ache in her head.

"Jewels and gold bracelets, I have—necklaces, too. If it's got real value, I'll take it. But I do know a few girls who've been paid with scripts of ownership. They're the most fortunate of all, for silver is gone once you've spent it, but a good piece of land can go on paying you handsomely for years. Those are all free girls, though—the ones whose patrons gave them estates." Archidike breathed a satisfied sigh. "One day, Duckling... one day. Freedom isn't so far off, believe me."

Doricha eyed Archidike carefully as she sailed down the street. The silver pieces Nikostratos had given her had long since disappeared, secreted away in some hidden fold or pocket of her dress.

"How far off is freedom, anyhow?" Doricha asked. "For you, I mean. I've only just started."

"You haven't even started yet, but I've no doubt you'll hold the record for shortest stay in the Stable. As for me, I expect I'll be out in half a year. Maybe a touch longer. I'm only glad it's easy work, so the time will go by quickly."

"Don't know as I'd call that 'easy,'" Doricha replied. "Seems you did an awful lot of work for the money."

"Oh, that rolling around and moaning isn't hard. It's all theatrics—like the shows the players put on, down in the amphitheaters. I can teach you how to do it; it's easy enough to learn." Archidike threw an arm around Doricha in an unexpected show of camaraderie. "I don't mind teaching you. You put on a good show of being sweet and innocent—that's your style, isn't it? But you're really a sharp girl, Doricha. I can tell; you've got watchful eyes. Someday, when we've both bought our freedom, we could work together, you know."

"Together? I've only heard tell of hetaerae being in competition. At each other's throats, like. How could we work together?"

"Most hetaerae work on their own once they're freed, I grant you that. But a few of them work together. There are all sorts of ways to do it. We could play off each other, make a big show of the contrasts between us—you're the pristine little farm girl, I'm the dangerous cat—that sort of thing. Or we could put on shows together, if you take my meaning. Might be, we can appeal to a wider group of men if we work together: you're the great dancer; my particular talents may be less refined, but they're in higher demand. Imagine: you dancing and playing the gentle flower for the men who like that sort of thing, who like to feel they've got real refined taste—and me taking them off to the nearest closet to relieve them of their silver."

"Do you think we really could go into it together?"

"Of course. Once we're free, we can do whatever we please. Who's to stop us?"

"But you'll get free ever so much sooner than I will."

"Don't lose sleep over it, Duckling. While I'm working out there in Memphis, a free hetaera, I'll find us a beautiful house where we can live, just the two of us and our servants. So by the time you're all done with the old pig Xanthes, it'll be straight to the heights of society for you."

They arrived back at Xanthes' house, to Doricha's relief. Archidike shouted for the guards to open the gate. The blue-robed men greeted her as she came inside, but the young hetaera made no reply, abandoning the candor she'd shown on the walk with Doricha and resuming her act as the haughty gem of Xanthes' stable. The garden shade swept its crisp blessing across Doricha's skin, driving off the terrible heat and cooling the sweat from her body. She sighed with relief and lowered the feather fan, letting Archidike lead the way back toward the Stable.

The big chamber was empty when the girls returned. "Middle of the day," Archidike said. "Most of the girls are off working by now, heading out to meet their first assignments. The newer ones will be out in the garden taking lessons—practicing their singing and dancing, that sort of thing. But since we worked today—" Archidike stretched luxuriously— "we're exempt from our lessons. Three hours at least until supper; if I were you, I'd use the time wisely, and sleep. There's never enough time to sleep, believe me."

Archidike stepped into her alcove and shut her curtain with an abrupt, suspicious jerk. A moment later, Doricha heard furtive rustling behind the curtain—Archidike extracting her money from beneath her clothing, hiding it away in whatever secret nook she'd found to hoard her growing fortune.

Doricha undressed. She hung the pink robe and green girdle on the hook beside her alcove; Amenia would collect the garments that night, check them for damage, and send them off to be cleaned. She plucked a clean kerchief from her shelf and wiped the sweat from her body, then settled on her bed with a sigh.

She wanted to sleep, and the gods knew she was tired enough that she should have nodded off easily. But now that she was lying still, in the quiet of the Stable, she found that thoughts of Aesop preoccupied her mind. Did Aesop know what had happened to her? Had Iadmon confessed what his secret weakness had cost him?

If only I could get some word to Aesop. He could find a way to get me back safely, and then I could become a hetaera on my own terms, without having to train in Xanthes' way, or live here in the Stable, or put up with Vélona's temper.

For a long while—hours, perhaps—Doricha thought of Aesop, dreaming up a hundred different ways to contact him...

and discarding each in turn, for every plan she made was more flawed and impossible than the last. Sleep evaded her in that grim territory of hopeless surrender to her fate. This was her life now—Xanthes, the Stable, trailing after Archidike as she flitted from patron to patron. She had best make up her mind to accept it, for there was nothing she could do now to change it.

As the afternoon wore on, its pervasive heat crept even into the depths of the Stable. The air grew closer; the clamoring smells of a dozen different perfumes hung more thickly in the room, reviving Doricha's headache with a vengeance. When the door banged open at the far end of the room, the sound was enough to make her wince.

A few of the newer girls, freed from their lessons, had come back to the Stable to prepare for the supper hour. Their voices were loud and tense, and their insistence on talking over one another set Doricha's teeth on edge.

"I swear to Isis, I never saw a worse dancer than you."

"Give over, you lumbering hippopotamus. Think you're the gods' gift to dancing, but—"

"You *would* swear to Isis. The Egyptian princess here thinks she's too good for any proper Greek gods."

"Proper? Whose land are you in, anyway? This is still Kmet, even if it's over-run with Grecian insects."

"*Kmet!*" one of the girls hooted with cruel amusement. It was, Doricha knew, the native name for Egypt.

"Better watch yourself, Bastet. Grecian insects have kept your precious Kmet from crumbling into nothing."

"We thank you, I'm sure," Bastet retorted, her voice dripping with sarcasm.

"You'd better."

Bastet spat a few Egyptian words at the other girl. "Ankh, wedja, seneb." Life, health, prosperity—it was the traditional expression of greeting and gratitude, delivered with an unmistakable note of irony. Bastet went on in Greek: "You pus-filled cleft. All praises to the Greeks, the saviors of Egypt!"

"The Greeks *did* save you ignorant beasts from yourselves. Don't forget it."

"Yes, we've been doing so poorly these past three thousand years. You call yourselves saviors; I call you invaders!"

There was a loud bump from Archidike's alcove, then the rattle of her curtain as she ripped it aside. "If you can't shut your ugly mouths, then go find some cocks to stuff them with! We're trying to sleep!"

"Shouldn't you be picking lice from your pubic hair?" one of the girls shouted to Archidike. "Everybody knows you're infested!"

Doricha crept to the edge of her bed. She peeked around the edge of the alcove. Archidike was on her feet, arms folded below her breasts, leaning casually against the wall. She watched the fight build with a lazy smile. The girls who had returned to the Stable gathered in a tense knot, milling and shouting. At the center, two stood almost toe-to-toe, bristling in one another's faces like cats in an alley.

"Invader!" one of them spat. Dark of skin and hair, she could only be Bastet, the native Egyptian dancer.

"Mindless pack-ass!" the other screeched. She had the lighter coloring that marked her as a Greek.

Bastet lurched at the other, swinging her fist. The Greek girl ducked, then dodged sideways and caught Bastet by the hair. They were both screeching now, like two eagles locked in aerial combat. They tore at one another with their talon-like nails, slapped and kicked with the violence of pent-up rage. Doricha gaped at the fight, but Archidike only laughed—coolly amused, unruffled by the force of the two girls' fury.

The door banged open again. Vélona strode in with plump Amenia close behind her. The mistress cleaved through the group of spectators like a knife through goat's cheese; she and

Amenia each seized one of the fighters and pulled them apart. Vélona shook Bastet hard, bringing her back to sense.

"Bléssed Aphrodite's glorious, golden tits," Vélona boomed, "what is going on here?" She didn't give either girl a chance to answer the question, but forged straight ahead. "How many times have I told you useless chits you're never to strike one another? How many times?"

The group of spectators had scattered to the edges of the room. Every girl wisely held her tongue.

Vélona turned Bastet roughly around and looked her over. The thin woman's cheeks hollowed even more as she frowned. Even from the other end of the Stable, Doricha could see that Bastet had taken a fist to the face. Her left eye was red and puffy; soon it would turn a hideous purple-black.

Vélona glared around the room for a long, silent moment, stabbing each girl in turn with the daggers of her eyes—even Doricha, still half-hidden in her alcove. Then she shouted through the open door: "Guards! Two of you in here, now—move yourselves, or Master Xanthes will hear why!"

"Please, Mistress," the Greek girl said. "We're sorry, aren't we, Bastet? We won't fight again."

"Keep your mouth closed, Efthalia, or I'll close it permanently."

Efthalia subsided and hung her head. Doricha could see how she trembled.

When the guards arrived, Vélona shoved Bastet and Efthalia into their hands, then led the way out of the Stable. She gave no command to the other girls in the room, but they were all quick to follow. Clearly, they had seen this before. Archidike jerked her head at Doricha, silently bidding her to come along. On numb feet, Doricha joined the rest of Xanthes' girls as they made their way out to the garden.

Vélona led her charges to a stone-paved courtyard, bare except for a fountain, which splashed gaily in the hot sun. The girls formed up in a half-circle; Doricha, terrified of incurring the mistress's wrath, took her place among them. Archidike fidgeted beside Doricha, shifting her weight from one foot to the other and sighing heavily, annoyed at having lost the chance to nap.

"Strip off your tunics," Vélona said.

Bastet and Efthalia complied. Neither lifted her eyes from the ground. All the girls stood in grim silence until Amenia bustled up with a wide leather strap in her hands. She passed it to Vélona.

"Turn around," the mistress said.

The two condemned girls reluctantly turned, presenting their backs to the mistress. Vélona swung the strap over her shoulder, paused, then cracked it hard across Bastet's back. Bastet jumped; a strangled cry ripped from her throat, but she quickly regained control. Efthalia was next; she flinched and shuddered under Vélona's blow. The mistress lashed each girl in turn. The smack of her strap against their exposed flesh played a hideous, mocking counter-harmony to the splashing of the innocent fountain.

Archidike leaned close to Doricha's ear. "Wide strap like that won't leave any lasting marks on their flesh. You know why they're being punished, don't you?"

"For fighting," Doricha whispered faintly.

Archidike chuckled, but not loudly enough to attract Vélona's attention. "Don't be a fool. No one cares if we fight. In fact, they expect it. No, Efthalia is being punished for giving Bastet the black eye, and Bastet is getting it for allowing herself to be marred. She can't work again until that eye's healed, you see. They've wasted the master's time and money, for now Bastet will be a useless mouth to feed until her looks have returned." Archidike's voice dropped lower still. Doricha couldn't decide whether she sounded menacing or humorous. "Take the lesson, little duckling: if you're going to hurt another hetaera, do it in a way that leaves no physical trace."

After ten lashes each, Vélona handed the strap to Amenia.

"Take these two to the baths and leave them there," she said to the guards. "Bastet, Efthalia: wash the tears from your faces and make yourselves presentable for supper. The rest of you: get out of my sight, and don't let me catch any of you striking or scratching one another. Am I clear?"

Archidike and Doricha turned back toward the Stable, but Vélona snapped her fingers at them, and Archidike paused.

"Yes, Mistress?"

"I've had a request for the two of you," Vélona said. "You're both to attend Good Man Diokles' party tomorrow night."

"Diokles... do you mean that young spice trader?" Archidike said. There was a note of hopeful excitement in her voice.

"The very same. His wife has just given birth to a son; he's in the mood for a grand celebration. You'll both see Amenia tonight after supper, to plan what you'll wear." Vélona narrowed her eyes at the bath house, into which Bastet and Efthalia had just disappeared. "Don't get any black eyes, in the meantime."

❧ 13 ❧

THE SPICE-MERCHANT'S PARTY

DORICHA AND ARCHIDIKE RODE TO THE SPICE-TRADER'S PARTY IN one of Xanthes' most beautiful litters, for Diokles' party was far across town, on the western edge of Memphis where the bustling city gave way to the peaceful, rolling fields and orchards of the farming district. The litter was gilded, as were most of Xanthes' possessions, its long carrying poles carved like outstretched harpy's wings, the upright posts that supported its silk curtains crowned with roaring lion's heads. Doricha reclined comfortably on dark-blue cushions, each one smelling faintly of the soft wool inside, and watched Memphis go by in the dusky tail-end of sunset. Vividly, she recalled her last litter ride—with Iadmon, on the night when he'd lost her to Xanthes. He had seemed so sad that evening—so wistful. Had he suspected he might lose Doricha? Had the gods whispered some dire premonition in his ear?

"You're quiet," Archidike said. "Are you sulking?" She lounged on the cushions beside Doricha, her dress pulled up so the cool air could caress her thighs. She looked lovely, in a forceful sort of way. The gown Amenia had chosen for her was flame-orange, a shade that bordered on the garish but reflected Archidike's brazen style to perfection. She held a tiny white clover blossom by its thin stem. She plucked out its tubular petals one by one, sucked the sweet nectar from the base of each, then spat it away with a puff of breath.

"What's there to sulk about?" Doricha said.

Archidike toyed with the end of Doricha's green sash—the girdle that marked her as untouchable. "This, for one thing. You won't have any fun at the party, poor thing. Won't make any money, either."

"Reckon my time for all that will come soon enough."

"Soon enough to pay for the use of this dress?" Archidike blew one of the clover petals onto Doricha's robe. It was an exquisite creation—ivory silk, embroidered all over with lotuses and ibis birds, picked out in golden threads. "Or this litter ride? Xanthes' best litter. You can bet it's costing us a small fortune."

"My situation's no different from what yours was, when you were my age." Doricha's pang of nostalgia, her longing for better days with Iadmon and Aesop, had made her snappish. "Why do you try to hurt me and frighten me, Archidike? I never did a thing to you."

Archidike tossed her head and laughed lightly, as if Doricha had missed some all-too-obvious joke. "That's just my way. You mustn't take it personally, Duckling. All the girls in the Stable know what I'm like." She fixed Doricha with a thoughtful stare. "You don't have to wait until you're officially made a hetaera, you know. You can start earning your money now."

"This says I can't," Doricha retorted, holding up the end of her green sash. "And what would Vélona do, if I came back with my girdle undone and silver in my hand? She'd beat me senseless."

"That girdle isn't a fortress. It's sewed around your middle, not between your legs. Or is that dress so heavy that it can't be pushed up?"

Doricha's face flushed. She said nothing. In truth, the same thought had occurred to her: the green silk sash was a very weak shield, and the threads that held its knot in place could be snapped as easily as one tears a spider's web from a garden path. If she wanted to remain untouched, she must place her trust in the men of Memphis. Would they respect the green sash, and leave her be? Could men of Xanthes' sort ever be trusted?

"If the men have any sense, they'll leave me alone," Doricha insisted. "They wouldn't want to cross Xanthes."

"Oh, all men respect Xanthes," Archidike said in a voice laden with irony. "What will you do, little lotus, if some of the men at the party want to have a go at you? Xanthes isn't here to protect you. Vélona isn't here with her leather strap, to drive them back. The men at the party might get other ideas, too, you know. They might all stand around and watch as you're mounted by a dog or a goat."

Doricha's stomach roiled beneath the tight green silk. "They wouldn't do such a thing." She was proud that her voice sounded steady, unafraid—for the gods knew she didn't feel that way. "You're only trying to frighten me, Archidike. It's not working."

Archidike shrugged. She sucked the last petal from her clover blossom, spat it out, and turned her face away to gaze out at the city. "I may torment you, because it's my way, but heed what I say all the same. Whether you've bled yet or not—that sort of thing matters very little to the great men of Egypt. Or of Greece. Or even men in Thrace, and yes, I know you think everything Thracian is superior, the very best the gods ever made. But this is the truth, Doricha: men don't care about us. They don't give a goose's shit, how their greed or their lust or their thirst for violence affects our lives. Best get used to that idea now, for it is the truth."

"Men respect hetaerae," Doricha said, startled by Archidike's sudden candor.

"I don't speak of hetaerae. I speak of us all—hetaerae, pornae, slaves. Wives and sisters and daughters. To powerful men—and even many weak men—women are nothing more than trade

THE SPICE-MERCHANT'S PARTY

goods. Just little bits of nothing, to be used in any way they please and discarded like trash afterward." She tossed the wilted clover stem off the side of the litter. It disappeared in the street below.

Doricha bit her lip. What Archidike said couldn't be true—or at least, it couldn't be the whole of the picture. Aesop didn't treat women that way, and he was a man. But then, Aesop was also a slave.

Still and all, it's a grim way to look at life, a miserable dark way of seeing half the people in the world. What terrible things had been done to Archidike in the past, Doricha wondered, to make such a young woman turn so hard and cynical? She almost felt sorry for the girl—but Archidike's warning prickled along Doricha's spine, and settled deep in her mind. She was too concerned now for her safety to give herself over to sympathy.

Archidike fell silent, watching the evening shadows creep across Memphis. By the time they arrived at Diokles' estate, Doricha's insides were so knotted up with anxiety that she could barely rise from the cushions and climb from the golden litter. Diokles' household steward came forward to greet them and usher them inside; it took all of Doricha's training in composure and confidence—training that good, dear, forever-lost Aesop had given her—to keep her country-girl expression of pleasant inno- cence fixed to her face.

But when they reached the modest andron, where Diokles' celebratory feast was already well underway, Archidike's typical pluck had returned. Diokles was young for a successful merchant —not yet in his late twenties, Doricha thought, to judge by his round, youthful face, lush crop of glossy curls, and the rather patchy state of his short-trimmed beard. His appetite for wine was boyishly robust, too. He sat upright on his couch, accepting the congratulations of his guests and eagerly taking a long draft from a very large wine cup each time someone called out, "Luck to Diokles!" or "A boy! A boy for Diokles!" The majority of his guests were just as youthful—a fact that was not lost on

Archidike. As the girls accepted festive flower garlands from a female servant, then allowed the woman to rub their bare arms with fragrant rose water, Archidike gazed about the andron with a satisfied air. She growled in appreciation as a group of energetic young men dashed past her, jesting good-naturedly as they went.

"Look at that one, Doricha, with the strong arms. No, not him —the dark-skinned fellow standing there beside the pillar. Couldn't you just...?"

"For someone who claims not to like men," Doricha said wryly, "you do enjoy staring at them."

"Who said I don't like men? I never did. I'm wary of them; that's all. And I'll have you know, I enjoy doing more to them than just staring. You won't see me marry some withered old fool once I'm free, I can promise you that. I'll keep working until the day I die. Some young ram like that one with the strong arms— he'll ride me right into the grave."

Doricha laughed aloud in disbelief. She was relieved to see Archidike's good humor returning, though. The hetaera's sudden shift into darkness had frightened her, and had made Doricha feel even more hopelessly beyond her depth.

"Listen, Duckling, and listen well: men only want to use us. It's nothing to cry over; it only means we've got to be clever enough to use them first. And take them for every last hedj they've got."

"Before they ride you to your tomb," Doricha giggled.

"Just imagine, if you can, what the walls of my tomb will look like." Archidike snatched a cup of wine from a passing servant's tray. She tipped it back and drank deeply until a trickle of red ran from the corner of her mouth. Then she raised the empty cup high above her head. "Rows and rows of cocks, adorning every wall, from one end of my tomb the other!"

Archidike linked arms with Doricha and led her off into the crowd. They weren't assigned to any particular guest at Diokles' party; they, along with several other hetaerae, were only there to beautify the place, to fill it with feminine charm as they flitted from couch to couch.

"This is my favorite sort of party," Archidike confessed. "It's a bore to be stuck entertaining one man all night long. But we can roam about and talk to everyone tonight. Make lots of friends—that's good for future business."

Archidike fawned and flirted her way around the andron. Plenty of Diokles' friends recognized her; several welcomed her with shouts and raised cups. Archidike was well known as the most game hetaera in Memphis, and her presence could only enhance a night of fun. Of course, the other hetaerae in attendance also knew Archidike. But not all of them were pleased to see her. Several whispered to their friends behind their hands, following Archidike with narrowed eyes as she blazed a trail of laughter and coarse shouts through Diokles' party.

Archidike was so engaged in greeting her many admirers that Doricha was left alone, standing uselessly by while the older girl worked the room. Doricha was left to introduce herself to the few men who spoke to her. At least there were no dogs or goats in the andron, she noted with relief.

In time, Archidike remembered Doricha. She plucked two honey cakes from a serving tray and handed one to the younger girl. Her skin seemed to glow with vitality; she was tense with a curious energy, a kind of wild fervor that only served to make her more attractive.

"When I'm working for myself," Archidike said, "I'll only have beautiful patrons—young lions like that fellow there, standing by the harp, or the one with the big, strong arms. I won't have to put up with any more ancients like Nikostratos. Though, gods bless good old Nikos for giving me so much money. He'll set me free years faster than I could have done without him. But—ooh, look at the chest on that one, Doricha. He's welcome to be my top patron, once I'm away from Xanthes. Once I can pick and choose whoever I please."

Despite her coarseness and her cruel tendencies—which Doricha felt sure were unintentional—Archidike did know how to charm men. Doricha watched the older girl with frank fascination. Archidike remade herself swiftly to suit the preferences of each new man she encountered. Now she was giggling and shy, now barking with laughter at a crude joke. For one man, she was dignified and polite—for the next, she licked her lips and ran a hand up her thigh in a way that made Doricha blush. She was like one of the little forest lizards from Thrace—the kind that changed from brown to green to brown again, matching whatever environment surrounded them. Young as she was, Archidike was already a master of her art. There was no trace now of the cynicism that had darkened her mood in the litter. Doricha herself could hardly believe that this pleasant, pretty young woman was the foul-mouthed, hard-eyed schemer of Xanthes' stable.

As the night wore on, Doricha began to attract her share of attention, too. A few of the men recognized her from the fateful New Year party at Xanthes' estate; they called out, "It's the Maiden of the Reeds!" and "Let's have another dance!" as she passed. But the frantic cheer inside the andron had begun to overwhelm Doricha. She edged closer and closer to the garden door until at last, she was able to slip outside.

The night air was cool, and sweet with the perfume of fruit ripening in the orchards. Doricha carefully dabbed beads of sweat from her brow with the back of her hand, breathing as deeply as the tight green sash would allow.

"Ho there, little dancer," a man said.

Doricha started in surprise and turned to face him. It was the fellow with the strong arms—the one Archidike had taken a liking to.

"I had to sneak away to the garden," she said. "I just love the smell of the flowers and the leaves at night, when the air turns crisp. Do you think Diokles will be angry that I've left the party?"

"What, Diokles? Nothing ever upsets him. You certainly never could, charming thing that you are."

Doricha lowered her eyes. "You're very kind to say so."

"I saw you dance at Xanthes' party, didn't I?"

"You did if you were there." *Wish I could forget all about that gods-cursed night.*

"Ra—a—mose!" Several men, leaning together from the andron's door, bellowed the name at once.

The fellow with the muscular arms laughed back at them. "I'm out here, you drunken fools."

"Luck of Horus," one of the men shouted. "Look what Ramose found! It's that dancing girl with the red hair."

The men spilled out into the garden. Doricha clutched the knot of her green sash. Alone in the garden with a pack of drunk men, and not even Archidike anywhere in sight. Who could help her, if these drunken oafs set upon her? She couldn't fight one of them off by herself, let alone all six of them.

The men quickly surrounded Doricha; she turned about, looking for some path to slip past them, but they stood almost shoulder to shoulder.

"Let's have a dance!" one of them cried, lifting his wine cup.

"Yes, yes! A dance!"

Pushing down her panic, Doricha eyed the men more closely. They were grinning, bouncing on the balls of their feet, as playful as boys in a swimming hole. There was nothing predatory about them; the wine had made them too merry for violence.

"Well, I can't dance for you," Doricha said, laughing. "No music, out here in the garden, is there?"

Another figure appeared in the circle of men, slender and dark-haired. Light spilled out from Diokles' house as someone opened and closed the andron door; the wash of lamp light flickered over the flame-orange dress. It was Archidike, lurking silently in the shadow between two broad-shouldered men.

Archidike's pale eyes lowered briefly to Doricha's sash. *Don't think that protects you*, said her dry, sober expression.

"We'll make music for you," Ramose said.

"You haven't got any lyres or pipes." Doricha hoped that would be the end of it. The circle of men, and Archidike's sudden appearance among them—Archidike's cool, judgmental silence —had made her far too nervous to dance. If she tried, she would only blunder about like a blind cow.

But the men were too keen on the idea to give it up. They began to clap their hands in a brisk rhythm; after a moment, they stamped their feet, too, a jaunty counterpoint to the clapping. They raised their voices in a ragged, off-key version of an old Egyptian drinking song—one Doricha had heard early in her career. It was, in fact, one of the earliest songs Iunet had taught her. The steps of that traditional dance were simple enough. Perhaps Doricha could satisfy them with a quick demonstration, and then they would let her alone. Feigning delight, she gave into their urging and began to dance.

The easy, rustic steps lent themselves to plenty of improvisation. As Doricha succumbed to the rhythm, she did her best to channel Archidike's slinking, suggestive style, and made her way around the ring, flirting with each man in turn, using her sweet, batting eyes and her innocent smile to great effect. Now and then she touched one of the men, sliding her hand down a strong arm or pressing briefly against warm flesh—and she found, to her surprise, that she liked the feel of their bodies.

She had intended the dance to be brief, but before long, Doricha was laughing with real joy. She didn't want to stop. She pulled one of the men into the circle with her, urging him to match her steps. Then she tried another fellow. None of them could dance with her, intoxicated as they were. She twirled away from one partner after another, putting on a great, humorous show of disgust at their inability to keep up. She tugged playfully at their short robes, and even dared to flip the hem of Ramose's kilt, almost revealing what he had underneath.

By the time the old Egyptian song was nearing its end, the men were so happy with Doricha's performance that they couldn't manage to sing the final lines. Instead, they burst into one great, wordless roar of approval, laughing and shouting, pounding on one another's shoulders, lifting their empty cups in salute.

Archidike, too, joined in the praise, and even embraced Doricha. "Marvelous," she said. "Really, Doricha. You've got such a talent for dance. And you make it look so easy, too."

Doricha could sense no cynicism in Archidike's words, but she couldn't quite make herself trust the other girl, either.

Ramose edged closer to Doricha. His grin was almost sheepish, his eyes reddened with wine. But he looked down at her earnestly—even hungrily. "How much to get you into bed?"

Doricha's cheeks heated like a smith's furnace. Couldn't he see her green belt? Surely, even in his intoxicated state, he understood what it meant. She opened her mouth and shut it again. She couldn't speak to the man.

"Look at that," Archidike said in playful rebuke. "You've ruined her complexion, Ramose. Now her cheeks are glowing so hot, I don't think they'll ever go back to white again. Master Xanthes will be very cross with you, for ruining his little dancer." Archidike pinched Doricha's cheek—gently, with a sisterly smile. She said to Ramose, "You can't have our little Rhodopis yet. She's too young. Didn't you notice her girdle?"

Rhodopis. Doricha blinked. The name meant "rosy cheeks."

Archidike pressed herself against Ramose's chest. Her playful mood evaporated, replaced by a seductive smolder. "You can have me, though. I've got no green belt, as you can see. I'm ready... and more than willing."

Ramose's grin widened. He didn't even glance Doricha's way

as his arm snaked around Archidike's narrow waist. He began tugging her toward a darkened corner of the garden.

Archidike looked over her shoulder, fixing Doricha with a firm stare. "Stay here. Keep talking with that country-girl charm of yours. And don't go off with *anyone*, do you see? I'll come and find you when my work is done."

Then she winked, laced her arm through Ramose's, and disappeared with him into the blue-black depths of the garden.

§▲

SOME HALF HOUR LATER, Archidike re-appeared, quietly slipping back into the circle of men that had remained in Doricha's orbit. They had lingered, apparently content to listen to her stories, chuckling indulgently over her rustic accent. They'd even coaxed her into teaching them a few simple dance steps, though some of them could hardly remain on their feet, let alone master the easy dances she had tried to teach them.

Now that her dancing had won their respect, Doricha found she enjoyed talking to the men. None of these fellows was likely to assault her, and the air was pleasant in the garden, rich and sweet and bracing, so far from the stifling center of Memphis.

All Doricha needed to do was talk, playing up her innocence, acting the unspoiled girl. Archidike re-appeared, tugging her dress back into place, and cozied up to another of Doricha's admirers. Minutes later, the older girl led him off into the night— and then, some fifteen minutes after, she pulled another man away, too.

By the time Archidike had parted ways with her third companion of the evening, Diokles' party was coming to its end. Most of the guests had already departed, riding their litters off into the night with the ragged ends of song still trailing from their lips. Archidike and Doricha kissed their hands to Ramose and his friends, and sank back against the cushions of their golden litter amid shouts of farewell from the men.

"Diokles had better invite you two the next time he throws a feast," Ramose called.

"You make sure he does, and we'll be there," Archidike promised.

The litter's curtains dropped; the bearers hoisted it to their strong shoulders. Archidike lay back, sighing with satisfaction. In the close air between the curtains, she smelled strongly of the work she had done, but she seemed to revel in it—proof of her own competence, her desirability.

"Three in one night. Now that's the kind of party I can enjoy. We make a good pair, don't we, Duckling? And do you see how easy it is, now? All you need do is just what you do best: dance like a swaying reed, and then hold the men captive with your silly little country girl act. Leave it to me to drag them back into the bushes and do what I do best."

"Why did you do it?" Doricha asked. "Stop them from taking me, I mean. You said yourself that this girdle doesn't go between my legs. That drunken Ramose could have gotten it off me if, he'd really wanted to."

Archidike turned to Doricha with another sigh, but this one was more exasperated than satisfied. She pinched Doricha's cheek again—but now, unlike in the garden, the pinch was hard. "I've told you a hundred times, Rhodopis: the work isn't as bad as you think. You'll have to do it someday, when Xanthes says so. In fact, you'll probably have to do it with Xanthes himself, the first time. So you'd best stop being terrified, and get used to the idea."

Archidike released Doricha's smarting cheek. She turned her face away, maintaining a pensive silence for the rest of the ride back to the Stable. Archidike was brusque—there was no denying that. But through her prickly exterior, Doricha thought she could feel a strange, hesitant friendship forming between them.

❧ 14 ❧

A NEW NAME

THE FLOOD WATERS ROSE, AS THEY HAD DONE IN EGYPT FOR thousands of years before. The first month of the new year slipped by while Doricha became better acquainted with the rhythms of life in the Stable. Xanthes' other girls were every bit as harsh, as ruthlessly focused on self-preservation as Iadmon had once warned Doricha they would be. As the newest and youngest among them—not yet even a woman—Doricha felt herself very much at the bottom of the heap, the lowest in the Stable's complex social order.

Vélona assigned Doricha to the best speech tutor she could find, for the mistress was driven to distraction by Doricha's unsophisticated accent. She was determined to force some polish onto Doricha, or perish in the attempt. Doricha did her level best to make Vélona happy, but she often found herself backsliding into old habits, and more than once her palms were whipped for speaking like a classless sheep-herder.

Pashon, the first month of summer, was drawing to a sweltering close. On a miserably hot and humid afternoon, Doricha crept to her sleeping alcove, her hands still stinging terribly from her speech tutor's rebuke. She curled up in her bed, a sour mood hanging over her, head aching fretfully. She felt vaguely ill and more than a little angry, though she couldn't say what exactly had upset her so. She curled her body into a tight ball, enjoying the silence of her alcove, hoping she would sleep long enough that the worst of her malaise would be gone by supper time.

The Stable door opened; a girl entered, humming the tune of a rowdy drinking song. It was Archidike, easily identified by the rough edge in her voice. She went to her alcove, rummaged inside for a moment, then paused. The hum abruptly died away.

"Doricha, is that you in bed? Are you well?"

For answer, Doricha could only groan.

Archidike appeared by her bedside, examining her with a critical eye. "What's the matter with you? You look green around the mouth."

"Don't know," Doricha said, not caring whether she sounded like a goatherd. "My belly hurts ever so much."

"Do you need the privy?"

"No; not that kind of hurting. It's... Oh, I don't know what's the matter, Archi. I've felt achy and sick to my stomach and just plain angry all day long."

"Ha," Archidike said. She smirked at Doricha. "I know what's the matter with you. You're about to officially become a hetaera; that's all."

Doricha's eyes opened wide. She caught Archidike's meaning at once, but she couldn't quite believe it was true. Yet when she reached down between her legs, she felt the telltale dampness, and knew it was so. She rose from her bed reluctantly, and in the dim light that filtered into her alcove, she and Archidike both looked at the smear of blood on her fingers.

Tears sprang to Doricha's eyes. She looked up at her friend, sniffing miserably.

"It's nothing to cry about," Archidike said. "It happens to us all. It's about time, don't you think? The pain will go away; you'll see."

"It's not the pain. It's... what I'll have to do now."

Archidike laughed dismissively. "That? You've seen it done countless times by now. What's to be afraid of?"

"I don't know. 'Spose I'm afraid it'll hurt."

"It never hurts any more than the pain you feel right now— the cramping in your belly. If you can endure that, you can endure a man."

But still, Doricha shuddered. She wrapped her arms around her body and wept. It wasn't only fear of the pain. Very probably, she thought, Archidike was telling the truth, and the ache in her belly was worse than the hurt a man's attentions might bring. The fear was something deeper, broader. She wondered at it, examining her anxiety from a distance even as she wept and sniffled in Archidike's arms. After a time, Doricha realized it was the change itself that frightened her. She was afraid of being a woman now. Childhood was gone forever—what little childhood she'd enjoyed. Now, ready or not, she must enter fully into the world of grown women. Worse—now she must compete with the other, more experienced, far more vicious hetaerae.

I'll never know enough to make my way among them, she thought frantically. *They're too mean, too hungry. They'll crush me if they can, eat me up like crocodiles... and I'll never be able to win my freedom.*

Archidike's embrace was some comfort, though. Over the past month, Doricha had built up a shaky trust in the older girl. She pressed closer, snuggling against Archidike's chest, hiding her eyes in her long black curls.

"Listen," Archidike said gently. "It won't be so bad. Shall I show you what I mean?"

"Show me?" Doricha pulled back, looking up at her friend in confusion. "What do you—"

Archidike kissed her, so suddenly that Doricha didn't even have the presence of mind to pull away. The kiss was pleasant— far more gentle and kind than she would have expected from

Archidike. The Stable was empty, save for the two of them, so Archidike led her across the room to her alcove. She slid beneath her covers, then held them up, beckoning for Doricha to join her.

Doricha hesitated, glancing back through the stable as if she expected Vélona to appear at any moment. But the great room was still. She crept into bed and lay beside Archidike, their skin warm and damp where it touched. It was strangely exhilarating, to lie in a bed that was not her own—like being in another country.

"It's nothing to be afraid of," Archidike whispered and kissed her again.

When Archidike pulled back, Doricha said, "But I'll have to lie with Xanthes. You told me, didn't you? That night of the garden party. You told me in the litter—"

"That's usually the way of things around here," Archidike said, waving a hand dismissively. "But really, it's a good way to start out in this business. If you can survive Xanthes, you can survive any man."

Doricha went cold. "Is he so terrible?"

"Terribly funny." Archidike smiled. "Terribly boring. And it's terribly hard to get through it without laughing at the doltish faces he makes, or the way he grunts. You've only got to think of Xanthes as a game. And once you win that game, then by the gods, you can win any game."

"After the way he got me, though," Doricha said, "tricking my master and all, when I'd been so happy living with Iadmon... I hate to think of having my first time with him."

Archidike's smile took on a mysterious air. "Who says your first time must be with Xanthes?"

"Why, you did." Doricha stopped, chewing on her lip. She blinked at Archidike as the older girl's meaning dawned on her. "Do you mean... you and me?"

"Why not? We'll be working together someday—remember? We might as well get used to it. Just think how much money we can make with that kind of act. We'll be so clever, all tangled up like a couple of snakes, we'll charm the silver right out of men's purses." Archidike stroked her shoulder, the touch gentle and reassuring. "We'll be so clever, we'll steal Xanthes' fun right away from him. We'll send you to his bed already broken in, and the old slobbering fool will never know it. What do you say? Shouldn't we put one over on Xanthes? It'd be the best possible way to get him back, for what he did to Iadmon."

Doricha laughed uncertainly. It seemed impossible that hard, cynical Archidike could truly be on her side, conspiring to get the better of their master. But hadn't Doricha sensed a strange kind of friendship growing between them? It would be pleasant to have a friend again—somebody she could count on. The gods had seen fit to separate her from Aesop, who had been such a good friend to her. If Archidike was the replacement the gods intended... well, then...

Doricha nodded her consent. Archidike wrapped her in a gentle embrace. It was warm and encouraging; it set a little ember of hope glowing in Doricha's belly.

Reckon I can get used to life in the Stable after all.

She kissed Archidike back, and allowed her friend to comfort her in the seclusion of the empty chamber.

DORICHA REPORTED her first blood to Vélona that same night at supper. It would have been impossible to hide the change from the sharp-eyed mistress, anyway. Vélona was pleased. "It's about time you started earning your keep," she said, and set to work at once, making plans for Doricha's first presentation to Xanthes. By the time her blood had stopped flowing, Doricha was scheduled for a night with the master.

She stood in the dressing closet, in a pool of bright light from two large oil lamps. Doricha followed every order promptly, holding out her arms just so, turning this way and that as Amenia draped her in silks and fine-woven linens, then stood back with Vélona to eye her critically.

"She needs more jewels at her neck," Vélona said. "She doesn't have much in the way of breasts—probably never will—so something big and eye-catching, to sparkle on her chest."

"I quite agree," Amenia said. "Archidike, bring that Egyptian-style necklace with the bird's wings made of agates. You know the one."

Archidike, acting as the chief dresser's assistant, hurried over to the shelves and lifted the lids of various casks until she found the piece Amenia had in mind. She carried it back to the circle of lamplight and held it up for Amenia to examine. The necklace was made of many long slices of well-polished, white agate, each one cut in the shape of a feather and shot through with delicate, moss-like twists of amber and green. The stones were luminous and delicate-looking; it was the prettiest necklace Doricha had ever seen.

While Vélona and Amenia handled the necklace, debating its suitability, Doricha and Archidike exchanged a sly, humorous glance. Over the past several days, Archidike had prepared Doricha in her own way for her night with Xanthes. She had taught Doricha everything she could think to impart about men in general—how to bring them to the peak of their pleasure quickly and efficiently. She had passed along many useful tips about Xanthes in particular, showing Doricha how to speed the ordeal to its conclusion so that the master would fall into a heavy sleep all the sooner. She had shown Doricha, too, how to hollow out a half of a citrus fruit, scooping out the flesh and fitting the cupped rind just so inside, to keep from falling pregnant.

The lessons had been amusing. Archidike made it all seem like a lark, and maybe after all it was. With Archidike's humorous lessons running through her mind, Doricha was already in danger of laughing, and she hadn't even been presented to the master yet. All her fear from days before had evaporated like a puddle of piss in the street. Now she was so thoroughly prepared —indeed, so eager to finally take her place among the hetaerae— that she thought she truly might disgrace herself by giggling at the master's exertions.

"Very well," Vélona said. "The agate necklace will do, I suppose."

Amenia hung the heavy piece around Doricha's neck. The coldness of the stones in their golden, wing-shaped settings pressed through the open-weave linen of her dress.

"You look suitable," Vélona said to Doricha. "You may go to Xanthes now. He will be expecting you. There's a guard outside the door; he'll take you to the master's chambers. But don't speak to the guard any more than is necessary, and don't you dare flirt with him. I shall know if you do."

Doricha nodded. She turned to Archidike. "Thank you for your help."

They shared tiny, mischievous smiles, and Doricha thought she saw a hint of real affection in Archidike's eyes.

"Be on your way," Vélona said. "It won't do to keep the master waiting."

Doricha left the dressing closet and crossed the great chamber of the Stable. As she passed the other girls' alcoves, their stares and whispers followed her. I'm one of you now, Doricha told them silently, moving with her head up high, the bangles on her wrists and ankles chiming with gentle music. *Or I will be, soon enough. Soon as this job of work's over.* The excitement of knowing that she had almost reached her goal—that she stood at the very threshold of her fate—blotted out any lingering fear Doricha might still have felt.

Outside the Stable door, the guard was waiting for her, just as Vélona had said. The man looked at Doricha in some surprise; she recognized the brief flash of desire in his eyes. She was a woman now in truth, and she knew she looked as fine and flaw-less as any hetaera.

"Take me to Master Xanthes," Doricha said

The guard bowed at her command. She walked along beside his left shoulder—not behind him, for although she was still the property of Xanthes, she was no longer a slave... not exactly. Now she had attained the status she had longed for since first meeting Iadmon.

Doricha walked calmly through the long corridors of Xanthes' house. Some of the halls and chambers, she hadn't seen since coming to the estate on that first, fateful day. Had it only been a month since she'd come here? The whole estate felt different to her now—not a house of oppression, but a domain through which Doricha would move under her own power, strong and confident, a woman on her way to freedom.

The guard halted outside a door, its surface carved with a rearing lion. The lion's mane and teeth were leafed in gold. Such an extravagant door could only lead to Xanthes' chamber, Doricha knew. The guard knocked, and after a moment, the master called for Doricha to enter.

She stepped into his chamber alone.

The room was strewn with chairs and tables made of the finest ebony wood; its floor was covered in one huge carpet, dyed brilliant blue and accented here and there with rich Tyrean purple. The carpet alone must have cost more hedj than most great men of Memphis saw in an entire year. Plenty of lamps burned brightly, without regard for the cost of oil; the light revealed every twisting vine and lily pool painted on the chamber walls with brilliant clarity.

Xanthes reclined on his huge sleeping couch—easily wide enough to hold three people, with legs carved like lion's paws, their gilded claws extended. He eyed Doricha in silence, taking in the fine, pure white of her linen gown, the grand necklace spread across her chest. His mouth curled slowly; he smirked at her with an obvious air or triumph.

"You do look lovely," Xanthes said, perhaps belatedly.

Doricha knew his hunger for her had nothing to do with the way she looked. All that mattered to Xanthes was that he had bested Iadmon, his old enemy... and now he would enjoy Iadmon's favorite slave.

I know you, she thought. *I know how your small mind works. You aren't a great man—no, not at all. You're nothing like Iadmon.*

But of course, it would never do to allow her feelings to show. Doricha lowered her eyes, pretending shy acceptance of her new master's praise.

"Look now, Iadmon," Xanthes muttered thickly—and so quietly, Doricha couldn't be sure she'd heard him correctly. "See who has taken the other's best slave in the end, you primped, oiled, flouncing goat."

Doricha swallowed a sudden lump in her throat. She hadn't expected to feel so shaken up by the mere mention of Iadmon's name, but memories of the life she'd left behind came rushing to her head.

Don't allow him to distract you, she told herself. *He's nothing but a boor.*

She imagined she could hear Archidike whispering in her ear. *All men are boors. And all men are the same.* What would Archidike do now, tough and hard as she was? Would she weep for what had been taken from her? Certainly not.

Doricha tossed her head, affecting a brazen, unconcerned air that would have done Archidike proud. "What do I care about Iadmon?" she said. "Isn't one man just like any other?"

Xanthes stared at her for a moment. Then he threw back his head, roaring with laughter. "No, little lotus. One man is not like any other. You'll find that out soon enough, now that you're ripe for working. But I'll be your first taste of this business—of loving and pleasing. I shall be the one against whom you compare all your future lovers."

Oh, do you think so? Doricha thought, remembering Archidike's ardent embraces. All at once, she found she had to bite the inside of her cheek to stop herself from giggling. *We pulled a clever trick on the master, after all, Archi. Didn't we just about fool him!*

"Take off that dress," Xanthes said.

"What, so soon, Maser? I only just put it on." Doricha fluttered her lashes, but she did as she was told straight away. *Sooner this is done with, sooner it's behind me. And then it's on to men who'll pay—men who'll pave me a path away from you, Xanthes. Just wait and see how quick I'm out of your Stable and off on my own!*

After all the time and effort and pointless fretting Amenia and Vélona had put into Doricha's appearance, it all came down to a crumpled heap of linen on Xanthes' fine blue rug. Doricha stepped out of the fallen dress, wearing only her sandals and the agate necklace. She faced Xanthes fearlessly, exposed before his eyes. What was there to be afraid of, after all? Hadn't she danced all but naked in front of Iadmon's household, and more times than she could count?

"I've stolen Iadmon's treasure," Xanthes said. "And what a treasure you are."

You haven't stolen a thing, Doricha thought. She kept her placid smile in place, and went calmly toward his couch. Xanthes shifted to make space for her, and Doricha set to work. She tended to her first assignment as a hetaera with a steadiness and professional detachment that did all her teachers—Aesop and Archidike included—most proud.

THE ORDEAL WAS over faster than Doricha had expected. Archidike's instructions had served her well; within minutes,

Xanthes was slumbering on his couch in a tangle of linen sheets, and Doricha was none the worse for wear.

She breathed a tiny sigh of relief, slid quietly from the bed, and dressed as best she could in the discarded linen gown. She stole toward the chamber door, sneaking on her toes, reluctant to wake Xanthes and reignite his appetite.

Doricha slipped through the door, out into the dim corridor. *Reckon this work will be easy enough to handle. And now I'm well on my way.* She was fully prepared, confident as the rising sun at the start of a new day. She even smiled as she addressed the guard. "I'm finished here. Take me back to the women's chamber, if you please."

She was quiet with satisfaction as she returned through the corridors. Xanthes had nothing to do with her happiness, of course. He had thought only of himself, seeking his own pleasure. Doricha had expected nothing else. Her satisfaction came from the knowledge that now, at last, she was moving forward. Now she had seized the future that was hers by right. In Xanthes' garishly bright chamber, Doricha had completed the last crucial part of her training. She had emerged from the tangle of his sheets like a butterfly breaking free from the confines of its cocoon. She was a hetaera now.

When Doricha returned to the Stable, she heard whispers and giggles behind its door. She pushed it open curiously, and was greeted by a great shout of "Luck! Luck to our new sister!" Every hetaera who hadn't gone off with a patron that evening was gathered there in the middle of the Stable. They had brought in a few small tables from the gynaeceum; each table bore trays of sweets and cups of steaming, spice-mulled wine.

Doricha stared around in awe. The girls grinned back at her; they waved colorful sashes in the air, whooping and singing in celebration. Even Bastet and Efthalia had set aside their animosity, for one night, at least.

"Is this all for me?" Doricha said, approaching the tables hesitantly as if they might vanish before her startled eyes—a mirage on a desert horizon.

"Of course," Callisto said. "Here, have some of these dates. They've got goat cheese stuffed inside."

"Yes, please, for the gods' sake," Efthalia said, "eat some of the dates before Callisto shoves them all down her throat. She's going to get even fatter if she keeps on like this."

"Our own little party," Archidike said, breaking away from the rest of the girls, pulling Doricha into a warm embrace. "Without any men to ruin the fun."

"I thought you *like* men at parties," Doricha said, laughing. "Really, Archidike, I can't keep you straight when it comes to men."

"We do this for every girl when she becomes a hetaera," Callisto said.

"It's ever so sweet." Doricha blushed.

The girls giggled and chattered around the tables, making short work of the honey cakes and stuffed dates. Callisto licked the stickiness of the last date from her fingers and said, "Come on, girls; let's take the mulled wine and have a soak in the bath. Vélona got some new bath oil, and I'm dying to try it."

Each girl hurried to her alcove, stripped off her dress, and wrapped herself in a long, plush linen towel. Then they went together to the bath house, easing into the large, sunken pool. Its water had recently been refreshed from the big kettles, which were suspended over hot coals in the fire pit outside. The pool was still quite warm; its welcome heat relaxed Doricha's body, adding to her pleasant glow of satisfaction. She sipped the spiced wine, enjoying the rare night of camaraderie. No girl picked on any other; no one hurled any insults, nor pulled any hair. The whole of the Stable was in a festival mood; Doricha was determined to enjoy it while it lasted.

"Let me take your hair down," Efthalia said. "Clumsy Xanthes has just about ruined the style, anyway. He pawed at it like a dog trying to bury a bone, didn't he?"

Efthalia carefully snipped the threads that held Doricha's braids and curls together, then combed out her coppery hair with her fingers. "Gods, but you've got pretty hair, Doricha. Wish mine was that color." She found a jar of rose-scented oil and began washing Doricha's locks, while Callisto massaged Doricha's hands.

Doricha was quite content to let herself be as pampered like a kitten on a silk pillow. The gods alone knew when her fellow hetaerae would ever be so kind to her again.

"Well," Bastet said, grinning over the rim of her wine cup, "Tell us what he was like."

"He was like Xanthes," Archidike said. "You didn't expect any different, did you, Bastet?"

Bastet rolled her eyes and grunted rhythmically. It was such a perfect imitation of the master in the throes of his pleasure that they all laughed until they were breathless. Archidike tried to mimic the face Xanthes always made when he reached his climax, and soon the girls were locked in a competition to see who could do it best.

"A real hetaera," Callisto said when the laughter had finally died away. "No more green girdle for you."

Bastet nodded. "Now that you'll be going out as a working girl, earning your keep and making your own friends, you'll need a new name."

"A new name?" Doricha sat up quickly, sloshing water over the edge of the bath. She remembered how, long ago, she had feared that Iadmon would take away her name. And wasn't her name still the only thing she truly owned? "But why? What's wrong with the name I've already got?"

"Nothing," Callisto said quickly. "Nothing at all. It's just the custom; that's all. We all changed our names when we started working. It's the way of hetaerae."

"You changed your names?"

"Of course," Bastet said. "No mother in Egypt has ever named her daughter Bastet. I was born Ahaneit."

"And my name was Hestia," Callisto said. "That's not glamorous enough for a hetaera."

"What about you, Archidike?" Doricha asked. "What were you called, before?"

The blue-eyed hetaera sipped from her wine cup, gazing regally into the distance. "Archidike has always been Archidike."

Efthalia splashed her. "Oh, come off it. She probably had some dreadful dull name, like Klotho."

The girls laughed, but Doricha chewed her lip, considering what they'd said. Now that she was a hetaera, she was entering a new world—one where she was the confident mistress of her fate, or would be, as soon as she'd earned her freedom. She was leaving behind the person she had been—child and slave. She was even leaving behind Thrace, for now it was certain she would never return to her homeland again. *Hope I'll leave behind the poverty of my family, too, and become a rich woman someday.* If ever there was a good excuse to take a new name, this was surely it. A hetaera was more than an ordinary woman, too—possessed of a privilege no other woman could hope to attain. Doricha the girl would have grown up to be Doricha the woman, essentially the same as she had been before. But the hetaera was another creature altogether. The hetaera could never be Doricha, the Thracian exile, the former slave.

As long as no one took her name by force, Doricha didn't mind exchanging it for a new identity.

"All right," she said gamely. "How does a girl go about choosing a new name?"

"You should call yourself what you hope to become," Bastet suggested.

"No, no," Callisto said. "Take on a name that describes you—

one that will make your patrons think of you instantly, the moment they hear it, and never mistake you for anybody else."

"Call yourself after a physical trait," Efthalia said.

"You should name yourself Copper," Bastet said. "No one will mistake you then. No other hetaera has hair like yours."

"Copper?" Efthalia stuck out her tongue. "That's what a soldier might name his horse."

Archidike snorted. "Good; maybe it'll inspire them to ride our little Doricha hard and often."

The girls went on arguing over the best way to choose a name, offering up suggestions and discarding each one. Doricha blushed ever deeper as their proposed names became more absurd, more coarse and vulgar until finally Archidike leaned forward and pinched Doricha's cheek, as she'd done the night of Diokles' party.

"I know the right name for this one: Rhodopis."

"Oh," Callisto sighed. "That's just perfect. Really it is; no more jests. It goes so well with your style, the way you play the innocent little country girl."

Doricha glanced around at the other girls, shyly. "Do you think so?"

"No man will be able to resist it," Bastet said.

Doricha grinned at Archidike. After what they had shared— not only the afternoon in Archidike's bed, but the party where they had worked so well together, Doricha was grateful to her friend. She was glad to take her working name from Archidike's suggestion.

"All right. Then I'm Rhodopis, from this moment on."

II

HETAERA

CHARAXUS

As the year advanced, each season brought new excuses for the wealthy upper class of Memphis to celebrate with feasts and parties. And with each new event she attended, the girl who had been Doricha felt ever more at home in the skin of Rhodopis, the confident and hard-working courtesan. At first, Rhodopis had been a mask for Doricha to wear—the costume she donned when she left the Stable for her assignments, the cloak she removed again when her alcove curtain was drawn and she crept to her bed in the small hours of the morning. But as her renown spread, and as she garnered praise even from Vélona, Rhodopis became just as real to her as Doricha ever had been. By the time the harvest season ended and another New Year loomed, a few short weeks away, the fourteen-year-old hetaera doubted whether she could still answer to the name Doricha as readily as she now answered to Rhodopis.

Her friendship with Archidike grew, too, over the course of that year. The two girls had become fast friends, attending most of their parties together. They were seen so often in one another's company that Memphis society now considered them part and parcel, going together like wine and honey, or bread and olive oil. Almost without exception, wherever one girl went, there would go the other.

Rhodopis had yet to establish a relationship with any dedicated patron; she was still being sampled, as it were, tested and tried by the elite of Memphis until she found the handful of clients who would take most strongly to her particular charms. Rhodopis felt no anxiety over her lack of steady clients—not yet. She could see how well the men of Memphis responded to her flirtations; she knew she was gaining a following. In time, that following would produce a patron or two. That was the way the business worked, Archidike assured her; and she'd only just begun her career. Patrons came with time, with the careful nurturing of a hetaera's unique style and reputation.

A few men had begun to express increasing interest in Rhodopis as the New Year approached, and so she looked forward to the good fortune the rising of the Dog Star would bring. Most of the men who had inquired about her were great fans of Archidike—which was to be expected, given how often Archidike and Rhodopis entertained together. Anyone could see the natural chemistry that existed between the two girls. Men seemed to especially enjoy the startling contrast between the two girls. Rhodopis was all wide-eyed naiveté and delicate, pale beauty—but Archidike was a carnal creature. Her dark hair, dusky Egyptian complexion, and strange, piercing blue eyes were as different from Rhodopis as the moon was from the sun.

Her reputation as a dancer had grown favorably, too. Indeed, demand for Rhodopis' dancing eclipsed her popularity as a bedmate. This did not displease her. She still loved dance better than anything else in the world, and welcomed any opportunity to perform before a crowd. Sometimes she was paid just as well for dancing as she would have been for other services; if she could have earned her freedom by dancing alone, she would have done so gladly.

Every party presented a new opportunity not only to dance, but to hone her skill as a conversationalist, too—and there she was also building a reputation. She often used the witty stories she had learned from Aesop to enchant men at feasts and celebrations. Something about her simple, uncultured speech, combined with the deeper intelligence of the tales she told, amused and delighted the most sophisticated men. Rhodopis nurtured her skill at conversation assiduously. She knew it took more than just bed-play to make a successful hetaera, and she intended to be the very best of them all.

But as the year came to its close, Rhodopis finally began to wonder when she would ever find her first patron. She confided her worry to Archidike, the only other hetaera whom she knew she could trust. Archidike was quick to comfort Rhodopis. "The offers will start pouring in, and soon, too. Don't worry, Duckling; sometimes even the best hetaerae have a slow start. Often it's only because the men can sense how good she is. Most of them think a truly dazzling woman is too far beyond their means."

Rhodopis was fourteen years old. She knew only a fool or a beggar would think a girl of fourteen was beyond his means.

One day, however, when the smell of rich, soil-laden water hung thickly in the air—a sure sign that the New Year was upon them—Rhodopis strolled into the Stable from the women's private garden to find Vélona waiting for her. Rhodopis had been practicing a new dance, with Archidike playing the flute; she was still dressed in her dancing belt, the skimpy silk garment hung with tassels of many colors.

Vélona clicked her tongue when she saw it. "I do hope you plan to wear something nicer tonight, Rhodopis."

"Why, Mistress? Are we to go off to another party tonight?"

"Not a party. I've received a private request for you."

Rhodopis smiled. "I'm glad to hear it, Mistress. We haven't done a private entertainment in a long while."

"Who is it?" Archidike asked eagerly.

Vélona paused, savoring her power to make the two girls wait.

"Oh, won't you tell them, Mistress," Callisto cried. "We're all dying to know, aren't we, girls?"

"It's Charaxus," Vélona said.

A murmur traveled around the room. "He's the brother of Sappho," Persephone said. "You know who Sappho is, don't you, Rhodopis? The famous poetess from Lesvos."

"Charaxus is as wealthy as they come. Lucky Rhodopis." Bastet didn't sound congratulatory; there was a venomous sting of envy in her words.

"Wealthy as they come," Vélona agreed, "but not yet the patron of any hetaera. This is a good opportunity for you."

Archidike tucked her flute under her arm. "We should get ready straight away," she said. "We'll want plenty of time to get the look right—a private event, with a man as rich as Charaxus!"

Vélona raised a hand. "I know the pair of you most usually entertain together. But Charaxus was specific: Rhodopis only."

Archidike wilted. Rhodopis turned to her friend quickly, just in time to catch the disbelief as it flickered across her face. But Archidike, professional as she was, banished the emotion.

Rhodopis took her hands. "I'm sorry. I wish it could be both of us together."

"No doubt you do," Bastet said. She waggled her two fingers at Rhodopis and Archidike, then dodged a cuff from Vélona, and ducked back into her alcove.

Archidike shrugged. She kissed Rhodopis on the cheek. "I'll make good use of a night off. I could do with a few extra hours of sleep. Make him happy, Rho. Maybe this Charaxus will become your first patron."

❧

WELL AFTER SUNSET, under a peaceful cloak of twilight blue,

Rhodopis was carried south along the river to Charaxus' home. To her left, the Nile lay smooth and dark, not yet reflecting the early stars that had just begun to bloom overhead. Far across that great expanse of water, pinpoints of golden light marked villages on the eastern shore. The peace of the night comforted Rhodopis, fortifying her confidence. It soothed away some of her regret over leaving Archidike behind.

Charaxus' home was located in an elite district on the southern edge of the city. The noise of crowded Memphis was so far behind her now that Rhodopis could hear the sweet monotony of frog song along the river bank and the sighing of the wind in the date palms. The streets of the southern district were still and serene; no one accosted her as she was carried through the dark lanes. The only other people she saw were the bearers of other litters. No doubt those litters concealed hetaerae like herself, drifting gracefully from one appointment to the next.

Reckon I could get used to visiting this place often. If I can make this Charaxus like me well enough, I should like to be his special friend.

Rhodopis thought back to all the parties that lay behind her, all the private assignments. Where had she met Charaxus before? Surely he could be no stranger to her. No man sent for a girl he'd never seen before. But she couldn't place him. Nor could she summon up his face, no matter how many times she repeated his name in her mind. She knew nothing about him, other than what Vélona and Persephone had told her.

Presently, the litter arrived at her companion's house. An erudite slave came out to greet her; the man put Rhodopis in mind of Aesop, and she wondered what that dear fellow was up to nowadays—whether he was managing Iadmon well enough, or whether Iadmon had sunk down deeper into his private shame.

Charaxus' slave led Rhodopis out of the courtyard, into the warm, well-lit, riverside house. The house was not large, but it was exceptionally beautiful, decorated with fine goods that were nevertheless displayed with admirable restraint. The house stood two stories above the river—a real luxury, for even in this wealthy district, most of the homes were only a single story in height, with rooftop courtyards open to the sky.

"Please make yourself comfortable," the slave said. "My master is concluding some business in his private chambers. He will arrive shortly."

Rhodopis nodded, and the slave departed. She drifted around the main room, examining the finely made furniture, the well-woven textiles, the clever little sculptures displayed in their wall niches. Everything Charaxus owned seemed to be of the highest quality—expensive, yet understated, a testament to his excellent taste and elevated class.

Two narrow doors stood open on a railed balcony. Rhodopis stepped outside. The balcony was small, and looked down on a garden that was hardly any larger. But even in the dark of night, the sweeping view of the Nile made up for whatever the small house and garden lacked. The water sparkled with the reflection of stars, and over that starry vista, the dark silhouettes of Egyptian boats drifted smoothly by.

"I must apologize for keeping you waiting."

Rhodopis turned. Charaxus stood in the doorway, framed by lamp light. He was tall and handsome—young, too, she noted with pleasure. He was no older than twenty-five, a startling age for a man to have attained so much wealth and success. He wore a red tunic and white chlamys, both free of any ostentatious embroidery, but Rhodopis noted the smooth sheen of the garments and knew they were made from the finest silk. He offered her a polite bow; his tumble of blonde curls ruffled in the river breeze.

"I'm pleased to meet you, Good Man Charaxus," Rhodopis said.

He laughed lightly. "Ah, but we have met before. Don't you remember?"

Rhodopis smiled at him timidly.

"Diokles' party—to celebrate the birth of his first son. My friends and I were shamefully drunk that night, but I remembered you. You danced in the garden, while we clapped and stamped like a noisy herd of bulls in a mud-wallow. How foolish you must have thought us!"

Rhodopis laughed. "Of course—Charaxus. How could I forget that night... or you?"

In truth, she had no recollection of Charaxus at Diokles' party. If he had been one of the drunken fellows whom she had danced for, he had done nothing to make himself memorable. But Rhodopis was too intelligent to let her companion know that she had never noticed him in the first place.

"You remembered me, after all those months?" she said. "You flatter me too much."

Charaxus stepped forward. He took both Rhodopis' hands in his own, staring down at her with a sudden intensity that took her aback. "I've never forgotten you, Rhodopis. You're all I've thought about since first I saw you. Business and family affairs have kept me out of Memphis for the better part of a year, but I am back now, and I intend to stay here for a good, long while. I've followed your career—seen you at a few parties, too, though propriety—duty to my hosts—kept me from approaching you. But believe me, I have longed for you since that night in Diokles' garden. And now at last, here you are: a hetaera without the green sash. The gods are good to me."

Rhodopis had no idea how she ought to respond to such an extraordinary speech. Charaxus must have thought about plenty of other subjects since Diokles' party. She was not vain enough to think she could occupy a man's thoughts to the exclusion of everything else. She gaped at him, at a loss for words. *Archidike would know just what to say—make some smart remark and set him to laughing. I'm no good at this business, no good at all.*

"Erm..." she shrugged helplessly. "Tell me what you do, Good Man. What is your business? This is such a lovely house, and right on the river, too. You must stay busy with your work."

The slave re-appeared, bearing two folding leather stools. He set them out on the balcony, then vanished again. Charaxus gestured to one; Rhodopis sat, facing the river, and listened as her host told his story.

"What do I do? Not much, if truth be told. Nominally, I trade in dyes. But I've turned over most of the business to the men who work under me. They excel at it; I never did. I'm afraid most of my wealth has come from society... that is to say, from being who I am. You do know who I am, don't you?"

"I've heard you have a well-known sister. Is that what you mean?"

"Yes." Charaxus smiled, but in the darkness, Rhodopis couldn't tell whether it was an expression of fondness or chagrin. Perhaps, she thought, it contained a little of both. "I am the brother of the great Sappho, the beloved poetess of Lesvos. Her star will forever shine brighter than my own, I'm afraid. But Sappho has always been dutiful to her family. She doesn't let me go hungry, as you can see."

"You're from Lesvos, too, then."

"Yes—but Memphis is my true home. The gods never made another city like it, not in all the world."

The slave bore a tray out onto the balcony. He set it on a small table between Charaxus and Rhodopis.

Charaxus picked up a cup of wine and sipped thoughtfully, watching the boats glide past. A watchman stood at the bow of each boat, holding up a golden torch. Now and then, one of their distant shouts traveled across the water. It was a lonely sound, but somehow the loneliness felt comfortable and pleasant, there on Charaxus' small balcony.

He turned to Rhodopis after a moment of pensive silence. "And what of you? That's Thrace I hear in your voice, isn't it?"

Rhodopis smiled rather sadly. The boatmen called again. *Ho, to the left. Ho, on the water!*

"Yes, Good Man. Yes, I came from Thrace... but that was a long time ago."

"I'm sorry; I shouldn't have asked. It was boorish of me. There's not a woman in the world who comes to this work by her own choosing, is there?"

"Oh, there must be some," Rhodopis said lightly. "But I don't know any, that's certain and sure."

She sipped her wine to hide her discomfiture. It was the finest she had ever tasted, rich as butter. She looked up at Charaxus, smiling in real delight. "Gods of the water and air, but that wine's good! Reckon I could drink it down by the skin-full, if I was some thirsty shepherd-girl out in the hills."

The next moment she covered her mouth with her hand, face burning hot. She was grateful for the cover of darkness, so Charaxus couldn't see how she blushed. "I mean to say," she amended, "what very fine wine you have, Good Man Charaxus."

He laughed heartily. "I take it your master doesn't like it when you speak like a Thracian country girl."

Rhodopis shook her head, giggling. "Not Master Xanthes—it's his mistress of women who can't stand for me to talk this way. Vélona is her name... or leastways, that's what we all call her. She can't beat the rough speech out of me, though gods know she tries."

"I hope she never succeeds." Charaxus set his cup down. He leaned across the table and kissed her—a long, lingering kiss, quite unlike the hungry, insistent kisses she'd grown used to receiving from men.

Now I have him, she thought triumphantly. She was well on her way to securing her first patron, and what a patron he would be!

Rhodopis rose gracefully from her stool. She came around the table and took Charaxus' hand in her own. He gazed up at her, waiting for her to speak.

"Why don't we go inside?" she said. She lifted a finger to her lips and sucked it briefly. She had seen Archidike do it many a time; it always seemed to encourage her men.

Charaxus sighed; he tugged his hand out of Rhodopis' grip and turned his attention back to the wine.

What did I do wrong? Rhodopis stood silently beside him, utterly bewildered by his change of mood. No man had ever responded so strangely before, withdrawing his interest as suddenly as a snuffed lamp flame.

Never one to be put off so easily, she rallied and tried again, this time twining her arms around Charaxus' neck and letting her breath tickle his ear. Charaxus shrugged irritably, as if she were a buzzing gnat.

Rhodopis threw up her hands with an offended huff. She marched back to her stool and slumped upon it, glaring out at the river. "You've a funny way of making a girl feel welcome, and no mistake. Reckon I'd have a better time back at the Stable, getting my eyes scratched out by Bastet!" She kicked a pebble that had been lying on the balcony floor; it sailed over the railing and plummeted into the garden below.

Charaxus lowered his wine cup, staring at Rhodopis with renewed hunger. She blinked back at him, as understanding dawned. *It's the poor little Thracian girl act that gets him going. He may be a creature of high society, but he only wants to bed a dirty little street urchin, jumped up to a hetaera's status.*

If the urchin was what Charaxus wanted, then Rhodopis was determined to deliver. She turned to him with a petulant pout and gave free rein to her shoddy grammar. "I'm not as pretty as the other girls back at the Stable. Reckon you're fixing to trade me in for another, one's as got more class than me. Guess there's nothing for it but to go home now—"

She turned away, but Charaxus jumped to his feet just as swiftly. He caught Rhodopis in a tight embrace, kissing her again in the same slow, gentle style. She was so taken aback by his shift in mood that she didn't need to pretend to be the flustered young girl, hopelessly out of her depth in the big city. Her stammering and shivery breaths were both unfeigned. She let him kiss her again.

"There, now," Rhodopis murmured when he released her. "Now perhaps you'll—"

"Dance for me."

She blinked at him. "What?"

"I want to see you dance." Charaxus panted a little as he spoke. He was tense with urgency, staring down at her with a strained expression of longing.

There were no musicians to be found in Charaxus' home, but, quick as always, Rhodopis perceived that her companion would like a simple country dance best.

"Very well, then," she said. "I'll teach you how to clap the rhythm, shall I? And you can be my accompanist. This is a dance from the Thracian hills—one real shepherd-girls do."

She soon had him clapping along as she circled and stamped in the little spill of lamp light that illuminated the balcony. With her hands up above her head, Rhodopis snapped her fingers, dipping her knees and twirling, twirling, so the skirt of her dress lifted gracefully around her. The dance was earthy, unsophisti-cated—and all the more so for being performed on a balcony in the dead of night, with only one man to keep the rhythm. But Charaxus was grinning by the time she had finished. She bowed to him, laughing, while he hailed her with his wine cup raised.

"Another?" she asked.

"By all means, yes!"

This time she performed a country girl's dance from his homeland of Lesvos. She hadn't done it but once before, and that was many months ago. Once she'd begun, she found to her mortification that she had forgotten half the steps. She was forced to improvise, but if Charaxus noticed, he didn't seem to care. In fact, her blushing face and slight hesitancy only seemed to delight him all the more.

When she'd finished and stood panting before him, laughing as she struggled to catch her breath, Charaxus captured her in his arms once again. His kiss was more insistent this time, hotter and hungrier.

He pulled back, gazing down at her with an expression of awe.

Rhodopis gently touched his face. "Do you want to take me to bed now?"

Charaxus smiled tightly. He released her, turning away. "I find I'm very tired," he said. "I had best send you home."

Rhodopis gaped at his back. A cold weight settled in her chest; she searched for words—a plea for an explanation, or even a shout of outrage to hurl at him. But nothing came to her.

Charaxus summoned his quiet, elegant slave; the man led Rhodopis to the door and slipped her pay into her hand. She closed her fist around the silver and stumbled through the darkness to her litter.

Only when the litter-bearers had lifted her and borne her away from Charaxus' home did she force her clenched fist open to count her hedj by the pale starlight.

Ten.

A meager ten coins. Cold horror suffused her veins. It was the smallest allowable payment for a hetaera, such a tiny sum that it was practically an insult.

Vélona won't believe me when I tell her this is all he paid me. She'll think I pinched some of the money for myself, to cut Xanthes out of his fee.

She would get the strap for sure. Worse than that, she had somehow offended Charaxus, lost her chance to secure the patronage of a rich and influential man.

How had it all gone wrong? She relived every moment of the night as she rode back to Xanthes' estate, but Rhodopis could identify no grave mistake, no obvious error on her part. By the time she reached Xanthes' courtyard, her face was slick with tears.

16

THE FEATHER MASK

Rhodopis was glad she arrived back at the Stable late into the night. She didn't think she could face the other girls. They would see the tear-tracks staining her face, and would know straight away that her night with Charaxus had been a disaster. They might pretend sympathy, but even kind-hearted Callisto would secretly thrill to know that Rhodopis had made a mess of things. Charaxus was fair game; his wealth and prestige remained available for any clever girl to seize.

She slipped into the great chamber, shutting the door softly behind her, and crept slowly toward her alcove. She placed each foot with exaggerated care, for she feared even to scuff the soles of her sandals against the floor tiles. Rhodopis would never live it down, if Bastet woke first and asked how the night had gone, then crowed over her miserable failure.

Archidike's dark head peeked out from her alcove as Rhodopis approached. She was smiling eagerly, but when Rhodopis shook her head, Archidike's smile faded. She glided across the room, gathered Rhodopis under her arm, and ducked with her behind the curtain.

Rhodopis covered her face with her hands in the darkness of

her alcove. She emitted the tiniest possible wail of mortification, but Archidike wasted no time comforting her.

"Come along; out of this dress," Archidike whispered.

She helped Rhodopis undress, then carefully took down her hair while Rhodopis sniffled and wept, swaying on her feet. Archidike scrubbed the paint from Rhodopis' face as best she could in the darkness, then climbed with her into bed. Only then did she allow Rhodopis to press her face against her shoulder, and only then did she circle her with her thin, wiry arms.

"Are those tears I feel?" Archidike whispered. "Enough crying, Duckling. Tell me what happened. He didn't hurt you, did he?"

"No—nothing 'cept my pride. Oh, it was awful, Archi. I'll never make my way at this rate!"

Rhodopis told her everything—the tender kisses, the eagerness Charaxus had shown for her... and then his inexplicable coldness as soon as she'd tried to coax him into bed.

"I admit I can't make much sense of it," Archidike said. "Maybe Charaxus likes men, but is trying to hide the fact for reasons of his own. Sometimes men from wealthy families, like the one he comes from, are expected to marry and have children. What's a man to do, if he doesn't respond to a woman's charms? Maybe he was trying to get used to the idea of taking a wife. It makes sense, doesn't it? Have a night with you, prove to himself he can stomach it. But then he couldn't go through with it after all."

Rhodopis shook her head vaguely. "I'm sure I can't begin to guess what he meant by it all. Vélona's going to be sore, though. He only paid me ten hedj!"

Archidike gave a quiet snort of disgust.

"Won't surprise me a bit if Vélona has me whipped for it," Rhodopis said, fighting back another flood of tears.

"She won't. Charaxus has never had dealings with Xanthes' girls before; Vélona doesn't know what to expect from him. For all she can tell, he's always just as tight with his purse-strings, whether he likes a girl or not. And anyway, there's a chance to do better. Don't you know what happens three nights from now?"

"No... what?"

"It's Iason's big feast! Iason breeds the best race horses in Egypt. He holds a big party at the same time every year, to commemorate his first stud horse, the one who started it all. It's the wildest, most exciting party you'll ever see. And you can be certain Vélona will send you to it. She's eager to show you off, good as your dancing is."

"I never went to this party last year."

"No; you weren't a working girl yet. Vélona would have thought you fragile back then; she wouldn't have risked you on such a wild night. But you're ready this year, for sure. And oh, Rhodopis, you'll love it. We always have such a marvelous time. Sometime—years ago—Iason held an auction, with all the men bidding on their favorite hetaerae. It was so popular that he did it again the next year, and the next. And now it's a tradition. The auction is the whole reason why most of these fellows still attend year after year—for after all, who cares about some old dead horse?"

"An auction," Rhodopis said uncertainly.

"Mm-hmm. All the girls wear the most intricate costumes you've ever seen. We dress up like birds and goddesses and creatures from the old stories. It's great fun. Highest bidder gets to enjoy his girl for the rest of the night. And Iason puts up a nice, fat bonus for whichever girl fetches the highest price of all."

"Oh, that sounds grand. If I can get a few bids, maybe I can make up the difference in what Charaxus might have paid me. Then Vélona won't be so angry."

"Just don't try to win the highest bid," Archidike said playfully. "This is my year. I haven't told anyone yet, Rho, but... I'm terribly close to buying my way free."

"Archi! You are? That's wonderful."

"I've only got a little more to earn, and then I'm free and clear. I intend to get the last of my silver at Iason's party."

Rhodopis frowned in the darkness. "And then you'll go off and leave me."

"Never. You know I never could. I'll stay right here in Memphis, and work on my own until you're free, too. Remember —just like we planned? By the time you're out, too, we'll have a grand estate of our own. Think of it, Rho: our own house, our own staff of servants. One day you'll see; it'll be simply grand. For now, just you focus on the party to come. It will make you feel better, I promise."

"What would I do without you, Archi?"

"Cry too much; that's what you'd do." She kissed Rhodopis on the nose. "Now forget all about that dolt Charaxus. He might not appreciate you in his bed, but I sure as Hades do."

❧

EACH OF XANTHES' girls attended the horse-breeder's party, for it was among the most prestigious events of the year. Vélona had no intention of squandering her chance to make so many lucrative connections; she deployed her master's hetaerae with all the strategy of a general, bedecking each one in a lavish costume. Hetaerae from every corner of Memphis would attend Iason's feast, and from other cities, too. Vélona was determined that no woman, no matter how wealthy or free, would out-shine any of her charges.

They had all arrived at the party together, in a caravan of litters. Xanthes' twelve hetaerae raised appreciative murmurs from Iason's guests and staff as they made their way across the wide, well-groomed estate. The annual party was so popular that no andron could hold it; crowds of men, draped in their best and brightest chlamys, milled about the manicured garden while women in the most astonishing and intricate costumes flitted from one man's arm to the next.

Rhodopis looked anxiously around the garden as Xanthes' girls dispersed into the crowd. "Do you think Iadmon will be here?" she asked Archidike.

"Would you like him to be here?"

"I don't think I would. It'd be terribly awkward, wouldn't it? I wouldn't know what to say to him, or how to act."

"Like you would with any other man," Archidike said. She pulled Rhodopis around to face her. "Here; let me straighten your feathers. They've gone all askew."

The costume Vélona had selected for Rhodopis was a marvel. The short tunic was sewn all over with overlapping feathers, cut from silk and gently frayed around the edges. The little scallops of white, black, and russet-red fluttered and swayed with her every movement. The skin of her bare legs had been stained black with kohl, leaving a suggestive band of pale, naked flesh at the top of each thigh, just below the hem of her tunic. Her arms were wrapped with beaded bracelets to match the colors of her feathers. A mask was pinned to her coiled braids so that it partially obscured her face. The mask bore a jutting black beak, sewn all over with tiny onyx beads, and the real feathers of a sewen, the Egyptian goose whom Rhodopis was supposed to resemble. It was simple, as costumes went. But the constant motion of her feathers, stirred by each unconscious, graceful, dancer's movement, drew every eye in the garden.

Archidike straightened a few of the feathers in Rhodopis' mask, then nodded in approval. "You look a perfect goose now, and that's the only time you'll ever hear those words as a compliment. Tell me again how beautiful I look."

"There's never been a prettier girl that the gods ever made," Rhodopis said sincerely.

Archidike had worked her influence over Vélona, convincing the mistress to send her off to Iason's party dressed as the element of fire. She wore a tight gown fashioned from strips of glimmering silk, in myriad shades of scarlet and orange, bright golden-yellow and deep ember-red. Hundreds of tiny gold beads glittered along her neckline and hem, and long strips of silk floated behind her as she walked, a colorful, drifting train. Archidike's black hair was bound up simply in a net of red carnelians. Instead of a mask, she had painted her whole face, from the bridge of her nose to her hairline, a brilliant orange. The ingenious disguise extended even to her scent. She had foregone the usual floral or musky perfumes and had instead burned a potent incense within the confines of her sleeping alcove so that the smell of smoke followed everywhere she went.

"You'll win the bidding for sure, Archi. Oh, you look like a flame come to life!"

"Come on, then," Archidike said eagerly. "If we're to win the highest bids, we'd best start making friends."

They threaded their way through the crowd, pausing to join the conversations whenever opportunity permitted. Rhodopis was fairly made dizzy by the variety of costumes she saw, dazzling and glittering in the late slant of afternoon light.

Every variety of bird strutted through the garden—some with real feathers, some merely draped in gowns of the right color. One stately hetaera wore a flowing, white linen robe and a close-fitting hood that completely covered her hair and hid her slender neck from chin to shoulders. The hood was stitched all over with yellow beads, and a crest of white feathers bristled at the back of her head. Rhodopis grinned when she recognized the costume as an Egyptian vulture, one of the traditional symbols of the Pharaoh's power. Iola, a hetaera known for her long, thin legs, played up her best feature to great advantage as a black-and-white stork. And one woman trailed a robe that must have weighed as much as her own body, for it was sewn with thousands of glimmering, blue-green faience beads. The beads caught the sunlight with a metallic flash as she moved slowly about the garden. The long jut of black beak she wore on her forehead, and the round orange patches painted on her cheeks, gave her away as a kingfisher.

There were plenty of butterflies, with graceful silk wings tied to shoulder and wrist. *And oh, wouldn't I be just about furious if I'd come as a butterfly, only to find so many others already here,* Rhodopis thought as she watched two of them stalk stiffly past each other. Goddesses of Greece and Egypt—even of Mitanni and Rome—flaunted transparent linen robes and the features beneath, or balanced great wreaths of grapes on their heads. There was Hathor, with her breasts bared and the horns of a she-cow rising from her head; there was Aphrodite, with roses in her hair and an apple in her hand. Bastet was dressed as the cat goddess she was named for, with silk ears and tail, and a collar of gems beautiful enough to make any woman sick with envy.

No one, though, looked quite like Archidike. Her fiery disguise was a perfect match for her temperament; admirers and old friends exclaimed over its originality—and declared it a perfect fit for Archidike. In the sun, she flickered like a flame as she went from one group of men to the next, heating their conversation and igniting their lust. Then she moved on as quickly as she'd appeared, leaving nothing behind but the lingering odor of smoke.

Rhodopis was content to follow after, keeping well out of Archidike's way, allowing her friend to shine like the fire she was. Nothing would please Rhodopis more than to see Archidike take the prize for the highest bid. She looked forward to the auction, and Archidike's victory, with pleasant anticipation that was almost strong enough to erase her unease, for she still had not decided what she would do if she were so unlucky as to meet Iadmon at the party.

Restlessly, she turned this way and that, searching the crowds of laughing men for Iadmon's unmistakable dark hair and upright, elegant bearing. She hung back as Archidike led her toward each new group of guests, cautiously peering at every face before she would approach herself.

That constant observation—and the protection of her feathered mask—allowed Rhodopis spot Charaxus before he saw her. The tall, handsome blond was standing quietly on the edge of a large group of men and their hetaerae, contemplating the wine in his cup with a despondent frown.

Rhodopis turned quickly away. "Blast!" she muttered. "Strymon blast him!"

"Step on something sharp? What's gotten into you, Rho?" Archidike had just worked her charms on a new group of men and was now drifting, smoke-like, across the garden.

"You won't believe, Archi. Worse than if Iadmon was here. I thought nothing could be worse, but this—!"

"You're banging on, Duckling. Or should I call you Gosling today? Steady, now. Tell me what's got you so upset."

Rhodopis leaned close to her friend. She whispered, "Charaxus is here."

"Oh, by the hairy balls of Zeus. Don't look back; I'll do the looking. You just stay inside your mask."

Archidike linked her arm with Rhodopis and glanced over her shoulder. "What does he look like? That man with the streaks of gray in his hair? No, there he is—I see him. Yellow curls?"

Rhodopis nodded.

"Come on. Iason has a big garden, and if we're quick on our feet, we can keep the whole thing between Charaxus and us all night long."

"But you can't, Archi. You've got to make friends. The auction—"

"I'll make friends easily enough. Don't think I'll neglect the auction; I've been waiting for it all year long. Good thing the mask hides most of your face."

"Not my hair, though. Everyone can see my hair, and there's nobody else with hair like mine."

Archidike scowled. "That's true enough." She hauled Rhodopis across the garden all the faster, turning now and then to wave and smile as hetaerae called out compliments for her costume.

They found some shelter behind a hedge of rose bushes and peered out at the party. Charaxus was now wandering from group to group, glancing into each small knot of guests and then moving on.

"Maybe he's looking for someone else," Archidike said.

"Can't imagine why he'd want to see me, anyway, after the way he treated me."

Several guests wandered back behind the rose hedge, roaring with laughter as they came. "Tell another one," a man shouted. "Kleitos has the best jokes in Egypt!"

"Nothing for it," Archidike said. "We'd best go over and make friends with Kleitos. If the jokes are coarse enough, maybe they'll keep the dandy Good Man Charaxus away."

The girls ingratiated themselves with Kleitos and his friends, and made a good show of appreciating the man's rather sophomoric humor. But after a time, Rhodopis saw Charaxus approaching from the other end of the rose hedge. Drawn by the raucous laughter, he had come to investigate. Rhodopis tried to shrink back behind Kleitos, but the man kept bobbing and weaving as he reeled off an especially theatrical story. Charaxus started when he caught sight of her and hurried toward the group.

"Ignore him," Archidike hissed, pulling Rhodopis close. She edged further into the group, maneuvering Rhodopis out of reach.

The men and hetaerae roared with laughter again, but as soon as it died away, Rhodopis heard an urgent whisper from beyond the group. "Rhodopis! Rhodopis!"

She groaned. Charaxus would not leave her be until she had

spoken with him; that much was clear. She gritted her teeth, pretending she hadn't heard.

But he went on calling to her, and soon the men in Kleitos' circle were laughing at Charaxus instead of at their friend's stories.

"What is it, Charaxus? Lost something?"

"Lost his dignity," somebody muttered.

"Come, now. Good Man Rax gets plenty of dignity from his sister. It's where he gets everything else."

Rhodopis' cheeks flamed. She knew it was silly to feel embarrassed on Charaxus' behalf, yet she did all the same. To spare him more mockery, she left the group abruptly and allowed him to follow her across the grass.

When they were well apart from the group, Charaxus took Rhodopis by the arm. She spun to face him and had to press her lips firmly together, stopping herself from hurling the insults and accusations she longed to fling in his face.

"You look beautiful," he said rapturously. "You're the most beautiful woman here."

"I'm dressed as a goose," Rhodopis said drily.

"But still the most beautiful. I've been searching for you since I arrived. I had to find you, and tell you..."

He hesitated, and for a moment Rhodopis thought he would apologize. But then he said, "I had to tell you... how lovely you are."

"You say that now," Rhodopis said bitterly. "Can't imagine why, when you were so cold at our last meeting." She was so stung by his inexplicable attention and the memory of how he'd shamed her that she let all pretense at sophistication slip. The pout she'd been holding back for days won out. She braced her hands on her hips and glowered up at him through the feathers of her mask. "D'you know what you nearly did to me? Got me whipped, you careless fool! Wasn't for this party, my back would probably still be red from the strap. Why, if I never was to see you again in this life, it'd be too soon for my liking."

Charaxus pulled Rhodopis into his arms and kissed her. Her fists clenched; she wanted to push him away, but she had already gone too far in chastising him. She was lucky he was kissing her now, instead of running to Vélona or Xanthes to report on her cheek. *You may not be a slave exactly, not anymore*, she told herself, *but you aren't free, either. Remember that, and don't slip up again.* She marshaled her control and pulled gently away from his embrace.

"Good Man Charaxus," she said with a coy smile, "if you want to pay to see me again, I would be glad to meet you." Her smile slipped. "And I'll do my best to make you happy, though I confess I can't imagine how I might go about it."

Charaxus opened his mouth, about to make some reply, but at that moment a great shout went up across the garden. Archidike waved to Rhodopis: "The auction is starting. Hurry!"

"I've got to go now," Rhodopis said. "You understand, don't you?"

"Of course." He lifted her hand to his lips. Rhodopis joined the other costumed women, who streamed toward the great central courtyard where the auction was to take place. She subtly wiped her hand on the fluttering feathers of her tunic, scrubbing away Charaxus' kiss.

Iason had appointed his chief household steward to run the event. As soon as the majority of Iason's guests had assembled, the steward stepped up on the low limestone wall of a flower bed and raised his arms to the crowd. Silence descended over the garden.

"Good men," the steward called, "my master Iason is honored that you should all gather here tonight, in remembrance of Night Star, the noble horse whose loss the master still feels." Jeers from the crowd mingled with salutes to the long-dead horse. Rhodopis couldn't decide whether the salutes were ironic or sincere. "And now, with no further delay, let us begin the one event the men of

Memphis anticipate all year long! Let the goddess Hathor come forward!"

The woman dressed as Hathor stepped up beside the steward while the crowd cheered her on. She waved gaily to the men, and the steward opened the bidding.

Rhodopis watched with delight as one hetaera after another presented herself before the crowd. The women turned to display their stunning garb, basked in the praises of their admirers, then joined their highest bidder, his dedicated companion for the rest of the night. No one referred to the hetaerae by name; they had assumed the identities of their costumes, and that illusion of anonymity—however thin—added to the thrill of the event.

Bids rose ever higher as the auction went on, for Iason's servants were everywhere in the crowd, filling guests' cups as soon as they emptied. One of the butterflies went for a handsome hundred and fifty hedj. A female incarnation of Dionysus, god of wine and revelry, took nearly three hundred; she let out a victorious shout entirely appropriate to her identity. The kingfisher and the vulture landed bids of three hundred and fifty apiece.

"Who do you think will take the prize for the highest bid?" Rhodopis whispered.

"It has to be me," Archidike answered grimly. "But it'll be hard to top three hundred and fifty."

At that moment, the steward called, "Let the Element of Fire come forward!"

"Luck!" Rhodopis whispered as Archidike stepped up on the garden wall.

The crowd's shout of approval was long and loud. The lowering sun shimmered on the golden beads at Archidike's neck, casting a triumphant light on her face. Her blue eyes looked brighter and more intense than ever among her mask of orange paint. She held herself regally still until the tumult died away. Then she nodded her assent to the steward.

"Let us hear the bids for twenty," he said.

It was the usual starting price, but far too low for the notorious Archidike. Her admirers knew that at once. "A hundred and twenty!" someone shouted.

"Ah!" the steward said. "It seems one among you is eager to get burned. Who else bids? Or are you afraid of the fire?"

Archidike wiggled her hips, making her trails of bright silk dance. The bids rose higher—and higher still. She beamed out at them, pure pleasure and gratitude melting away the habitual hardness of her face. It was rare that no trace of anger or cynicism tainted Archidike's expression; Rhodopis had seldom seen her friend genuinely happy. She grinned and clapped her hands every time a new bid came in; by the time Archidike's bid reached three hundred and seventy hedj—the highest of the night—Rhodopis was dancing from foot to foot with joy.

The steward took the final bid—three hundred and eighty—and Archidike hopped down from the wall to roars of approval. Hetaerae kissed her cheeks in congratulation; men slapped the winning bidder on the back with rueful expressions—for who among them wouldn't like a night with the very personification of a wild, leaping flame?

When the crowd quieted, the steward called, "And now, the little russet goose. Where is she?"

Rhodopis swallowed a sudden lump in her throat. She didn't know whether anyone would bid on her tonight. No hetaera had yet failed to win at least a few bids, but Rhodopis was still little-known in Memphis, and had spent the party yielding to Archidike, helping pave the way for her victory. *It would be dreadful to only get twenty hedj*, she thought as she stepped shakily up onto the wall.

The steward raised his hand, ready to speak. But before he could even open his mouth, Charaxus stepped to the front of the crowd. "One hundred!"

The guests laughed. "Well," the steward said. "No one told me that Good Man Charaxus has taken up cooking. See how eager he is to stuff a goose!"

There was more laughter—from everyone but Charaxus. He stared at Rhodopis with a steady, sober expression, as if willing her to leap from the wall and into his arms.

Should have known he'd bid, she thought, forcing herself to smile at him. *At least this'll be an end to it. A hundred hedj is a respectable price, too. Thanks to the gods, and get me down from here!*

But Charaxus' opening bid was not the end of Rhodopis' ordeal. Kleitos, it seemed, was in the mood for more of his jokes. He, too, stepped from the crowd, leered at Charaxus for a moment, and then shouted, "A hundred and twenty!"

"One hundred fifty," Charaxus said at once.

Rhodopis' wide-eyed stare darted from one man to the other. *Gods, don't let this be real. Put a stop to it now!*

"Come on," somebody shouted from the crowd. "Make Rax work for it, Kleitos!"

Kleitos raised his wine cup. "One hundred seventy."

"Two hundred," Charaxus said coolly.

Rhodopis shifted uncomfortably, swaying from foot to foot. She cast a glance of mute appeal toward Iason's steward, but the man only grinned back at her, pleased with the bids.

"Two hundred and fifty!" Kleitos said. His friends bellowed with laughter.

Charaxus' jaw clenched; he tore his eyes from Rhodopis only long enough to glare his hatred at Kleitos. "*Three* hundred and fifty."

It was such a leap of a bid that the crowd gasped collectively. *Let it end there,* Rhodopis prayed to the indifferent gods.

Kleitos tipped back his wine cup. For a moment, Rhodopis thought the gods had heard her, and the jokester was ready to surrender. But when he lowered his cup to reveal a drunken smirk, she knew the ordeal had not yet ended. "Three hundred sixty," Kleitos said.

"Please," Rhodopis muttered. "Please, enough."

Charaxus dashed his wine cup to the ground; the dark dregs spilled out across the paving stones. The crowd exclaimed over his sudden show of temper.

He raised a clenched fist toward Kleitos. "Four hundred!"

Kleitos shrugged casually and turned to his friends. "It seems our friend Charaxus is determined to pluck this goose. Who am I to stand between a man and his meal? Enjoy, Rax—enjoy."

"There it is, then," the steward proclaimed. "Bidding is closed, at four hundred hedj."

Rhodopis had gone numb with shock. When Charaxus grabbed her wrist and pulled her down from the garden wall, she stumbled weakly after him. She only looked back once—and all she could see was Archidike's disbelieving stare. Those blue eyes, vivid in their mask of carnelian paint, watched Rhodopis with all the pain of betrayal... and all the promise of retribution.

17

HIGHEST BIDDER

RHODOPIS COULDN'T ERASE ARCHIDIKE'S STARE FROM HER MIND AS Charaxus pulled her out of the garden and into Iason's house. She had never expected the bidding war to erupt. She prayed viciously for the gods to curse Kleitos with eternal impotence, for having the cheek to prod Charaxus into over-spending. How could she have known Kleitos would do such a thing? Yet now, the sensitive and easily angered Archidike surely thought Rhodopis was a traitor to their friendship. Archidike had thought herself so close to winning her freedom—and at such a young age, too! Rhodopis would have wept for her friend, but she couldn't afford to do it now. She must put on a show of flattered happiness, for Charaxus' sake—when all she wanted to do was cuff him and scorch him with her tongue.

Four hundred hedj! It was an astounding sum... a *ridiculous* sum. Rhodopis had only recently debuted as a hetaera; she was not yet a known personality, and far from an established commodity. Certainly, she was not as popular as Archidike, even though they had often worked together. Archidike had worked so hard, and for so long, to nurture her reputation, cultivating a brazen style that no one else in Memphis possessed. Hadn't she earned her freedom by now?

And haven't I robbed it from her? Though the gods know I never intended to do it.

Another thought occurred to Rhodopis as Charaxus led her from one chamber of Iason's house to the next, checking for an empty room. *If I wasn't known before, I will be now. Every hetaera in the city will gossip about the simple little goose-girl who fetched four hundred hedj at Iason's auction.* Every man of means would wonder what secret the goose-girl was hiding—what Charaxus knew that no one else did. *My reputation's made, all right. And how will I ever live up to it? Sweet gods have mercy on me now.*

Charaxus found an empty chamber; he impatiently kicked the door closed. The room was small—not much larger than her old room back at Iadmon's estate—but prettily appointed, with two small clay lamps already conveniently lit, a couch spread with fresh linen sheets, and the air scented by burning cones of sandalwood incense.

As soon as the door was decently shut, Charaxus set to work undressing Rhodopis. It seemed the auction had enflamed him like nothing else—having almost lost out on her, Charaxus could wait no longer to possess her.

Rhodopis stepped back as he removed her feather mask. She stared up at him, utterly lost in confusion.

Charaxus reached for her again, but then he hesitated. At least, Rhodopis thought wryly, he was unwilling to force her compliance.

"I don't know what to make of you," she said, making no attempt to culture her voice. The Thracian girl was on full display now. "Playing me cold like you did back at your house, and then behaving a perfect fool, right in front of everybody. Really, Charaxus—what's a girl to think of a man like you?"

"Whatever do you mean?"

She pressed her lips together for a moment, and only spoke again when she could be reasonably certain she wouldn't shout at him. "When you invited me to your house, you seemed to like me well enough. But then you went cold on me the moment I suggested we go to bed. What had you brought me for, if not for that? And then when you sent me off, you paid me so poorly! I don't know how I could have offended you, but it's sure enough I did. And now there you were, bidding on me as if your life depended on winning me. You played right into Kleitos' hands, Charaxus! I'm not worth four hundred hedj. You over-spent on me, and that's just what Kleitos intended. But really, Rax: ten hedj one night, four hundred the next... you've completely tweaked my wits, and no mistake!"

To Rhodopis' surprise, Charaxus fell on his knees before her. He clutched both her hands in his own. "Since I first saw you at Diokles' party—since I saw you dance, I haven't been able to get you out of my mind."

"You told me as much already," Rhodopis said. She tried to free her hands, but Charaxus held tight.

"You're not like the rest of the hetaerae," he said, "cunning and calculating, only thinking how they might better themselves. You're real, Rhodopis. There's nothing false about you, in a world where everyone, everything is false! Your innocence, your fragility... they're all I've ever wanted in a woman. And I know I was cold to you when you came around to my place. I shouldn't have been; it was wrong of me. I just couldn't face the fact of what you are, darling. When you were so direct... when you asked me about... well, about lying together... the beautiful illusion shattered, and cruel reality came to me. You aren't a free woman, whom I may court and marry. You aren't what I want you to be— what I need you to be. The fact of it depressed me, I'm afraid, for I'd so set my heart on you. You mustn't mind my moods; it's the curse of my family, you see. Sappho is just as moody as I, but she can use it to her advantage, to write beautiful poetry. I'm a poor beggar; I've no such skill. I'm a creature of my moods, Rhodopis. I wish it weren't so, but it is. I've no words like my sister's, none to tell you how I feel. All I can tell you is... well..." Charaxus burst out with sudden, loud passion, "No other woman will do, none at all! Yet how can we be together as I want us to be—as I need us to be—when you are who you are, and what you are?"

Rhodopis was silent. For a moment, her quick mind was struck blank and dull by Charaxus' startling revelation. Finally she said, "But I can only be who and what I am."

He climbed to his feet, still clutching her hands. "And I can only be what I am: a man who loves you passionately."

"Loves me?" Rhodopis nearly laughed. "Darling, we hardly know each other! How can you love me?"

"It's just as I told you: my family is passionate and love-lorn. It is our curse, I suppose. I cannot write you poetry, Rhodopis—I cannot tell the world how you make my heart soar and how you haunt my dreams at night. But this love is no less agonizing to me. And so, when I saw Kleitos bidding on you, I couldn't let him win. We may be fated to be forever apart, but still I cannot stand the thought of another man having you, even though I know you are..."

"A hetaera."

Rhodopis finally tugged her hands free and turned away from Charaxus. If the chamber had had a window, she would have stood beside it, gazing out at the garden as she had so often done, in her own private room at Iadmon's. There, alone with her thoughts, she could have pondered over Charaxus' strange confession and what it might mean to her. But there was no window—only the two small lamps. Rhodopis stood beside one and watched its flame dance, bending and swaying, fluttering each time her breath disturbed it.

It was plain that Charaxus couldn't truly love her. She was

only fourteen years old and new to womanhood, but Rhodopis had enough good sense to know that Charaxus' proclamation of love was absurd. Yet there had been real sincerity in his eyes. He believed every word of what he'd said. This silly idea of love was real to him—truth to him—whatever Rhodopis may think of it. And if the results of the auction were any indication, then his feelings were strong enough to drive him into any sort of foolishness.

The flame twisted and bowed again. With a lurch of regret, Rhodopis thought of Archidike. What would she do, if she stood in this chamber with Charaxus—if she had received this outrageous pronouncement?

Reckon it's time I start thinking more like Archidike, and less like the Thracian urchin.

Especially now that her alliance with Archidike was uncertain. Rhodopis felt a twinge in her rib, in exactly the place where, on the first night they'd met, Archidike had pressed her sharp nail into Rhodopis' skin. For all she knew, Rhodopis was on her own now, left to navigate the world of the hetaerae with no oar but her own.

Charaxus is one of the wealthiest men in the city. I can use his wealth to my advantage. Play him right, and I'll secure the best patron a girl like me could hope for. But can I play Charaxus at all? Oh, it's so much simpler with other men! All they want is my body—not my heart.

She knew at once that Charaxus would not be easy to please. If he were to become her patron, he would expect more from Rhodopis than she might be able—or willing—to give. But if she could win his generosity, then his patronage would bring her freedom all the faster.

"Rhodopis?" Charaxus said uncertainly.

P'raps I'll just have to run the risk, and let him love me... and deal with the consequences when they come.

What other prospects did she have? Inexperienced as she was, she could never live up to the expectations set by the four hundred hedj. It must be Charaxus or no one.

Rhodopis turned back to him, offering her warmest smile. "Darling, you must forgive me. It's only that no man's ever said such things to me before, and... well, I didn't know how to take it. Imagine, a simple country girl like me—and owned property, too. I never thought I'd have the affection of such a great man."

"It's more than affection," Charaxus insisted.

Rhodopis lowered her eyes shyly. "Love," she said.

Suddenly, Charaxus tore at his blond curls in a display of hopeless longing. "Oh, but what's the use of it? We can never be together. The gods are so very cruel!"

The moment had arrived. Rhodopis went to him, laying one trembling hand on his chest to calm him. "But we can be together... after a fashion. What if I were to see you special?"

Charaxus released his grip on his hair. He lowered his hands, staring fixedly at the wall. Finally he said, "You want me to become your patron." He didn't sound as if the idea appealed.

Rhodopis pressed her lips together again. She struggled to keep her anger from flaring up. *What does the silly ass want me to say? I am what I am: he said himself. Not 's if I have any say in the matter, not 'til I've got all the money I need.*

She made herself take his hands in her own. She lowered her eyes again, and let the heat of anger flood her face—a passable substitute for a girl's shy blush. "I wish it could be different for us. I wish we could be free to love each other without any cares in the world. But until I'm freed from Xanthes..."

"Perhaps I can buy you," Charaxus said hastily.

Rhodopis fluttered her lashes to keep herself from rolling her eyes. She was certain that even a man as wealthy as Charaxus wouldn't be able to meet her master's price—especially not once word of the auction reached Xanthes. Now the shrewd old bull was sure to consider Rhodopis more valuable than ever before. He would set her price high—whether that price was for another man to buy her, or for Rhodopis to purchase her own freedom.

"But if you buy me, then I'll still be owned, won't I? And we'll be in the same fix."

"I'll free you!"

Rhodopis thought quickly. "But you'll always know that you had to buy me first. Everyone else will know the same. It will only taint our love—poison it—and I couldn't stand for that to happen. Won't it be better, dear, if I continue as a hetaera for a little while longer? I'll make my future in the usual way, earn my freedom, and all the respect that goes with it. Then, perhaps, everyone in Memphis will think I'm good enough to be your bride."

She stroked his knuckles with her thumb. "If you're my patron, Charaxus—if you contrive to see me often, then I'll earn my freedom in no time."

He pulled his hands from her grip, turning away. "But in the meantime, other men will have you."

"Only for a while, dear... only until I'm freed and we're together. And then we'll forget all about those men, for they mean nothing to me... nothing at all! Only you matter. Oh, please say you will! Without you, I'll never hope to get free. And I want to be free... I want to marry a respectable man, and be a good, honest wife. Save me from this fate, dear Charaxus!"

Rhodopis played the role of the helpless innocent so well that Charaxus' passion returned. It swept over him in a hot gust, scorching away the last of his resistance, the last of his fears. He reached for Rhodopis hungrily, pulling her into a kiss. She returned the kiss, as if the same fire burned in her heart, in precisely equal measure.

Still kissing her, Charaxus stumbled toward the couch. But just before he pulled her down onto it, Rhodopis pushed back from his embrace. She gazed up at him, wide-eyed and pleading, until at last he blurted out the promise she sought.

"Yes, yes, I'll do it. I'll be your patron. You know I would do anything for you, Rhodopis!"

❧

AN HOUR LATER, Rhodopis was finally able to extract herself. Charaxus' passion had taken a long while to exhaust itself. He was inclined to savor the moment he had dreamed of for so long. He had drawn out their play so excruciatingly that Rhodopis wanted to scream with frustration—and was tempted more than one to take control of events, employing one of the tricks Archidike had taught her to finish off any man with speed.

But a show of haste would never do. She had to convince Charaxus she was sincere—make him believe that she loved him as much as he loved her, and that she longed to be his wife above all else.

When at last the deed was done and Charaxus drifted off to sleep, murmuring with satisfaction, Rhodopis counted to one hundred to be certain he was truly gone. Then she sprang up from the couch, collecting her tunic, sandals, and mask from the chamber floor. She pulled the tunic on over her mussed hair, jerked it straight around her body, and smoothed the silken feathers as much as she could. She stood over the couch for a moment, frowning down at Charaxus.

She hadn't liked to make all those promises, for she knew she could never live up to them, and felt instinctively that it was a great and terrible wrong—an affront against the gods themselves —to swear love where none existed.

But what else could a girl like Rhodopis do? *Got to look out for myself now. If the gods are angry, then they've no one to blame but themselves. It was they who made me a slave, after all—and a hetaera.*

She turned toward the door, but paused, casting one last,

regretful glance toward Charaxus. He had been fumbling in bed, and rather silly with all his proclamations of love. But he had touched her face gently after the deed was done, in a way that had gone straight to Rhodopis' reluctant heart.

The self-serving hetaera—burgeoning hour by hour inside the shell of the Thracian urchin—only hoped she hadn't left her companion too satisfied. *I wouldn't do for Charaxus to feel entirely sated.* He must never quite have his fill of her, or he would soon transfer his affection—his *love*, as he insisted she call it—to another girl. Rhodopis had no doubt that he would do just that, the moment another woman caught his eye. Charaxus was not in love with Rhodopis. He was in love her act—her style, as the women of the Stable called it.

And it was an act, indeed. Charaxus wanted a simple little country girl, but Rhodopis was not that. She had been separated from Aesop for two years, but she was still Aesop's pupil—careful and canny, always alert for any twist in fortune's road, any new path, however rocky, that would lead her ever closer to her goal: freedom.

Still, because she was careful and canny, Rhodopis knew she couldn't let Charaxus slip from her grasp until he had served his purpose.

I can't go off and leave him like any old hetaera would—in and done, and thanks for the pay, see you at the next party.

If she hoped to maintain the illusion of love, she must part as a lover would. Briefly, she considered leaving a piece of jewelry with Charaxus, so he would know she had been thinking tender thoughts as she'd slipped through the door. She quickly dismissed that idea. Jewelry would have to be paid for, and Amenia knew every bead and pearl in the collection.

Instead, Rhodopis plucked one of the russet goose feathers from the side of her mask. It was soft and delicate, just as she was, within the pink mist and sweet perfume of Charaxus' fantasy. She placed the feather carefully in his half-curled fist. He would find it when he woke.

Rhodopis let herself out of the chamber, closing the door softly behind her, and hurried back along the corridors to the garden. She could hear the party in the distance, bursting with laughter, vibrating with rollicking song. The sun had set; a pale purple twilight hung over the garden, dimming the former brightness of the hetaerae's costumes and disguising the far boundaries of Iason's estate in shadow.

Rhodopis searched every face in each new crowd as she made the rounds of the garden. All she could think of now was finding Archidike, explaining to her what had happened—that she'd had no part in the bidding, it had all been the fault of that fool Charaxus. But Archidike was nowhere to be found.

She came across Bastet, purring as her companion for the night stroked her silk cat ears.

"Where's Archidike?" she whispered.

"Don't know," Bastet snapped. "I'm not her keeper."

"Please, Bast; it's ever so important."

"Last I saw, she went off with the fellow who'd bid for her. But that was long ago. You know Archidike; she finished him off quick like she always does. I can't say where she might be now."

P'raps she's gone back to Iason's guest rooms with her man. Archidike liked to work quickly, but she was always game for another round. Rhodopis started back toward the wing of guest chambers, but she halted halfway there. *Last thing I want's to find Charaxus coming out of his chamber. He'd never let me get away again.*

Rhodopis skirted the side of Iason's massive house instead, working her way through a side garden where grape vines grew in profusion, climbing up the trunks of whispering date palms. She stumbled now and then in the darkness, and once cried out as she stubbed her toe against a half-buried stone. But the side garden was empty, save for herself; no one tried to stop her.

She reached Iason's front courtyard a few minutes later. The guests' litters stood rank upon rank in orderly rows, waiting to carry their owners home. Dozens of litter bearers had gathered by the estate's front wall; Iason had provided them with lamps, and they crouched around the pools of light, amusing themselves by throwing dice, or with games of senet, the playing boards scratched into the dust. Rhodopis wandered among the litters. In the twilight gloom, they all looked nearly the same. She searched for the one that had carried Archidike and herself to the party—the one with the harpy's wings and lion's heads—but it was nowhere to be found. With dread rising rapidly in her gut, Rhodopis scanned the groups of litter-bearers. Here and there, she found men in Xanthes' dark-blue robes, but not the fellows who had carried her to the party.

"Do you need any assistance, my lady?"

Rhodopis turned. It was the steward—the one who had run the auction. He carried a clay lamp in one hand. Its flame illuminated an earnest, intelligent face, and Rhodopis longed for Aesop with a terrible, cold pang.

"I'm looking for Archidike—the girl dressed up as fire. Have you seen her?"

"Ah," the steward said, "she went back to Xanthes' place some half an hour ago, perhaps more. Are you Rhodopis?"

"Yes, that's me." She pulled the mask from her face.

The steward offered a small bow. "Your friend said you would be returning to your master's house in Good Man Charaxus' litter. Is that no longer the case? Shall I make other arrangements for you?"

"N—no; no, thank you," Rhodopis said quickly. "Charaxus will see me home."

The steward bowed again and headed off across the courtyard, to deliver the extra light to the dicing litter-bearers. Rhodopis ducked back into the shadows of the side garden, watching. When the steward had vanished again inside Iason's house, she marched stiffly across the courtyard, past the litters and the dicing men, and walked right out the front gate.

The trek back to Xanthes' house was longer than Rhodopis had expected. If the two estates hadn't lain along a straight path, at opposite ends of the long market street, she could certainly have lost herself somewhere in Memphis. But she followed the market road faithfully, ignoring the men who called out to her. She could only pray that no one would assault her. Her thoughts were dark—very near despair—and her bleak mood distracted her. She didn't notice the turmoil brewing in the street until she was well into the thick of it.

"If you don't like the king, then why don't you get out of the country?"

Rhodopis looked up quickly. She was in the center of a wide square—the site of the great market, during daylight hours. There were no peddlers' booths or farmers' wagons in the square now. Instead, groups of men lounged about the corners, leaning against buildings, drinking from skins of beer, and tossing dice in the wan moonlight. Five or six fellows came out of a nearby wine shop, singing loudly and laughing. A pair of garishly dressed pornae approached them, but the men waved them off.

The fellow who had shouted was one of the dicing men. He pointed across the square to the men with the beer skins. They all wore the short white kilts of Egyptians.

"Get out of the country?" a kilted man shouted back. "This is still Egypt, for all the Pharaoh tries to turn it into Greece. You get out, and take all the rest of the boy-buggering Greeks with you!" His friends hooted in appreciation.

"Fucking Egyptian dogs don't know what's good for you!"

The group of Egyptians barked at the dicers, then howled to the moon.

The dicers were on their feet now. Rhodopis could see how they stumbled as they rose. They were perilously drunk, spoiling for a fight. She picked up speed, hoping to cross the square and slip back into the shadows of the market street before any violence erupted.

The men in the white kilts stopped barking—stopped speaking in Greek, too. They flung insults at the dicers in their native tongue. Rhodopis understood just enough Egyptian to know they offered dire offense. The dicers came on faster now; she saw the glint of honed metal as they slid daggers from their belts.

"Gods have mercy!" Rhodopis gasped. She forgot her dignity and ran from the square. Behind her, the bristling men clashed; shouts filled the night, from the fighters and from those looking on. She clenched her fist around the ties of her mask, wishing she held a knife instead. A man's agonized scream cut through the darkness; Rhodopis pushed herself harder, running as fast as her legs would move, deeper into the cold dark of Memphis.

By the time she returned to Xanthes' house, Rhodopis was footsore and hopelessly out of breath. The guards on Xanthes' gate stared at her, startled.

"Let me in, for pity's sake," she cried. "Can't you see it's me?"

The gate squealed open; Rhodopis flung herself into the house and along the corridor until she reached the door of the Stable. She leaned against it, covering her face with her hands, heaving until her breath had finally slowed, until it no longer burned in the back of her throat. Then she pushed the Stable door open and crept inside.

All the girls save Archidike were still at Iason's party; they weren't expected home for hours yet. None of the lamps had been lit. Rhodopis made her way down the long chamber by feel, counting each alcove as her outstretched hand found it, until she reached Archidike's bed.

Rhodopis pulled back the curtain. She could tell by the rhythm of Archidike's breathing that she wasn't asleep.

"Archi, it's me—Rho. I didn't know that fool Charaxus would do what he did. I didn't want it to happen."

The silence stretched on.

"Archidike, please. Won't you talk to me? Haven't we always been good to one another?"

The only response from Archidike was a sniffle in the darkness. Then her bed creaked and the mattress crackled as Archidike shifted to her other side, turning her back on her friend.

❧ 18 ❧

A PATRON, AT LAST

RHODOPIS SOON LEARNED THAT SHE WAS ON HER OWN IN THE Stable. Archidike hardly spoke to her, unless occasion—or Vélona—required it. Vélona was quick enough to note that the girls' alliance had crumbled; she tactfully turned away summons for Rhodopis and Archidike to entertain together, and within a few months, all such requests ceased.

Rhodopis didn't know how she ought to feel about losing her partnership with Archidike. On the one hand, she was grateful she didn't have to pretend. It would have been agonizing to go to parties arm in arm with Archidike, making believe their friendship had never ended. But on the other hand, Rhodopis missed her friend terribly. She longed for a chance to make everything right between them, to mend and rebuild what they'd once had... though she hadn't the first idea how she might go about it.

A certain pall of fear hung over Rhodopis in the months after Iason's party, too. Archidike could be a dangerous enemy; she knew that instinctively. The gods had never made a harder girl. Archidike had learned long ago that success only came to those hetaerae who cared for themselves—first, last, and always. A girl who succumbed to the pleasantries of friendship was a girl who ended with her heart broken—or worse, a knife in her back. Rhodopis knew full well that Archidike had the strength of will— and the raw cunning—to achieve whatever she wanted. She could only hope that whatever Archidike wanted now, it wasn't to revenge herself upon the friend who had inadvertently betrayed her.

As Rhodopis had grimly foreseen, the story of the four-hundred-hedj bid spread rapidly through Memphis society. She was isolated in the Stable—a complete outcast now, despised by all the girls, who envied the high bid and took Archidike's outrage as a convenient excuse to shun Rhodopis. But beyond the walls of the Stable, her star was at last beginning to rise. The men of Memphis clamored for their chance to make the acquaintance of the shy new hetaera. It seemed every wealthy man sought to uncover her secret, to learn what subtle magic had inspired the astonishing bid. Rhodopis was busy almost every night—and was grateful for it. The more parties she attended, and the more beds she visited, the less time she spent in the Stable, where Archidike's simmering hatred and the other girls' envy made life a misery.

Nearly eight weeks after the auction, Charaxus finally lived up to his promise. He wrote to Xanthes, proposing an official patronage for the hetaera Rhodopis, along with the gift of an emerald necklace. The necklace was exquisite—three stones the size of hedj coins, set in discs of gold. When Vélona presented it to Rhodopis, even Archidike had to admire its beauty.

The emerald necklace was only the first of Charaxus' gifts. As the offerings came from a true patron, Rhodopis was allowed to keep them, rather than surrendering the goods to Amenia and the dressing closet. But Charaxus' taste in presents was as confusing and ever-changing as his moods. Some of the things he sent—silver bracelets, ivory hair combs, ankle cuffs of lapis lazuli —had real value, and added to Rhodopis' growing store of personal wealth. Others were only the silly sentiments of a hopelessly besotted man. He sent her honey cakes and bouquets of flowers, valueless bracelets made from colored thread. Rhodopis was dreadfully afraid that he'd send her a kitten or a puppy, and what would she do with a pet? But whether the gifts he sent were valuable or had no real worth at all, Charaxus sent something to Rhodopis nearly every day. Soon Rhodopis thought it best to seek discretion. She asked Vélona to pass Charaxus' gifts to her only when the other girls weren't anywhere nearby, for she was frightened of what might happen to her if their jealousy boiled over.

Her new patron's largesse presented another problem, too. Rhodopis was running out of places to hide the wealth she was accumulating. Long ago, when she'd first arrived at the Stable, Archidike had told Rhodopis that all the girls had a secret place —a hidden nook where they stashed away their money, protecting it from theft until they'd accumulated enough silver to buy their freedom. The only hiding place Rhodopis had yet devised was a slice in the bottom of her mattress cover. She knew it was too obvious a spot, and vulnerable to raiding. Besides, she could no longer sleep soundly at night, for Charaxus' many affections filled her mattress with lumps and hard, awkward edges.

The solution came to her one day when Vélona held her back while the other girls went off to the gynaeceum for their breakfast.

"Another gift from your patron," Vélona said. She opened the dressing closet door, stooped inside, and presented Rhodopis with a clay amphora.

Rhodopis accepted it with some confusion. It was the size of a large melon, with two looped handles beside its narrow neck and a stopper in its wide mouth. It was heavy, too—full of something that sloshed as Rhodopis shrugged.

"Bath oil," Vélona said. "As if we don't keep you oiled enough here. As if I don't know the business of running a house full of hetaerae."

Rhodopis sighed. "Charaxus doesn't mean any insult, Mistress. He's just... a bit silly, that's all."

"Silly or not, you certainly have charmed him. You've done well, Rhodopis. Now take that stuff off to the baths—there's enough for a whole year's worth of bathing in that jar—and hurry along to the gynaeceum. You're working this afternoon, so be sure to eat well."

"Yes, Mistress."

In the bath house, Rhodopis pulled the tight stopper from the amphora. She sniffed the oil within. The smell was lovely, redolent with spices and myrrh—but even the finest bath oil wasn't worth much. She sighed again; another sentimental but ultimately useless gift from her patron. *Charaxus keeps up this foolishness, and Vélona will cut him off entirely.* Bath oil was the kind of present an honest woman would receive from her lover or her husband. It was not the sort of offering a serious patron would give a hetaera.

Annoyed, Rhodopis left the jar sitting beside the bathing pool. But she paused on the threshold of the bath house, and turned back, tapping her chin thoughtfully.

The oil wasn't worth much, but the amphora itself could be of real value...

Rhodopis rummaged on the supply shelves until she found a few empty jars. She poured the bath oil into these, draining all she could from the heavy amphora. Then, pausing at the door of the Stable to be sure Vélona was not still within, she hurried back to her alcove with the amphora tucked beneath one arm.

Quickly, Rhodopis raided her mattress, scooping out every bracelet and bangle, every necklace and collar and hair comb. She found the little linen bundle that held the smallest items— the earrings and finger rings Charaxus had sent—and then the larger bundle, containing the silver she had earned from other men, including the prize money Iason had sent for garnering the highest bid at his auction.

Everything went into the amphora. She estimated the value of her treasure as each piece plinked down into the jar. It made a merry music, and when she tamped the stopper down and hefted the jar to her hip, she was pleasantly surprised at its weight.

Won't be long before I'm out. One more year, maybe, and then I'm free.

Rhodopis carried the amphora well out into the garden. She must find someplace to hide it—where no one would ever think to look. And she must do it soon, before the girls finished their breakfast and came out into the garden to start their lessons.

She passed the big circular pond, raised partway above the ground in the old Egyptian fashion, walled with white-washed mudbrick. Lotus lilies covered the water in bright profusion, the spiky blooms sweet and fragrant among their flat, floating leaves. There was a bit of brick missing from the wall, just there—a perfect way to mark the place.

Rhodopis leaned over the edge of the pond. It was difficult to judge the depth, for the water between the lily leaves reflected bright sunlight, obscuring the pond's bottom. Glancing around to be sure no one saw her, she lowered the amphora carefully into the pond. She kept a fierce grip on one handle, afraid the jar would sink beyond her reach. But it came to rest on the silty bottom, and Rhodopis slowly withdrew her arm from the water. The lilies hid the amphora perfectly.

A job well done, Rhodopis thought, and hurried back to the Stable.

The morning after she'd sunk the amphora, Vélona made her usual rounds of the Stable, stalking down the room with her arms held stiffly behind her back, shouting commands to each girl. The girls had presented themselves, as always, in their plain white tunics. Vélona eyed them sharply, inspecting their beds for neatness and order.

"Callisto," Vélona barked, "stand up straight or I swear to blessed Isis, I will pay a metalsmith to melt an iron bar to your

back. You are off to Good Man Sophos tonight for private entertainment. If I hear that you slouched in his presence, it's the strap
for you. Archidike, Tarasios the boatwright is entertaining his
friends who have come up from Thebes. You and Bastet will
attend. The party will go late, I understand, so look alive. But first,
this afternoon, you're to visit Xanthes.

"Rhodopis—" Vélona pulled a small, lidded basket from
behind her back. She held it out to Rhodopis. "Your patron wants
you to dance at his party tonight. You're to wear these—a gift."

Rhodopis blushed. She didn't like to receive the gift in front of
all the other girls, but as it played a part in her assignment, she
supposed Vélona couldn't be blamed for having done it. She
lifted the lid of the basket—and gasped.

"What is it?" Callisto called.

Wordlessly, Rhodopis tilted the basket so the other girls could
see. A pair of slippers lay inside, snuggled into a nest of pink silk.
The slippers flashed as she tipped the basket, catching the lamplight, for they had been fashioned from rose gold.

"Gods be merciful," Persephone muttered.

Rhodopis lifted one delicate shoe out of the basket, examining it more closely. It was made in the Egyptian fashion—a flat,
sturdy sole that narrowed and curved at the toe, arching up and
over the foot. Open at the top, it would be held in place by a
thong that ran between the first and second toe, looped around
the ankle, and tied to the high-backed heel. The edges of the sole
had been etched all over with Greek keys, graven firmly into the
precious metal. A cluster of engraved grapes decorated the
upcurved toe, and in the center of the sole, just where her foot
would rest, was the image of a goose feather.

A tiny curl of papyrus lay in the basket. Rhodopis spread it
between her fingers and read Charaxus' note: *Rose gold, to match
your hair, my love.*

After so many strange and disappointing gifts from her
patron, the remarkable quality of the slippers—their obvious

craftsmanship, their unique appearance—struck Rhodopis speechless with awe.

"They are beautiful," Bastet said, grudgingly. "Lucky you."

"All right," Vélona said, "enough gawking. You have your assignments for the day. Get to work, all of you—and Rhodopis, I'd keep those shoes somewhere safe, if I were you."

❧

EVENING WAS APPROACHING. Rhodopis stood alone in the bath house, combing some of Charaxus' myrrh oil through her long, wet hair. The heat of her bath was dissipating from her skin, leaving behind a pleasant, subtle chill. Two hours hence, she would be at Charaxus' party, dancing for his guests—*And oh, won't I just about enjoy his company now!* The gift of the exquisite slippers seemed to prove that he'd learned the role of a patron at last. Rhodopis glanced at the slippers, waiting for her on a stone bench beside her tunic and belt. She smiled.

First those pretty shoes, and next...? Perhaps another necklace like the first he'd sent—the emeralds set in golden discs. She didn't know what the value of the slippers might be, but surely they had added significantly to her private cache of wealth. *Charaxus, you good soul—you dear, silly thing! How glad I am to have met you!*

"Rhodopis? Rhodopis!" It was Vélona, calling for her with increasing annoyance.

Rhodopis dropped the comb on the stone bench and pulled the tunic over her head. "Here I am, Mistress, in the bath."

Vélona leaned head and shoulders into the steam-filled bath house. "Xanthes wishes to speak with you immediately."

"Xanthes?" Nervously, Rhodopis tied the belt of her tunic in a sloppy knot. She hadn't gone before Xanthes since the first time, on her entrance into womanhood. The master had left her alone since then, only trotting her out to perform now and again at his supper parties. "Isn't Archidike with him now? I thought—"

"He wants to speak with you, not bed you. I don't know what you've done, but he doesn't seem best pleased."

Stumbling with sudden fear, Rhodopis stepped into her rose-gold slippers. She hadn't let them out of her sight since she'd received them that morning. She would have to find someplace else to hide them, for they certainly wouldn't fit inside the amphora, and in any case, Rhodopis didn't know whether pond water would damage rose gold.

I haven't done a thing to anger Xanthes, the thought. *I've been perfect, absolutely perfect since he first stole me from Iadmon.*

But the fact that the master had no just cause to be angry was small comfort. "Look sharp," Vélona said. "It won't do to keep him waiting." Shivering, as much from fear as from her wet hair, Rhodopis hurried after Vélona as she led the way to Xanthes' chamber.

The rearing, gilded lion still decorated Xanthes' door. Vélona knocked, and Xanthes barked, "Come."

Rhodopis entered alone, bowing as she went. She was aware that she looked disgraceful, with her wet hair hanging limply across her shoulders, her white tunic marked with splotches of water. All she could do was try to comport herself with dignity in spite of her appearance.

Xanthes sat upright on his wide couch, rolling a wine cup absently between his palms. A blue robe covered his broad shoulders, but hung open at the chest, revealing a forest of dark hair. A book of accounts lay open on the bed beside him, but Rhodopis was under no illusion that Xanthes had been hard at work. Archidike sprawled naked across his bed, one leg bent at the knee, her dark hair fanned out around her. She toyed with the long, slinking chain of a silver necklace. She had unfastened it from around her neck. She lifted it high in the air, then lowered it to pool in her navel. She cast a lazy smile in Rhodopis' direction.

"You wished to speak to me, Master?" Rhodopis said quietly.

"You've a patron now, I hear."

"Yes, Master. Charaxus of Lesvos. He's the—"

Xanthes stopped her with a wave of his hand. "I know who he is. How long have you been seeing him?"

"He has been my patron for three weeks now, Master. I visit him two or three times a week, whenever he sends for me."

"And before that?"

Rhodopis blinked at him. "Before that? I... I don't understand what you mean, Master."

"How did you come to know this Charaxus fellow?"

"He won me, Master, at Iason's auction. Before then, he called for me once, to go out to his house. But he didn't seem to like me then. I never knew him before that night. He says we met at a party, but I don't recall it."

Xanthes stood. He stalked toward Rhodopis, his great, dark bulk towering above her. She bit her lip and looked up at him, praying she looked calm.

"These gifts he sends you... they make me wonder. Is this Charaxus truly your patron? Or is he something more?"

"Something more, Master? Do you mean—my lover?"

Outrage burned Rhodopis' face. She refused to meet Archidike's eye, but she could feel the girl's smug grin, her lazy, dimpling triumph twisting around the room—around Rhodopis —like a snake's coils. Of course, it was Archidike who had planted the thought in Xanthes' mind.

"Tell me," Xanthes said. His voice was dangerously low.

Rhodopis lifted her chin, in what she hoped was a good show of haughty offense. "Master, Charaxus is nothing but a besotted fool. I've no feelings for him—in fact, I find him quite a bore. As for the gifts he sends me—I'm only doing my job, aren't I? Isn't that my purpose—to win men's hearts, and gather in their wealth? That's what your business is all about."

Xanthes looked her up and down. Rhodopis refused to quake

before his eyes—and refused to give Archidike the satisfaction of seeing her unsettled.

"Your patron gave you those shoes, didn't he?"

"Of course," Rhodopis said, tossing her head as if she didn't care one bit for the slippers. "He's given me many gifts, Master. I'd turn them all over to Amenia, for they're nothing to me, but as you know, Master, with him my patron and all—"

Xanthes held up a hand again. Rhodopis fell silent.

"Do not take a lover. Ever. If I hear again that you've done so, and I find out it's true, I won't be pleased, little lotus. Until you've raised enough money to strike out on you own, you are still my property. And your heart had best not come between my property and my profits. Am I clear?"

"Of course, Master," Rhodopis said lightly. She bowed, forcing a careless smile, and even managed to giggle coyly as she left Xanthes' chamber.

But as she stormed back toward the Stable, Rhodopis smiled no more.

Archidike, she thought sourly. *I'll win my way free before you ever will, you double-crossing, mean-hearted bitch. Just wait and see if I won't.*

AN EMPTY VESSEL

RHODOPIS DIPPED A SOFT LINEN CLOTH IN A PITCHER OF COOL water, wrung it out, and wiped the sweat from her neck and shoulders. Then she dropped into a chair, arms and legs sprawling, and panted, trying to recover her breath.

She had finished her performance for Charaxus and his friends. She could scarcely recall a time when she'd danced for so long, or so vigorously. She was exhausted, as wrung out as the linen cloth draped across the handle of the pitcher. But she had danced beautifully, and she was proud. Rhodopis was alone in the small chamber—Charaxus had thoughtfully set it aside for her exclusive use so that she might recover from the performance in peace. She could still hear the applause of her patron's friends, muffled by the chamber's walls, but she didn't need to hear how they'd loved her to know that she had done well.

Rhodopis had been the focus of the entertainment at a small, select party. The musicians Charaxus had hired were first-rate; the poignant beauty of their music had transported her far away from her troubles with Archidike. But it had been she who'd captured the attention and the hearts of Charaxus' guests.

She had opened with the joyful, clapping, stamping shepherd

dances Charaxus so enjoyed, and then eased, song after song, into far more elegant pieces. Clad only in the traditional fringed belt of an Egyptian dancer—and, of course, the beautiful rose-gold shoes—Rhodopis had enchanted the men and their hetaerae for more than an hour.

When at last she struck the final pose of her last dance, her small but appreciative audience had sent up a clamor of praise that must be audible in the village across the river. To Rhodopis' surprise, the hetaerae in attendance—all of them older than she, more established and mature—had been the first to applaud, and their delight in her performance seemed genuine. Perhaps that was because they were already free women, beholden to no master. No longer locked in competition for clients, they could be free to treat other hetaerae with kindness and respect.

What a change that'd make at the Stable, Rhodopis thought wryly. Then she silently promised the older women, *Someday I'll be among you—someday soon.*

Charaxus' servant tapped on the chamber door, then carried in a cup of some sweet-smelling liquid. "Melon juice with salt and mint," he said. "It will help you recover."

"Thank you."

Rhodopis gulped the salty-sweet mixture greedily. A light river wind drifted through the chamber's small window. It cooled her pleasantly; Rhodopis finished the cup of juice and leaned back in her chair, giving in to the simple pleasure of the breeze's caress.

Soon another knock sounded at the door. "Come," Rhodopis said, straightening in her chair.

Charaxus entered. Rhodopis stood, though her tired body protested. Nude save for the fringed belt, she faced him unashamed, leaving off her usual pretense of the shy country girl. She was proud of herself tonight; she had no need to blush or hide from anyone.

"You were glorious," Charaxus said, eyes glowing. "Better

even than I'd expected you to be. The gods blessed you, my love... and they blessed me."

He held out a small basket. Rhodopis could see that it brimmed with silver coins. Her eyes widened; there must have been at least two hundred hedj in the basket.

"From my guests—and from me. Their companions, the hetaerae, also contributed. You've impressed them, Rhodopis. I knew you would."

She shook her head uncertainly. "But you don't want me to sleep with all of them... do you?"

"No, never!" Charaxus laughed. "You charming, innocent little thing. They expect nothing more from you. Not all men are that way, you know—like Xanthes, I mean, and his friends. Some of us are more refined. Some of us appreciate a woman for her talents."

"Xanthes appreciates women for their talents," she said with a giggle.

"But only their talents inside the bedchamber. My friends and I—we know there's more to you than just that."

Tears of gratitude blurred her vision. "And the other hetaerae —they contributed, too? Why, it's so much money." *This will cut six months at least off my earnings, and no mistake.*

"You deserve it," Charaxus said. "You dance like a goddess. I couldn't be happier for my friends to see you, beautiful and talented as you are."

Rhodopis could see that Charaxus had thoroughly enjoyed showing her off to his friends. That pleasure gratified him almost as much as any other. Why shouldn't they all recognize the quality of his tastes? Why shouldn't they envy what he had: access to this exquisite, rare young hetaera?

She was so grateful for his help that she would have lain with him then and there, if there had been a convenient couch, or even a tabletop large enough to support them. But of course, Rhodopis knew her sentimental patron better than that. He glanced over his shoulder, back toward the andron. No doubt he felt pressure already to return to his guests, and play the role of the gracious, attentive host.

"Keep that money for me in your chamber, won't you?" Rhodopis said. "We'll be there together later, when they've all gone home."

"I'm looking forward to that." Charaxus kissed her, long and deep. "Come back to the party only when you're ready. The gods know you've earned a rest."

࿎

RHODOPIS WAS THOROUGHLY WORN out by the time she returned to Xanthes' house. The party had stretched on into the middle of the night. Afterward, Rhodopis had found herself in no hurry to leave Charaxus' bed. For the first time in their acquaintance, she had taken real delight in lying with him. He was not a skilled lover, but his generosity had moved her, and it made her glad to entertain him

Dawn was just beginning to break as the litter-bearers set her down in Xanthes' courtyard and drew back her curtain. Rhodopis' eyes were gritty and sore; she couldn't stop yawning. But she couldn't return to her bed just yet. By the pale light of earliest morning—the pink flush that tints the sky just before sunrise—she hurried out into the garden with the basket of hedj under one arm.

Rhodopis went briskly to the pond, and sat on its edge for some time, looking carefully around the garden to be certain she was unobserved. Then, as the birds woke in the trees overhead, she ducked her arms under the lotus leaves and heaved the amphora up from the pond.

It had taken on water, and was heavier than she'd expected. Rhodopis pried the lid free, then poured out the water that had seeped inside, letting it soak the short grass. She reached into the jar, satisfying herself that her treasures were still safe inside. Then she tipped the basket of silver coins into the amphora, re-sealed it as tightly as she could, and sank it in the pond once more.

Faint morning light rippled over the pond's surface. Rhodopis, nearly asleep on her feet, watched the enchanting patterns of pink light and blue shadow. She stood staring at the water until the ripples stilled, musing comfortably on her future. Two hundred hedj added to her fortune. How close was she now to obtaining freedom? Perhaps she need spend a few more months with Charaxus, and then she would be free.

A grim realization snapped her out of her sleepy reverie.

Once I'm free, I'll have to deal with Charaxus directly.

He was kind, to be sure—but nothing about him made her heart race. She would have to let him down easy once she was out from beneath Xanthes' heel, for there could be no question of settling down as Charaxus' wife.

With any luck, he'll find another woman to fall in love with, and forget all about me. She prayed that it would be so, and the sooner the gods made it happen, the better for them both.

A great yawn cracked Rhodopis' jaws and shook her frame. *I'm for bed now,* she told herself. *Time enough to sort the problem of Charaxus in the morning.*

Rhodopis headed back toward the Stable. Her steps dragged; the rose-gold slippers scuffed along in the grass. She could get two or three hours' sleep, she thought, before Vélona came and woke her up.

"What in Seth's name happened to you, Rhodopis?"

She looked up in alarm. Bastet was slinking toward the bath house, a long towel draped over her naked shoulder. But she stopped in her tracks, staring as Rhodopis came through the garden.

Rhodopis felt the drops of pond water still clinging to her arms, the splotch of wetness soaked into the chest and belly of her tunic. She didn't dare to look down, didn't dare confirm Bastet's suspicions.

"Who's awake already?" Rhodopis said acidly, "and going to the baths, no less?"

Bastet snorted. "You look like you've been in the baths yourself."

"I've just come back from my patron's," Rhodopis said.

"Did he ride you right into the river? Or doesn't he know where to drop his seed?" Bastet laughed harshly at her own joke.

"Don't see what there is to stare at," Rhodopis snapped, then turned abruptly and hurried back into the quiet of the Stable.

In her alcove, Rhodopis stripped off the damp tunic. She wrung all the pond water she could from the garment, then flicked the dirt from its linen. When it looked as innocent as she could manage, she hung it on the peg for Amenia to collect later that morning.

She still had no safe place to keep her slippers, so Rhodopis placed them under her pillow and sank into bed. If the gods were good, Rhodopis thought as sleep claimed her, Bastet would soon forget their strange encounter in the garden.

❧

THE WEEK CREPT BY, and although Bastet cast plenty of suspicious glances at Rhodopis, nothing came of their encounter in the garden. Rhodopis was gripped by a desperate anxiety, plagued with worry for her treasure. But she avoided the pond carefully, in case Bastet had spilled out the story to any of the other girls.

One morning, Vélona woke the girls earlier than usual. They scrambled from their beds and stood naked beside their alcoves, blinking and yawning, shivering in the cold morning air.

"You're all to dress in your house tunics," Vélona said, "and meet in the entrance hall, outside the andron, in half an hour's time."

"What's going on, Mistress?" Callisto said.

Vélona smiled, cool but pleased. "Today you will witness one of your own put forward the silver to buy her freedom. May it be an inspiration to all of you; may you all work just as hard."

The Stable rippled with conversation as the girls hurried to dress and comb their hair. But as Rhodopis reached up to take a fresh tunic from her shelf, her eyes traveled to the empty alcove across from her own.

Archidike was not there. She alone, of all Xanthes' girls, was absent from the Stable.

A sickening weight settled in Rhodopis' gut. She dressed as she was directed, tying her belt with numb, trembling fingers. She retrieved the rose-gold slippers from beneath her pillow and pulled them on her cold feet, then followed the other girls to the entry hall. Rhodopis did not join in their excited chatter. Archidike's name was on everybody's lips, for by that time they had all noticed her absence from the Stable.

The girls filed into the entry hall. Vélona fussed among them, arranging them in a half-circle. When she had finished, she called for silence, and the flurry of gossip died away.

Xanthes entered from the direction of the andron. He was dressed in his finest chlamys—a rich midnight-blue embroidered with red leaves along its hem. He looked as refined as that big, broad man ever could.

Behind him, Archidike moved with a grace and confidence Rhodopis had never seen in her before. She was dressed in the same provocative, scarlet-and-turquoise dress she had worn on the occasion of their first meeting—the transparent linen hiding nothing, revealing her beautiful, slender form for all to see. Her black hair coiled in several thick braids around her head, and the kohl around her eyes only heightened their victorious glow.

Several household slaves walked behind Archidike, each carrying a lidded basket. She turned to face Xanthes, and the slaves set their burdens at her feet, then backed away, bowing.

Vélona edged forward. "Master, this woman has served you loyally for many years. Now she comes before you to beg your consideration and grant her freedom."

"Can you pay the cost?" Xanthes said to Archidike.

Archidike bowed low, but as she did, she glanced over at the girls and winked. One among them shuffled on her feet—Bastet. The weight in Rhodopis' stomach turned cold as a winter wind.

"For every year of my service, Master, I have collected one thousand hedj." Archidike spoke clearly, boldly, reciting the words of the ceremony. "Or goods of equal value. Thus I shall repay you for your kindness in my keeping."

Xanthes gestured for Archidike to show him the pay. She lifted the lid from the first basket. It contained only coins, which Xanthes pawed through briefly. He was adept at estimating, by feel and sight alone, how many coins a basket of that size and shape could hold.

Archidike lifted the lid from the next basket. One by one, she took up the goods it contained, holding them up for Xanthes' approval.

The breath seized in Rhodopis' throat.

There was the necklace Charaxus had given her—the three emeralds set in their golden discs—and there, the lapis lazuli ankle cuffs. There were the pearl earrings, the ivory hair combs, the golden bracelets inlaid with turquoise.

She's robbed me, Rhodopis thought frantically. *Gods save me, the treacherous beast has found my hiding place and robbed me!*

She cut a stare toward Bastet, who only smiled sweetly back at her. Rhodopis could do nothing but watch as Archidike—who had once been her friend, and more than that—presented every coin and bauble Charaxus had given her to Xanthes.

She robbed me... robbed me!

There was nothing to be done about the theft or the injustice now. In any case, Rhodopis knew full well that neither Vélona nor Xanthes would care. To keep herself from crying—from screaming with rage—she lowered her face, unwilling to watch any longer as her stolen goods were presented in Archidike's hands. All Rhodopis could think of was the amphora. It was nothing but an empty vessel now; everything she had was gone. Everything but the rose-gold slippers she now wore. They were the only wealth that remained to her.

"It is sufficient," Xanthes said. The words of the ceremony came to Rhodopis as if from under water, bubbling and rippling, obscured by the rushing in her ears. "I free you; go out into the world with my thanks for your loyal service."

A terrible pain squeezed in Rhodopis' chest. She couldn't draw a breath, couldn't move, couldn't believe the gods would be so cruel.

You were a fool to trust Archidike, Rhodopis told herself. *You were a fool to like her. She drugged Iadmon to help Xanthes steal you away. She was never a good person, never was your friend. She only used you, and would have gone on using you forever, because you're a fool—fool, fool!*

There in the entry of Xanthes' estate, bitterness sprouted in Rhodopis' heart. Its roots found purchase where once only sweetness could grow. But it flourished quickly, sprouting thorns—and the thorns were sharp indeed.

Wearily, she tried to calculate how long it would take her to regain everything she had lost. Another year at least as Charaxus' special friend… probably more. She faced three more years in the Stable—three at the very least. Four or five seemed more likely.

It's not all that long. Rhodopis tried to comfort herself with that thought. *Many girls live in bondage far longer.*

But after her certainty that freedom was close at hand, it seemed an inexhaustible eternity.

❧ 20 ❧

THE FALCON AND THE RIVER

LIFE IN THE STABLE CARRIED ON AS BEFORE. RHODOPIS STILL KEPT her engagements, still visited Charaxus often. But the atmosphere of Memphis grew ever more tense. Soon she was half convinced that the cloud of anger and despair that had clung to her since Archidike's betrayal had grown to envelop the whole city.

Parties were no longer the elegant, jovial affairs they once had been. Men argued easily now; tempers were short. There was always someone willing to come to blows over a disagreement about the Pharaoh and his policies—or worse, willing to draw knives. At one party on the western edge of town, a hetaera had gone home early, for her companion had drunk too much wine and ended with a sick belly. Not a quarter of an hour later, the woman had come running back to the host's estate, tears streaming down her face, her beautiful linen dress smeared with dung. She had met a pack of Egyptian men on the road, and they had accosted her—cursing her Greek appearance, accusing her of enchanting the Pharaoh with her feminine wiles. They had pelted her with donkey droppings, picked up from the street. She had come back to the party for safety's sake and begged the host to give her guardsmen to see her safely home.

There was no doubt in Rhodopis' mind that Memphis grew more dangerous with each passing week. She couldn't forget the raw anger in the men whom she'd encountered the night of Iason's party, when she had foolishly walked home alone. How quick they had been to insult one another, how eager to pull their knives! Almost every night, one the girls in Xanthes' Stable had another chilling tale to tell—fights breaking out at parties, or gangs of Egyptian youths who fell on Greek men in the streets, pounding them with their fists and leaving them injured in dark, cold alleys. Worst of all was the night just before the harvest festival, when a messenger arrived from Good Man Sophos' house. The messenger's tunic was ripped and bloodied. Callisto and Bastet were taking shelter at Sophos' estate, the messenger had said, and would be there until well past sunrise, for a riot had broken out on the north end of town, and no one could navigate the streets safely, not even in a litter.

"What could it all mean?" Efthalia wondered. "What's it all leading up to?" For it was clear to all of them that tension in the city was building to some grand and terrible climax.

"If Bastet were here," Rhodopis said, "instead of hiding out behind Sophos' walls, she'd say it means the Egyptians have finally had enough."

"They're about to liberate Kmet," Persephone said. She laughed ironically. "Liberate Egypt—from what, the Pharaoh? From Egypt itself?"

Rhodopis shrugged. "It's clear they're angry. Have been for a long time."

"Rhodopis knows," Persephone said, "with all the wisdom of her fourteen years."

"I'm only repeating what I've heard the men say," she muttered defensively.

Persephone waved a dismissive hand. "This will all blow over, like a sand storm."

"I wish I could be so sure of it," Efthalia said quietly. "Amasis has never been a well-loved king. He does his country no good, in favoring Greeks over Egyptians. And I'm afraid it's gone on too long for it all to be forgotten."

The Pharaoh Amasis, however, soon restored his reputation —among Xanthes' hetaerae, if nowhere else in Egypt. Several days after the riot in the northern stretch of Memphis, Vélona swept into the Stable, beaming openly as that pinched, sour woman never had before.

The girls, sensing good news, scrambled out of their alcoves and stood waiting.

Vélona brandished a scroll of papyrus. "None of you will believe what I've got here. Do any of you recognize this seal? No? Well..." She opened the scroll with an exultant air and read: "Pharaoh Amasis, in celebration of the harvest to come and in fellowship to those who have been unfortunately affected by the insurrection in Memphis, will host a grand feast, one day hence, to begin at mid-day, in his own great house."

The girls stared at the mistress, wide-eyed. "The messenger told me," Vélona said, "the feast is to honor the great Greek men whose contributions to Memphis have made it a city to be reckoned with, all the world over. And to do equal honor to the Egyptians who have worked hand in hand with the Greeks, and not spurned them."

"What does it mean for us, Mistress?" Bastet said.

"Xanthes is certainly a great man of Greek extraction. He has been invited personally. And he intends to bring you girls, too, so that you may find more friends among the Memphis elite."

Squeals of excitement filled the Stable. Xanthes' girls had gained entrance to many a great man's house, but none had yet set foot inside the king's palace. They set about planning at once, rifling through the dressing closet under Amenia's watchful eye, discussing how they ought to comport themselves in the company of the king, and practicing their various talents—for all of them hoped they might have the chance to perform for the king and his court. Only the gods could say what doors might open for a woman who sang or danced for the pleasure of the King of Egypt.

The cloud that hung over Rhodopis for weeks lifted in her excitement. Now, at last, she would make more influential friends than just Charaxus. If she was to earn back all the wealth Archidike had stolen—and do it before she was a withered old woman—she would need more than one patron. As the Stable hummed with activity, Rhodopis sat on her bed, rubbing her rose-gold slippers with oil and a soft cloth, carefully buffing away scuffs and scratches. If the gods were good to her—and the gods were long overdue to bring Rhodopis a measure of good luck— she would dance before the king, and win the admiration of countless powerful men.

The girls stayed awake late into the night, chattering over their plans for the next day's feast. All their habitual animosity was forgotten—for the time being, at any rate. They lacquered one another's nails and tried new hairstyles, and told bawdy jokes until they were shrieking with laughter—and finally, Vélona marched into the room, shooing them off to their beds.

Bastet crept in behind Vélona; she had come from a party that night and was still sore over having missed most of the fun of preparing for the king's feast.

Vélona snuffed the lamps and shut the door on the Stable; moments later, the girls were back out of their beds, congregating in the middle of the room to whisper over their plans.

"I hope you greedy cows left a few good dresses for me," Bastet said. "If you only left me the plain tunics, I'll never let you forget about it."

"Stop fretting," Callisto said. "You know Amenia's got

hundreds of gowns. She'll be sure you look your best. How was the party?"

"Dull. Than's parties are always dreadful. He wouldn't know fun if it kicked him in the cock." Bastet elbowed Rhodopis in the ribs. "I saw Charaxus there. Your sweetheart."

"He's not," Rhodopis said patiently. "You know that."

"He was properly peeved. It seems he wasn't invited to the Pharaoh's party."

"What?" Callisto said. "Not invited—a wealthy Greek?"

Bastet leaned farther into the circle, relishing her gossip. "It seems Charaxus' sister—that poet Sappho—wrote some verses about our good king Amasis. A copy of the poem made found its way from Lesvos to Memphis. Needless to say, the Pharaoh found Sappho's opinion of his royal self quite disagreeable."

The girls giggled softly, but Rhodopis felt a prickle of dread. Long after they had all finally gone off to their bed, Rhodopis lay awake, staring at the dark ceiling of her alcove. Charaxus, not invited... what would it mean for her? Nothing, surely. There was no reason why Rhodopis should be barred from the party, even if her patron was.

In the morning, though, when Vélona roused the groggy hetaerae from their beds, she brought the news Rhodopis had been dreading.

"You may stay abed, if you like," Vélona said as she passed by Rhodopis' alcove. "Your patron is not attending the king's feast, and has sent for you to entertain him instead."

Rhodopis sat up slowly, chilled to her marrow. "What, Mistress?"

"I am sure you heard me perfectly well, Rhodopis. Now, the rest of you—up! Up and off to breakfast. You must all be dressed and in your litters an hour before mid-day."

"No," Rhodopis said faintly.

Vélona turned to her with a hard, affronted stare.

"No!"

Rhodopis leaped from her bed. Wounded as she was by Archidike's betrayal, Vélona's news shattered all the fine control Aesop had once taught her. She raced down the length of the Stable, her fingers bent like claws, teeth clenched so hard her jaw ached. She grabbed Bastet by the front of her tunic and hauled her out into the great room.

"You did this—you!"

"Let go! Get her off me!" Bastet cried.

"You've always envied me because I'm the better dancer! You convinced Charaxus last night—told him to call for me today, so I couldn't go to the Pharaoh's feast!"

Bastet made no reply; she only stared coolly into Rhodopis' eyes.

A moment later, Vélona's hand clenched in Rhodopis' hair; she shrieked in pain and rage as the mistress dragged her away from Bastet.

"You're lucky you didn't mark her," Vélona spat, shaking Rhodopis hard, "or it would have been the strap for you. Back to your bed—at once! And the rest of you, get dressed before I keep you all back, and make you scrub out the privies!"

Rhodopis flung herself across her bed, sobbing miserably into her pillow. Her scalp ached from Vélona's terrible grip, but it was nothing next to the pain in her heart. Archidike had taken her money, and now Bastet—or Vélona—or that damnable, blind fool Charaxus had taken this grand chance to start her fortunes over again, to fight her way up from the depths of this pit. She would never forgive them—never—not a single one of them!

Soon the girls, glittering in the best finery Amenia had to offer, were filing out of the Stable. Vélona herded them through the door, then looked back over her shoulder at Rhodopis, who sat huddled miserably on the floor beside her alcove.

"Charaxus will be sending his litter around for you soon. I want you ready by the time he arrives."

Rhodopis made no reply, and Vélona left, slamming the door hard behind her.

Rhodopis did not prepare herself for a day with her patron. She remained crouched on the cold floor, all her bright hopes shattered around her. By the time Vélona returned to the Stable, some two hours later, Rhodopis was still hunched in her plain white tunic, and its linen was damp with her tears.

"Get up, girl," Vélona said, not unkindly.

Rhodopis didn't move; after a moment, Vélona took her under the arms and jerked her roughly to her feet.

"The litter is here, but I can't send you off to Charaxus looking like this. I shall just have to send word that you've taken ill."

She nodded mutely.

"I know you're disappointed," Vélona said, "but this behavior will not be tolerated a second time. You may have the day off to recover your... mood. But I expect you alert, compliant, and ready to work on the morrow. Am I understood?"

Again, Rhodopis nodded.

"Good. Now get out to the baths and clean yourself up. You look like a mouse mauled half to death by a house-cat."

Rhodopis left the Stable, but she did not go to the bath house. She ran through the garden, half-blinded by her tears, past the pond that had once hidden her precious hopes. She ran through the courtyards and flower beds, past the stand of sycamores that filtered the wind from the river.

Rhodopis could have run on forever, but the land had given out. She had reached Xanthes' private quay. His boat waited, moored to the stone, just beyond the bed of reeds where she now stood, panting.

Doesn't matter where I want to go, what I want to do—the gods always stop me, she thought miserably.

She sank down among the reeds, kneeling in the damp earth, and wept until her eyes were dry and scratchy. Then she tore helplessly at the innocent green reeds, ripping them from the river's bank, shredding them in her angry, powerless fists.

Rhodopis looked up to the sky, her hands full of the broken reeds. The scent of their crushed stems rose all around her, green and sharp. High above, in the pale-blue arch of the mid-day sky, a single bird turned lazily on the wind.

I danced the Maiden of the Reeds once. Maybe I ought to be the Maiden of the Reeds.

She pictured it—her small body in the river, lifeless from the terrible force of her despair. Drifting north on the river's current.

North—that way lay Iadmon's house. Iadmon and kind, patient Helena, who was a slave, too. And the little messenger boy with the split lip, and Iunet with her sharp tongue and quick, lashing stick.

And Aesop. Rhodopis missed him more than anyone else. More even than her family, for they were a distant memory now, abstract and far away. She wanted her friend again—Aesop, the only true friend she had ever known.

"I've got no friends at all," she said softly. She let the broken reeds fall from her hands.

She had no one to confide in, no one to love. She had only Charaxus, clumsy and embarrassing in his affections.

That's all I've got to look forward to, for years to come. Charaxus, and no one else.

Rhodopis leaped suddenly to her feet. She kicked off one of her rose-gold slippers, seized it, and hurled it out over the river.

She had thrown with all her strength. The slipper flew up and up, and seemed to hang immobile for a moment at the peak of its trajectory. Then, just as it began to drop toward the water, a streak of blue-gray fell from the sky, quick as a bolt of lightning, and collided with the slipper.

Rhodopis stopped her weeping; she stared in awe. The blue-gray streak was a bird—a falcon. It threw out its sharp-pointed wings, pulling out of its swift dive mere inches above the water.

The falcon climbed through the air on powerful wing-beats. As it rose, the sun bounced up from the surface of the Nile and glinted on Rhodopis' slipper—clutched tightly in the falcon's feet.

She shook her head slowly. *Hadn't seen it with my own eyes, I never could believe...* The falcon must have mistaken her slipper for a bird—a duck or a pigeon.

She turned to watch the bird as it flew away, shading her eyes with one hand. It was fast on the wing, and growing smaller by the moment. But still she could make it out, a black dot against the hot blue sky. The falcon passed back over Memphis, heading steadily toward the Pharaoh's palace.

Rhodopis slid the other slipper from her foot, but she did not throw it. Instead, she clutched it to her chest, turned away from the river, and ran back to the Stable.

§.

NEAR DAWN, the girls returned to the Stable, breathless with their tales of the party. Rhodopis sat, calm and composed, on the end of her bed. She listened silently as they clamored to tell her everything—how glorious the palace was, how fine the food, how beautiful and regal were Pharaoh's many wives and concubines, who sat on dignified display in a railed gallery near the throne. And, of course, the array of powerful men in attendance—all the finest, wealthiest men in Egypt.

"Tell me about the dancers," Rhodopis said. "I would have so loved to see them."

"The dancers were fine enough," Callisto said, "but they weren't the most exciting entertainment."

"Jugglers? Magicians?"

"None of that," Bastet said. "The best part of the feast, the Pharaoh hadn't even planned."

"What do you mean?"

Efthalia leaned toward Rhodopis, her eyes alight with mystery. "In the midst of the entertainment—I think it was while some woman was singing—one of the king's trained birds flew into the feast hall."

A thrill of certainty raced up Rhodopis' spine. She said nothing—only waited.

"It was a hawk," Efthalia said.

Bastet rolled her eyes. "No, you witless fly, a *falcon*. Can't you tell the difference?"

"Anyway," Efthalia said, with a sideways glower at Bastet, "the bird circled the whole vast room—and the room was simply huge, Rho, with hundreds of tables and couches."

"It had something shiny in its talons," Bastet said. "I thought it was a fish at first—the thing in the falcon's talons, I mean. But then the bird flew right over the king's throne, for it recognized him, you see, and dropped what it was carrying in his lap."

Rhodopis nodded silently, encouraging them to go on.

"The king held it up. It was a shoe—a gilded slipper."

"It looked like one of yours, Rhodopis," Callisto said. "Like the pair what-his-name sent you."

"It couldn't be my slipper," Rhodopis said quickly, her cheeks heating. "I got rid of those old things."

"You never did," Bastet said. "You were wearing them this morning."

"I was wearing a different pair, and they aren't anything like the ones Charaxus sent me. Don't be silly."

"They must have come from the same shoe-maker, then," Callisto said, "for the slipper the king held looked every bit like your old ones."

"What did he do?" Rhodopis said. "It can't be a thing that happens every day—a falcon dropping a shoe in the king's lap."

"No, I suppose not. Well, the Pharaoh held that slipper for a very long time, and just... looked at it. He set it on his table, there among the wine cups and the dishes of food, and wouldn't let any of his servants take it away. For the rest of the night, I hardly saw him glance at anything else—not the dancers or the acrobats, not the men who approached to bow at his feet. Nothing. He was entirely taken with that slipper."

"It was an omen," Bastet said. "A sign from the gods."

Efthalia rolled her eyes. "What do you know?"

"Plenty, being Egyptian. Falcons are sacred—symbols of the god Horus, from whom the power of the throne descends. Any gift a falcon gives you has real meaning. Ten times as much, if you happen to be the king."

"Amasis has forgotten he's Egyptian," Rhodopis said. "He thinks he's a Greek—or he wants to be Greek, so the men say."

"Ah," Bastet sighed. "But he can't deny he's Egyptian now, can he? A sign delivered by Lord Horus himself. No Egyptian can ignore such an omen."

"What did he do about the shoe, then?" Rhodopis asked.

Bastet shrugged. "I couldn't say. By the time the entertainments had finished, we were all too busy playing the crowd—making new friends. I never saw what he did with the shoe. I suppose he must have it still."

The Stable door banged open; the girls scuttled for their beds, while Vélona bawled, "Not a word from any of you—not a whisper, not a sneeze! The night is quite late enough. I want you all asleep, or you'll regret it in the morning."

Rhodopis settled back in her bed. Her long day of weeping had drained her, but the strange sight she had witnessed at the river—the omen, if Bastet was to be believed—remained vivid in her memory, warding away her dreams. She found she couldn't drift off on sleep's currents until she had slipped her hand beneath her pillow and touched the rose gold of her one remaining slipper.

Then, at last, sleep took her, but her dreams were strange and shadowed. Vague, fragmented visions haunted her—Charaxus drawing a knife from his belt and fighting with the king; naked

Archidike lifting the silver chain, dropping it into her navel, lifting it again; the falcon's wings reflected upside-down in the surface of the water, a great, golden fish in its talons.

And over each strange, indecipherable vision, she heard the tap-tap-tap of Iunet's stick, the rhythms she had used when she'd first taught Rhodopis how to dance. And then, clear and vivid, echoing in her ears, she heard Aesop say, "Now—" in that way he had, that simple but distinct way—the way that meant, "Begin."

ROSE GOLD

V ÉLONA ALLOWED ALL THE GIRLS TO SLEEP IN LATE THE NEXT morning, for the excitement of the Pharaoh's feast had surely worn them down. Rhodopis was the first to wake, long before the Stable came to life. She climbed from her bed, checked to see that her slipper was still beneath her pillow, and dressed in the morning dimness of the great chamber.

She leaned against the wall for an hour or more, watching the morning light fill the wind catchers and pool petal-pink along the floor. She thought of falcons—of omens—and of Aesop's voice in the darkness.

When Vélona pushed open the door, her brows raised to see Rhodopis already standing beside her alcove curtain. But she nodded with satisfaction: clearly, Rhodopis had overcome the dark mood that had gripped her the day before, and was ready to resume the life the gods had laid out for her, with the quiet dignity that suited a woman of Xanthes' stable.

The girls rustled from their beds when Vélona called them, and stood yawning to receive their assignments from the mistress.

"It seems you all worked hard and well at the Pharaoh's feast," she said. "I've already had several requests from new admirers. Well done, ladies."

But before she could dole out the day's work, a clamor came through the wind catchers—shouts and the rumblings of a great crowd, rising up from the other side of Xanthes' walls. The crowd was chanting the Pharaoh's name: "Amasis! Amasis!"

Vélona glanced back through the Stable door, a new strain around her dark eyes. Rhodopis had never seen the mistress worried before.

"What is it?" Bastet said. "Another riot?"

"Let us pray it's not that," Vélona said. Then she raised her voice. "Guards!"

Callisto began to sniffle. "Mother Isis have mercy! Riots—and so close!"

"Quiet," Vélona snapped. "Keep your wits, all of you, no matter what may come."

A blue-robed guard did appear then, but he was grinning broadly. "Nothing to fear, Mistress," he said to Vélona. "In fact, I think you'll be most pleased." He handed her a scroll.

Vélona looked at its seal—then her eyes widened. "Gods bless me. It's another message from the Pharaoh."

Fear gave way at once to excitement. The girls flocked around Vélona, urging her to open the scroll, to read out the king's message.

"Very well; get back, now, all of you. Give me some room." Vélona unrolled the papyrus, read it over silently. Then she shook her head—in confusion or amazement, Rhodopis couldn't tell.

" 'To all the great houses of Memphis,' " Vélona read, " 'let it be known that the Pharaoh has received an omen from the gods.' "

"The shoe," Bastet whispered to Callisto.

Vélona went on: " 'The king, in his wisdom, has consulted his priests and turned to the gods in prayer. The holy falcon of Egypt has given the king the gift: a woman's slipper of most perfect beauty and artistry. The Pharaoh shall appear in each district of Memphis on this day, until he has found the woman to whom the slipper belongs. That woman will he take into his household, by command of Horus, Lord of the Skies, Wellspring of Power and Guardian of Egypt. Be it so.'"

The Stable erupted with chatter, which Vélona tried unsuccessfully to quell. Rhodopis heard none of it. There was a strange rushing in her ears, a rising pressure in her chest. Her limbs had gone cold and shaky. She thought, *Has my fate turned again? Or are the gods only toying with me?*

The sharp clapping of Vélona's hands brought Rhodopis out of her daze. The mistress was hustling the other girls down toward the dressing closet—toward Rhodopis, who still lingered beside her alcove.

"We have very little time," Vélona cried. "Where is Amenia? Somebody go and get her—be quick! Open up the dressing closet; we shall have to get started without her. Make yourselves look as beautiful as you can, girls. I won't have the house of Xanthes outshone today."

❧

THE MARKET SQUARE was emptied of peddlers and farmers, just as it had been on the night when Rhodopis had crossed it alone. But it was daylight now—hot mid-day, sweltering and heavy with the scent of dust and bodies and the sun-struck bricks of the city's rooftops.

Xanthes' girls clustered together under the great cloth canopies of sun shades, borne by their master's blue-robed servants. They certainly were not the only women in the square. Every great house in central Memphis had sent its ladies to the square—providing they were unmarried and young or beautiful enough to catch the Pharaoh's eye. For what family would not love to see one of its daughters placed in the king's harem—and what master wouldn't like to charge the Pharaoh the replacement cost of one of his best hetaerae?

Every woman wore her most beautiful garb—robes of linen and gowns of silk were everywhere to be seen, trailing in the dust, trodden by the crowd, dulled and stained by sweat. A glint of gems and flash of gold came from every corner.

Rhodopis was not surprised to find Archidike among the women. She stood apart, attached to no particular household now that she was free, in the company of no particular friends—for Archidike had ever been a solitary creature. Rhodopis watched her from the other side of the market square. She couldn't help but think Archidike looked beautiful, flawless in a pale blue robe, her hair twisted and curled atop her head. A simple silver chain circled her throat, and she stood without fan or sun shade, apparently untouched by the heat. Freedom suited her well. Rhodopis regretted that she couldn't wish good luck and good fortune on the girl who had once been her friend. But the bitterness that had grown in Rhodopis' heart had never uprooted itself. It had grown to fill her; she had no room left for any kind feelings toward Archidike. All she felt now was the ache of the freedom she herself had lost.

But perhaps today, Rhodopis would have a new chance at freedom. The other women of Xanthes' house had decked themselves extravagantly, scrambling for the best dresses and jewels in Amenia's closet. Rhodopis had been content to dress more humbly. She wore a silk dress, simply cut and dyed a pale pink hue, with a sky-blue sash looped several times around her waist. She wore no gems. She needed none, for concealed in the folds of the blue sash was the only treasure she required. She kept her hands folded at her waist, to help hide the strangely shaped bulge of the rose-gold slipper beneath her clothing.

The afternoon grew hotter, and the crowd more restless, but still the Pharaoh did not appear. Murmurs began to circulate—rumors that he had already found the woman whose foot fit the miraculous, god-given shoe, somewhere in another district of Memphis. Rhodopis tried to shut her ears to the rumors, but as the day wore on, they became harder to ignore. Perhaps, after all, her chance had passed. It wouldn't be the first time the gods had taunted her.

But then, with a fanfare of reed pipes and drums, the king arrived. The crowd parted, making way for the royal presence.

A massive litter carried him into the market square: sixteen bearers to the front and back, each wearing the striped blue-and-white kilts of the king's service. The litter's arms were gilded, and so well polished they made Rhodopis squint. The throne of Egypt sat upon that great platform, a chair of elegantly simple design, yet its every surface as covered in gold.

King Amasis himself sat upon the throne, regally still, a man in his fifties with soft, somewhat troubled eyes. The towering double crown of Egypt, white on red, was balanced on his brow.

The crowd in the market square bowed, murmuring their respects, as the litter sank to the ground.

A small, thin man with a shaven head stepped out in front of the king's conveyance. Rhodopis took him for a royal herald, for he unrolled a scroll and began to read from it, shouting out his instructions.

"I, the king's steward, am in possession of the blessed object, the gift of Lord Horus. Each woman who wishes to present herself to the king must wait her turn in line, for the royal presence will tolerate no insult to our dignity. Each woman will have but one chance to prove the slipper is hers, and if it is a match for her foot, then she will be welcomed to the Pharaoh's household. Such may it be, by the will of Lord Horus."

Vélona shepherded her girls toward the line, but it had formed rapidly—the women pushing and shoving as much as they dared, before the eyes of the king. By the time they reached the queue, Rhodopis was well back from the throne.

Patience, the counseled herself. *The gods can't abandon you now.* She hoped it was true.

Rhodopis craned her neck to watch as, one after another, the steward tried and rejected the women at the head of the line. She was not surprised to spot Archidike there, standing among the first of the women. True to form, the girl must have dodged to the front of the crowd and slipped to the head of the line just as it was forming.

The steward tried another woman's foot, and then another. Each left in disappointment, red-faced and grumbling.

Then Archidike faced the steward. She gazed up at the king for a moment, resplendent in her blue silk. She bent her head in a graceful bow, and even at a distance, Rhodopis could see the radiant smile on her face—a look of sweetness that was not hers by nature.

Archidike's foot slid neatly into the shoe. King Amasis leaned back on his throne, smiling with satisfaction and no small amount of relief.

"No!"

Rhodopis would not allow Archidike to steal what was hers—not again. She dodged out of line, leaping from the cool sanctuary of the sun shades to the full heat of the afternoon sun.

"Rhodopis!" Vélona's angry shout cut through the crowd's murmur of surprise. "Get back here, girl!"

Rhodopis ignored her. She ran down the line, the hem of her pink robe flapping, shouting, "Wait, my Pharaoh! Please, wait!"

She heard Vélona bellow with rage again, but Rhodopis pressed on. She couldn't falter now, couldn't give up. If it was already too late to claim the slipper as her own—or if the king simply didn't accept her proof, then Rhodopis would accept her fate. The dull drudgery the gods had planned for her, even Vélona's most savage beating. But she wouldn't surrender her newfound hope until she was certain it was well and truly lost.

The king's soldiers moved to block her; Amasis himself scowled down at Rhodopis as she ran gracelessly toward him.

She fell on her knees in the dust, as close to the throne as the guards would allow. "Please hear me, my king!"

Amasis leaned from his throne, consulting quietly with his steward. After a moment, during which Rhodopis heard nothing but her own ragged breath rattling in her throat, the steward gestured for her to rise.

Rhodopis climbed to her feet. The guards parted; she came forward, until she stood shoulder to shoulder with Archidike. The other girl's blue eyes held all the familiar hurt and pain— Archidike's savage spirit, glittering out from her heart.

"What is it?" the king said from his throne. "Speak, girl."

With Archidike beside her, Rhodopis could not have spoken to save herself from damnation. Instead, she reached into her sash and pulled out her rose-gold slipper. She held it up before her face, offering it to the Pharaoh.

Amasis jerked his head, a silent command—the steward whisked the slipper from Rhodopis' hands. A moment later, it was in the Pharaoh's grip. He stared at it, silent, contemplative, turning it over to examine it from every angle.

"Please," Rhodopis whispered. Beside her, Archidike growled deep in her throat, a groan of pure loathing.

The king rose slowly from his throne. He parted his guards with a steady hand, then approached Rhodopis, his soft eyes questioning, wondering. Archidike sank to her knees before him. Rhodopis tried to do the same, but Amasis caught her gently by the chin and held her, so she had no choice but to look up into his eyes.

She blushed—and how could the king resist her then? She, timid and beautiful, soft as a petal—the very picture of an ideal Greek girl. No Greek-loving king could turn away from that magical charm.

"What is your name, girl?" the king asked.

She swallowed hard, certain her voice would betray her. But when she spoke, the words carried. "Rhodopis, my lord. Rhodopis of Thrace."

Amasis raised his arms to the crowd. "The god Horus has spoken," he cried. "He has brought this girl to me, to serve in my harem. Let the god's will be done: Rhodopis of Thrace, Horus wills that you join the house of the Pharaoh."

The king took her hand in his own. Every man and woman in the square—noble and lord, merchant and soldier, servant and slave—bowed low before her.

THE END

The story continues in *Persian Rose*, Book 2 of the White Lotus trilogy, available now from your favorite bookseller.

ABOUT THE AUTHOR

Libbie Hawker writes historical and literary fiction featuring complex characters and rich details of time and place. She lives in the beautiful San Juan Islands with her husband and two naughty cats.

When she's not writing, Libbie can be found road tripping, decorating cookies, and working on her podcast about Jem and the Holograms.

Connect with her below, and don't forget to join Libbie's mailing list (at LibbieHawker.com) to receive updates about new books and get exclusive previews of works in progress.

Printed in Great Britain
by Amazon

30847507R00158